Love and Agita

GRAYSON AVERY

FARCICAL PRESS

To my amazing wife who chose me despite my wacky Italian family…
G.A.

CHAPTER
One

FAMILY IS LIKE LASAGNA. At least my family is. Pasta. Meat. Sauce. Cheese. All ingredients have their own unique characteristics, a role to play, and interact differently with each other. My parents are the pasta, firm enough to set boundaries, but can soften under some heat. My siblings are the meat. You'll understand when you meet them. Nonna is the sauce, adding a little spice and sometimes making things go down a little smoother. And I'm pretty much the cheese in my family, tasty with a little bite, keeping the rest of it together.

Done well, lasagna is a wonderful recipe. All I can tell you is that my family is not always done well...Lasagna is easy to assemble, but under too much heat, things get messy. And the heat was about to get turned up. We're not talking normal, run-of-the-mill 350 degrees. The oven was about to go nuclear and the cheese that holds everything together was about to be stretched to its limits.

But we're getting ahead of ourselves here. Let me introduce myself. My name is Leo Donati, although my mother calls me Leonardo when she's angry. Thwacks from a wooden spoon and an unleashing of Italian curses usually accompany the wrath. Even at thirty years old, the damn things still sting like, well, like a mother... It's because her forearms are like bricks, built by millions of revolutions stirring the marinara sauce.

If you haven't figured it out yet, my family's Italian. And if you're gonna hang with us, you should know our rules. We only have a few, but they're not to be broken unless you want to become acquainted with the aforementioned spoon.

1. You must attend Sunday family dinner. It's at 2:00. Nobody knows why.

2. You love your mother.

3. You never tell Nonna you're full. Unless you have a death wish.

4. You marry Italian.

5. Family comes first. Always. Friends come and go, but family is forever.

These rules are etched in stone. There's also an unwritten rule that states women must have half their wardrobe in animal print. I don't necessarily agree with that one, but the rest are legit, and I lived by them every day. Or tried to. I was single with not a whole lotta luck in the lady department, despite my rugged handsomeness and world-class charm. Surprising, I know.

There's one more thing to know about my family before you meet them. As wacky as they are, I love them more than anything. They're fun, loud, exciting, albeit slightly embarrassing, but I couldn't imagine being anywhere else when I'm with them. Most of the time, I love being a part of the Donati family. Being a part of something bigger than myself. Having people I can count on. Most of them. Some of them. Well, my mother and grandmother. And Pop when we're not clashing at work.

We own a print shop, or actually, a bunch of them. Donati Printing. My grandfather started the business, then gave it to my father, who has run it for the last twenty-two years, and

I'm eagerly awaiting my turn at the helm. I'm only thirty and I've been in the business almost twenty years myself. I started way back when child labor was an acceptable practice. I was what they call a Printer's Devil, doing just about everything: changing ink and paper, stacking boxes, collating projects, and even making local deliveries on my Mongoose bike. Now, I'm the Vice President, in charge of the operations of seven shops spread across Long Island.

It's probably best to start this story on the Friday morning before I got our October financials. It's what really turned up the heat on said lasagna. After a client meeting with The Hampton's magazine that I hosted at our eastern facility in Riverhead, I headed into our first shop and de facto head-quarters in Huntington at about noon. The acidic smell from the print facility grappled with Rebecca's sweet-smelling perfume. Rebecca worked the front and was one of the few non-Donatis employed at HQ, not because I ran out of cousins, but because we needed people to actually work. Most of our employees were some sort of relation and saw their paychecks as more of an allowance than for services rendered.

Rebecca looked up when I entered. "Hey, boss." She was about six inches shorter than me at 5'6" and thin, with over-sized red glasses. She wore a vintage 'I love 80s hair bands' t-shirt with tight jeans and her brown hair in a ponytail. She was cute, but more in a sisterly kind of way. I actually liked her more than my own sister most of the time.

"How's it going in here?"

Rebecca huffed. "Frankie's late on the Grappolo job. Again. Claims the machine is slow. But it's only 'slow' for him," she said, heavy on the air quotes.

I nodded. "I'll look at the machine and have a chat with him."

"None of them listen to me," she admitted, slumping into her chair.

"Join the club," I said, laughing.

The door burst open behind me. My mother's voice boomed through seemingly half the town, "I'm here!"

My beautiful mother enjoys making a good entrance. The first thing I always notice about her is her thick, wavy black hair and blue eyes. And the halo floating above her head on most days. Always dressed to the nines. That day, she wore black pants with a white blouse covered by a white apron that tried but couldn't hide a shiny gold belt. Her black high heels were a size below circus stilts and her earrings of linked crosses dangled to her shoulders like small weathervanes.

"Give me a kiss," she said, admiring my handsomeness, and then engulfing me in a hug.

I did as I was told.

She pinched my cheek and said, "Such a handsome boy. Is it wrong of me to say since you look like me? It's a wonder you're not married already."

I groaned, wondering if she just broke the record on how quickly she brought up my lack of a life partner. "Please, not today, Ma. Why are you still wearing your apron?"

My mother pulled Rebecca in for a hug. "Your father likes his veal nice and hot. I took it straight from the oven."

"You cook in this?" Rebecca asked, admiring her blouse.

"When you find the one you love, you want to take care of them and be wanted by them. Plus, I have to save my animal print for when I'm feeling frisky."

I threw up in my mouth and then managed to say, "Tell him to put it in the microwave. You're gonna kill yourself running around in those shoes. And me with your T.M.I."

My mother nodded to me as she spoke to Rebecca. "He used to try on my shoes when he was a kid. And my bras."

Rebecca laughed while I said, "Thank you for that, mother. Always so helpful."

"I want to take care of your father. Someday you'll have a

wife who cooks for you like I do for your father. The key to an Italian man's heart is through his stomach."

"I don't need to know that, Ma. I need to know the key to a woman's heart."

Rebecca said, "It's through his tongue."

My mother chuckled. "She's not wrong. Your father, well, he's not the best down there, but—"

"Ma, please. Geez, can we talk about something else? Let's get Dad his veal before it gets cold."

She headed toward the door, key fob in the air. "Help me get the food."

My mother didn't cook for us every day. It was Fat Friday. At least that's what I called it. My mother brought lunch for the entire crew every Friday. Trays and trays of salad, pasta, and something parmigiana-ed. It didn't matter what it was. Throw some breading, sauce, and cheese on it and it was amazing.

We stepped outside into the crisp November air, a blue sky overhead, and made our way toward her black Cadillac parked illegally in front of the building.

"So, how's Natalia?" my mother asked, popping the trunk. Her halo faded.

I was too annoyed to enjoy the marvelous scent of my mother's sauce emanating from the trunk. I answered in a huff, "Ma, I told you we're not together. We're just not compatible." I prayed to Saint Monica, the Patron Saint of Patience, who is also pretty much out of patience with the rest of my family.

"I thought you were going to propose?"

I grunted as I picked up a box of four tin catering trays. Even though I'm in great shape, she cooked for a small army. "I was absolutely NOT going to propose to her. I don't love her. We broke up months ago. You know this."

"I'm waiting for you to realize you made a mistake." She

held the door for me as we returned and then lovingly slapped the back of my head.

I held back a growl. "I won't settle just because you want me to get married. I haven't found the right person. I want to love and live my life fully. Do you want me to get divorced?"

My mother led me into the break room, waving my concern away. "We don't get divorced. We make excuses that the church will accept for annulment. Don't worry, you'll meet the perfect Italian girl. I just know it," she said with a twinkle in her eye.

I navigated two large tables and plopped the food on the counter beside the tiled sink.

I turned to my mother to see a dartboard with my face on it, the likely doings of my brother, Benny (Benito), and cousin, Frankie. "Can we talk about something else? What's going on in your life?"

"Oh, don't get me started. Your father ate some of Nonna's mustache removal concoction. Again."

I rolled my eyes. "Why don't you just buy the Nair stuff in a tube? Why does Nonna have to cook it on the stove? You know he can't resist what you both cook."

"It's more potent. After an Italian woman turns forty…we grow hair in places…just forget about it."

I pushed the thought from my mind and began opening the containers while my mother grabbed the plates and silverware from the cabinets.

"So, what happened with Natalia again? She's pretty and sweet, and from a good family."

I sighed and waited for my anger to subside before answering. "Ma, I think we need to take you to the doctor to get your memory checked. We've been over this. Twice just this morning. I don't love her. She doesn't love me. I want to feel more than physical attraction to a nice person. I want to find a love where you just know you have to be with that person forever. Where you're just...drunk in love with that person."

"Your father farts the alphabet in his sleep. Is that intoxicating love for you or what?"

I slapped some salad onto my plate. "Seriously, Ma. Where you would do anything for that person, anything just to be with that person."

"Your Papa was like that. He used to stare at Nonna's meatballs, hearts in his eyes. You know, the ones stuffed with gabagool. With a little ricotta on top."

"I'm serious."

My mother removed her apron and tossed it across a chair. "Okay. Okay. And Natalia doesn't do that for you?"

"With Natalia, there's no gabagool. No ricotta. Yeah, she's got the meat, but I want it all. We both agreed we weren't right for each other. I promise you, I want nothing more than to have kids and get married."

"Not in that order," she said firmly.

I laughed. "I didn't list them in order. Ma, I gotta go. Thanks for lunch. I can't eat with the family today. I need to prep for a meeting with Pop."

"Make sure he respects your ideas. You're such a smart boy. You'll be running this place one day. I'll see you on Sunday, my love."

I filled the rest of my plate with veal and a little linguini, kissed my mother goodbye, and headed back out front to Rebecca like a salmon swimming upstream, slipping around and between the salivating lunch crowd.

"Becs, can you bring me October's numbers before you grab lunch? I gotta prep for my meeting with Pop."

She held a stack of papers up. "Not sure you want to see these."

"That bad, huh?"

She just scrunched up her nose as a response and handed them over. At least she didn't fake hurl.

"Why are they so bad?" Rebecca asked.

"PremaPrint is discounting heavily. We lost two accounts."

"We gotta do something."

I nodded. "That's what my meeting with my father is about. We have to get with the times and start advertising online."

"Good luck with that."

I headed into my office and pored over the numbers while I ate. Nonna would've been upset with how little I ate, but the numbers were that nauseating. I couldn't remember the last month they were that bad. The silver lining was that at least it gave me ammo to help me shift my father's thinking, and I was gonna need a lot of firepower.

One thing you have to know about my father is that he's old school. There's a certain way to do things and you don't change them. Even if the business is getting pummeled, apparently. He is a tough man to get to know and to get through to.

But I had to stand up to him. I promised myself I would. It was time he allowed our business to enter the next generation. Our new reality. Printing was a tough business. Consolidation going on all around us. Rising paper costs. Geographic borders widening. And that was before the family drama.

Just before the meeting, I slipped into the bathroom, splashed some water on my face, and stared at myself in the mirror. "It's my time. Be strong. You're a smart boy." I rolled my eyes, and tried to shake my mother's voice from my head.

A voice echoed from the stall behind me, "You got this, bro!"

I nearly crapped in my pants. "Jesus, Benny. Why are you always in here?" Meet meatball number one, my brother, Benito.

"I have irritable bowels."

"You're allergic to hard work is what it is." I shook my head as I left.

"Good luck, bro! You got this!"

Just as I was heading into the meeting, my phone rang. It was meatball number two, my sister Gianna.

"Yo, sis."

"Can you watch the kids tonight? Sal and I want to go out."

"Hello, to you, too. Can't tonight. I'm going out."

"Please? We never get to. I already have reservations at Alberto's."

"You always go out. And Mom's on my case again about getting married."

"So, go out tomorrow night. Please? I'm begging. I need a break. You love the kids, don't you?" She went straight for my jugular. I adore my nieces and nephew.

"Of course. More than you. Like your kids are Alberto's and you're Olive Garden."

She whined a drawn out, "Pleeeease?"

I huffed and let out a retaliated, "Fiiiine."

"Thanks, big bro. You're the best."

"Mm, hmm." I stuffed my phone into my pocket with another huff and whispered, "Just livin' my best life. Can't even stand up to my sister."

I took a few minutes for myself outside, psyching myself up. I headed back in at 2:00 and smacked myself in the face. *I gotta do this. For my future. For the family's future.*

The spectacular feast of Fat Friday was often dampened by a contentious meeting afterward with my father, current, but hopefully soon-to-be outgoing, CEO of Donati Printing. Today would be worse than usual. As I walked into the meeting room, my father grunted his typical caveman greeting from his seat at the head of the table. casual Fridays did not exist in my father's world. He wore a blue pinstripe, double-breasted suit and a five o'clock shadow that had been casting since breakfast.

I leaned over and kissed him on the cheek as I passed behind him. We Italians are complex beings. We're tough on the exterior, but not afraid to kiss another man. I don't really know why that is.

He grunted, which in the old tongue means, "Good tidings, my favorite child. You are a blessing to us all." Or at least that's my translation. He then added, "The toilet's clogged. Your chooch brother dropped a strunza." Actual translation: your dumbass brother clogged the toilet with an enormous shit. Take care of it.

Fabulous. I slipped into the chair caddy corner to him. "We have a shittier situation to deal with, Pop. October financials."

"What are you wearing?" He eyed my jeans, sneakers, and t-shirt with distaste.

"What? It's casual Friday."

Pop furrowed his brow. "What is that?"

"We've had casual Fridays for six years."

He ignored my response. "Where's your suit?"

"I haven't worn a suit here on a regular day ever, let alone a Friday."

"Where's your pinky ring?" His eyes darted back and forth between my hands.

"Men my age don't wear pinky rings, Pop."

"Oh, forgot. The thumb ring. So chic." He pronounced it chick.

"I don't wear jewelry, except for my gold cross. Pop, you're stalling."

He rubbed his hand across the top of his thinning hair. "How bad are the numbers?"

My knee bounced with nervousness. "We need to shake things up. Do something different. I haven't seen numbers this bad since the last recession. We're behind in the market-place. We have to eat or be eaten. Have you seen how many small and medium-sized print shops like ours have been bought up?"

"Donatis don't give up. We fight for what's right. For what's ours."

"You can still wear your double-breasted suits, but we have to join the 21st century and use the tools that are available to us. And that our competitors are using against us."

Pop looked down at his suit jacket. "What's wrong with double-breasted?"

"Well, nothing if you're a woman, but in suits? They went out with John Gotti in the 80s. And the more important issue is the business. We need to invest in online advertising at a minimum, new digital printers, maybe even 3-D printers as a new business line. I want...we need five thousand dollars for a social media campaign."

"No."

I threw my hands into the air. "No? Why not?"

"Because we build relationships with our customers. One on one. We don't share sauce recipes on FaceTwit."

I laughed. I think he was kidding, but I'd bet he didn't know the real names anyway. "First of all, Mom would kill me if I posted her sauce recipe online. I think she has it protected by blockchain now. But seriously, though, it's to *advertise* on social media. We can slice and dice our audiences in a way that advertisers salivate over. Not recipes. Not dumb videos of people dancing. We can put our business offering in front of likely customers and measure the response. We can stop wasting money on billboards or placemats at the diner. We can calculate an actual return on investment for our advertising. Not just guess."

"Are you stunad? There's no relationship with online advertising."

"I'm stunad?" I stood up, attempting to control my anger, but failed miserably. My voice rose two decibels. "You can generate leads online and then meet them in person, ya chooch!"

"No."

I slumped into my chair and stared at the ceiling. "No? $2500. I can at least give you some proof of concept for that."

"No."

He's always stubborn, but this was extreme. "Why? It's only $2500. We waste that in Benny and Frankie's salaries each week."

"Should we go out back and burn $2500?"

"How do you know it won't work unless you try it?"

"I know shit tastes like shit without taking a bite."

"You're stuck in the past, Pop. Everything you worked for is going down the tubes."

"I got it under control. And we made more money this year than last."

I shook my head. "We had to fire two people at the south shore facility. How long can we cut costs before we cut into bone? Cutting costs is not a way to prosperity. We need to grow," I said, place heavy emphasis on the last word.

My father just stared at me, so I continued, "This business is killing you, Pop. At least taking your hair." I nodded to his Charlie-Brown like patches atop his head. I didn't want to say it, but I forced myself to. "It's my time to run this business. We have to adapt. We need more technology. It's the natural time for me to take over."

"Is that so?" Pop asked, leaning back in his chair, arms crossed.

"Papa came here with nothing. Worked on the docks in Brooklyn, then started this business. Gave it to you. You took us from two facilities to seven. Now, it's time for me to lead us into the digital age. If we don't, everything you built is going to crash and burn. I've done everything you've ever asked. You want me to unclog the toilet. I do it. You want me to go on a date with an Italian chick I have nothing in common with. I do it. You need me to fire two people because we failed. I do it."

I pushed the financials in front of him. "Look at these numbers! Tell me I'm wrong. Tell me we'll be here in two years if we keep going down this path. The economy is booming, yet our numbers are worse than the 2008 recession. What gives?"

My father looked at the numbers and grunted.

"Pop, can you elaborate a little? I know you find communicating tough, but maybe your caveman self can toss a painting up on the cave wall once in a while so the rest of us could figure out what's going on?"

He studied the numbers for a long while. "Leo, you've always done great work here. I'll think about it," was all he said, pushing the financials back to me.

I tried to hide my excitement. It was my time. Pop was always quick to say no, so when he didn't, it was usually good news. I grabbed the papers and kissed him on top of the head. "Love you, Pop." The thing about my family was that no matter how heated it got, we still loved each other, and we tried to keep it that way.

CHAPTER
Two

I KEPT a low profile for the next week, awaiting my father's response, but he was barely around. My mother had no info for me, either. She wouldn't know until the rest of us did. My guess was that the good news would be a family announcement. Could it be at Sunday dinner? We rarely talked business at the dinner table, but it was the gathering place for all big Donati family announcements. And this was big. I was going to be CEO of our family business. The business that made the American Dream a reality for our family.

But before we get to dinner, I have to tell you something pretty classified. The government suppressed a scientific fact many years ago and has kept it hidden from the public for decades. It's called the 'Italian family dinner effect'. It's like the butterfly effect but amplified by tons of spaghetti with meatballs stuffed with gabagool. Why is there a rise in global warming? It's not fossil fuels. It's the demise of the Italian family dinner. So much hand gesturing goes on at a family dinner, that it changes weather patterns. As Italian Americans move away from the family dinner, less wind had been created to cool the world. Everyone is focused on shutting down pipelines and emasculating themselves by driving

Priuses when we should reestablish the importance of the Italian family dinner. So, tune up your reflexes, because the hands are about to take flight, and get ready to mangia.

My parents live in the house I grew up in. It serves as the meeting place for Sunday dinners and all family holidays. The white colonial sits at the end of a cul-de-sac, well kept, but plain, minus the enormous Italian flag that flapped in the fall breeze. The inside of our house also doubles as a shrine to the Virgin Mary with statues and pictures of Her at every turn. I'm not trying to say I'm as important, but it would be nice if there was a picture of me somewhere around the joint.

I took the stairs two at a time, a little extra sauce flowing through my veins, excited for the potential promotion, and headed inside. The sweet, pungent smell of sizzling garlic danced through the air. I kicked off my shoes at the door and headed into the kitchen.

"There he is!" my mother yelled, stuffing a tray of chicken parmigiana into the oven.

I gave her a kiss and headed toward Nonna, dressed all in black, who greeted me by launching a fist full of spaghetti at my head. Well, I'm not sure she was really aiming for me. I ducked and smiled as the spaghetti splattered against and stuck to the cream wall. "Hey, Sandy Koufax," I said, referring to the great Brooklyn Dodgers pitcher. "Don't mess with the hair."

I leaned down to give Nonna a kiss. My Nonna is one of the sweetest women in the world, short and stout with grey, curly hair, and fewer wrinkles than you might expect for a woman in her 80s, but she also has the grip strength of a mountain climber. She grabbed my neck with her vice grip and kissed me on both cheeks. She spoke in a broken English accent, "Leonardo, I-va missed you."

I pretended like I didn't need a neck brace and a round of physical therapy and said, "Nonna! You been working out? I feel like you might be able to pop a soda can with your bare hands." *Or my head.* I produced a white paper bag from my back pocket. "I've got your pills."

I tossed her medicine onto the table and plopped into a seat at the kitchen table while Nonna and my mother navigated the sizzling and boiling pots and pans on the stove.

I said, "You wanna hear something weird? I thought I saw Uncle Michael at the pharmacy."

My mother dropped a wooden spoon dripping with sauce onto the counter. She signed the cross. "God rest his soul."

Nonna muttered curses in Italian.

I rolled my eyes. "Ma, he's not dead. He just married a Jew."

My mother returned to cooking. "He's dead to me. And she was very Jewish. Your grandmother died that day."

"Ma, she did not."

"She's dead inside. Look into her eyes. There's nothing in there."

I pointed to Nonna. "Don't be so dramatic. She's as adorable as always. What do you have against the Jews, anyway?"

"Nothing! Nothing. I just don't want your uncle's soul to burn in hell for all eternity. Every day, I pray to St. Anthony for your uncle's lost soul." My mother signed the cross again.

"Eternity. That's a long time."

"Shut up." My mother turned to me, pointing the spoon between my eyes. "Promise me you'll never do that to me."

I suppressed a smile. "Burn you in hell for all eternity? I would never do that to you."

My mother smirked. "Marry a sweet Italian girl who knows her way around a kitchen. I don't want to die like your grandmother."

"Okay. I promise I'll find a girl who knows her way around Italian meatballs and sausage."

She rolled her eyes and signed the cross again. "And you're the mature one."

Benny entered, nearly filling the doorway with his wide shoulders. He was a touch shorter than me and more muscular, but other than that, we looked a lot alike. He also fashioned enough hair product to keep a small manufacturing facility in a low-wage nation humming.

Benny's deep voice asked, "What's going on in here? You don't say hello?" Sometimes, I think he's faking, just to sound more manly. It's hard to tell, because, yes, he's that much of an idiot.

I shrugged. "I just got here, and we live together." I nodded to his tight black t-shirt, which was adorned with the customary Donati gold cross. "It's nice to see you're making sacrifices given the world-wide cotton shortage."

Benny flexed his pecs one after the other through his shirt, making them dance back and forth. "I need to share my art with the world."

My mother shook her head and then pointed the wooden spoon at me, sauce dripping from it. "Your brother is plotting to kill me."

I scoffed. "I am not."

Benny shrugged. "No, that's cool. Let me know if I can help."

My mother raised an eyebrow. "And then who would do your laundry for you at twenty-seven years old?"

"Good point. I'm out, bro. I can no longer be an accomplice to your heinous plan." He pronounced it 'high-anus' and then laughed. "What'd you do?"

"Nothing. I was just talking about Uncle Michael."

"Ooh. I want no part of this. Arrivederci, dumbass." Benny disappeared, which was often one of my favorite things he did, especially since he and Frankie moved into my apartment with me.

My mother's comments stung. They weren't right, and I wasn't finished. I knew she wouldn't budge, but maybe Nonna would. They came from the same Sicilian stock, so it wasn't overly likely, but I tried anyway. "Nonna, you're telling me...it's 1957, the Brooklyn Dodgers are moving to L.A. A very Jewish Sandy Koufax is down on one knee, his golden left arm and boyish grin beaming in the sun, and he says, 'Nonna, come with me. Marry me. Let's make beautiful, but religiously confused babies together.' You say no?"

"I-a do."

My voice rose an octave. "Because he's Jewish? That's ridiculous. He's Sandy Koufax."

Benny called out from the other room. "I'd marry Sandy Koufax."

I threw my hands up. "See? Your son would be gay for a Jewish man. God, I'd hate to see how you'd handle that." I turned to Nonna. "You're holding firm on this? I thought you were the reasonable one here."

Nonna weighed my question. "If he convert, I-a think about it."

I waved her words away. "Ah, blow it out your ass, Nonna. You're full of it. If he was Christian, you'd be all over Sandy Koufax like sauce on spaghetti."

Nonna smiled and picked up a wooden spoon, brandishing it menacingly. "You wanna the spoon, eh, you mamaluke?"

I nearly fell out of my chair. "Hey! That's not right. You know how much physical and psychological damage that spoon has caused me since childhood?"

My mother slipped the chicken parmigiana from the oven and lay it on top of a trivet. "Kids today. They need more spoon. You see how wild your sister's kids are?"

"Ma, it's not because she doesn't beat them with a spoon. It's because she's a terrible parent."

My mother shrugged. "Maybe it's both. Dinner is almost ready. Gather everyone at the table."

I did as I was told. There were thirteen of us for dinner every Sunday. My parents, Nonna, Benny and me. Gianna was married to Sal, and they had three kids: Viola, 6, Mia, 5, and Matteo, 3. Then there was Uncle Freddy and Aunt Franny, and my cousin, Frankie, who worked with us and lived with me, typically rent free.

Everyone gathered around the table amid laughter and loud conversation. I helped Matteo into his seat as the girls climbed into theirs. My mother and Nonna slipped into the room with overflowing plates and bowls.

My mother eyed Benny, Frankie, and me. "Stay away from the corners."

Benny rolled his eyes. "Ma, we know."

"I don't need any bad luck. I need you three married."

I don't believe in any of it, but apparently, it's bad news to be single and sit at the corner of a table, at least according to Italians. My father always sat at the head of the table with Nonna and my mother at his sides. The single men sat in the middle and everyone else filled in around us.

Matteo took his napkin and threw it onto the floor with a giggle.

"Hey, you," I said with a smile, before picking it up and placing it on top of his wavy black hair, so it covered his eyes. More giggles. I slipped into my seat, ready to mangia like a gavon, or savage to the non-Italian.

My mother continued, "It's bad enough we have thirteen seated around this table. We need a bigger family." She looked directly at me, because, well, if you added up the maturity levels of both Benny and Frankie, you might get into double digits in age.

Benny raised his eyebrows at me. "Last one seated, bro. That makes you Judas."

I forked some sausage onto my plate. "Sure. Whatever." Just so you know, thirteen is actually a lucky number for Italians, unless sitting around a table. I know, it's weird. Supposedly, it's because Jesus had twelve apostles, and as the Last

Supper began, Judas, the man who betrayed Jesus, was the last one seated. This is how we live our lives.

We all dug into our meals as conversations broke out in different sections of the table, as forks, knives, and spoons clanked against china. Mia stared at the food on her plate.

"What's wrong, sweetheart?" I asked.

"My cheese is too gooey. I don't like it."

Nonna interrupted, "It all-a go down-a the same-a way."

"What does that mean?" Mia asked.

Gianna said, "It means Nonna said to just eat it."

Mia made a face, but did what she was told.

As soon as we licked our plates clean, my father cleared his throat and said, "I have an announcement."

I straightened up. My pulse thumped. This was it. This was my moment. All I've ever known, all I've ever wanted, everything I had worked so hard for, was about to become mine. I suppressed a smile as the conversations petered out and we turned our attention to our patriarch.

My father swirled what was left of his red wine and downed it. "I'm selling the business."

My mother's eyes widened in shock. Aunt Franny gasped. My siblings were dumbfounded, although that is kind of their default. The children demanded cake.

I, on the other hand, couldn't move. Couldn't breathe. I'd never felt anything like what I felt at that moment. Pain. Anger. Confusion. All amplified and intertwined. Have you ever been disemboweled? Well, neither have I, but this is how I imagine it would feel like. Then the fury pushed the pain and confusion to the side, like 'Hold my beer, bitches,' as my brain tried to compute the relentless stream of questions surging into my head. *How could he do this to me? Why would he do this to me? Why doesn't he ever listen to me? What's wrong with me?*

"And when were you going to tell us?" my mother asked, glaring at Pop.

"I just did."

I blurted out, "How could you do this to me? To us?"

"This is what's best for the family."

I spat back without thinking, "Oh, it is, is it? Well, maybe it wouldn't have been had you actually listened to my ideas to build the business. I came into this business because you wanted me to. I could've studied anything. Done anything. I did this for the family. And this is what you do? Make me dedicate the last ten years of my life to this dying business because you asked me to and now you're gonna sell it out from underneath me just before it's my turn to take over?"

I stood up, slammed my hands on the table, and swallowed a colorful array of curse words for the children's sake. Plates and silverware clanked. Matteo burst out into tears.

"Leonardo," my mother gasped.

My father's voice boomed, "Sit. Down. I said this is what's best for this family. End of story."

I had to fight my desire to flip the entire table as my whole family stared at me like it was the World Cup and I was about to take a penalty kick to decide the game. I wanted to storm out of there and just be alone, but everyone looked to me as an example. I took a deep breath and did what I was told. I sat down slowly. Painfully slow, eyeing Pop with the Sicilian Stare, the most intense glare found anywhere around the globe. I crossed my arms and decided then and there that I would quit the business as soon as possible.

CHAPTER
Three

REBECCA PICKED up coffee from the new place around the corner, Sugar Cube, to drown our sorrows in. I would've preferred my mother's garlic butter Italian sausage sandwich, my go-to comfort food, but whatever. Caffeine has magical powers, too. I'm sure my mother would've fired up a grill in the fire lane outside the building had I asked, but it was 8:00 in the morning on a frigid Monday in November.

"I just don't understand," Rebecca said.

I don't know what the stages of family betrayal are, or if there are any, but I'd moved from anger to apathy. I stared at the logo of a sugar cube on my cup. "The old man has lost his mind. I have no other answers."

"What did he say?"

"He said, 'I'm selling the business. Kiss my ass, Leo and future Donati generations.' And then he gave the kids double middle fingers and said, 'That means you three, you little bastards.'"

Rebecca chuckled. "He did not."

"Maybe I'm exaggerating. A little. He only tripped Viola. And then rubbed her face in the carpet, yelled, 'Eat it!' and finished with a maniacal laugh."

"Seriously, what are you gonna do?"

"I'm quitting. Giving him six months' notice." I shook my head, uncertain. "I don't know how this is all gonna play out. With me gone, you'll be a lot more valuable, but if you want to leave, I'll support you. Whatever you decide." I sighed.

"I'm not leaving you."

"Maybe I can convince him to change his mind, but if I don't, I'm outta here."

"To do what?"

I shrugged. "Become a shepherd. I feel like nobody's doing that anymore. It could be lucrative if people buy their own livestock again. Or maybe I'll shave my head and become a monk."

"Your hair is too nice for that."

"I know. It's fitting, though, as it will just add to the tragedy." I downed my coffee and tossed it at the garbage pail but missed. "Just livin' my best life." I nodded toward my father's office through the wall. "He'll be here soon. I think he wants to address, well, pretty much you, since nearly everyone else was at dinner yesterday afternoon."

"Why do you eat dinner at 2:00 again?"

"Nobody knows. You just stop asking questions after a while. There's too much to keep track of with all the rules and superstitions. Anyway, don't be surprised if he wants to chat with you, and I promise you, I have some words for him."

Rebecca stood up and patted me on the shoulder. "Well, good luck. Let me know what he says."

"You'll probably just hear us screaming."

Rebecca laughed. "What else is new? That's pretty much our de facto communication system around here." She feigned a conversation. "Did you get the memo? Yeah, I heard Pop and Leo screaming about it."

Twenty minutes later, I burst into my father's office, anger replacing apathy for the moment, with a resignation letter tucked inside a manilla folder. He looked up at me like it was just another Monday. Not the Monday after he ruined my life.

I slipped into the leather chair across from his desk.

"You don't say hello to your old man?"

"I have other things to say. Pop, we have to talk more about this sale. Why are you doing this?" I demanded.

My father banged the wooden desk with a smack of his hand. "Are you that stunad that you can't figure it out? The industry's changing."

"I've been saying that the whole time! I'm the stunad? You never listen to any of my ideas. You keep doing old economy shit in a completely new world. You gave away my future. I earned this."

My father rubbed his face with his hands. "Sorry. I'm a little on edge. Your mother is pissed at me. You don't cross that woman."

"Thirty years and you're just figuring that out now?" I laughed, pathetically. "She has a right to be pissed. So do I, Pop. We can make this place better. I can make it better. I really don't understand why you're doing this."

He shrugged. "It's time to get out of this business."

"Just like that?"

He nodded. "Proprio così."

I bit my lip as I figured out what to say, but all I could come up with was double middle fingers.

My father stared out the window and said, "Batti il ferro finché é caldo. Chi troppo vuole nulla stringe. We made hay while the sun shined, but you can't get too greedy."

"I don't understand why this is happening."

Pop said, "My grandmother used to say, 'Non tutte le ciambelle riescono col buco.'"

I scratched my head, confused. I never really spoke Italian, just picked things up from my elders. "Not all doughnuts come out with a hole? What the hell does that mean?"

"Not everything turns out as planned."

I took a deep breath to steady my emotions. "So, what *is* the plan?"

My father shrugged. "Cash out and buy a place in Sicily for the winter, or maybe Boca."

"Raton? Have you lost your mind?" I threw my head back and stared at the ceiling. "Oh, that's rich. Mom's going to retire to the Jewish capital of America after everything that happened with Uncle Michael? Ridiculous."

I leaned forward, resting on the edge of my father's desk for one last plea. I didn't want to quit. I didn't want this place to be sold. "Pop, you've earned the right to take a step back and enjoy the fruits of your labor. Take Mom to Boca if that makes you two happy. But let me handle the business. You can't take this away from me."

"I've already given you my answer. End of story." He straightened his already-perfect tie. It was his power move.

"It's always 'end of story' when you don't want to talk anymore." I locked my eyes on his, but he looked away. *Is he hiding something?* "What are you not telling me?"

"There's nothing more to tell."

I swallowed hard and stared at the folder in my hand. I slipped the resignation letter in front of my father. My voice shook as I spoke. "Well then, I have no other choice than to quit. Rebecca can step up if you want me to leave immediately, or I can stay on for a few months until you find someone to replace me."

His face contorted, but he said nothing. We sat in silence for a moment until he spun the paper back my way. It slipped off the edge of his desk and floated to the floor.

My father spun his pinky ring and eventually spoke. "You can't quit. Caleb and I had an agreement that my kids would still be employed."

"If I don't want to be here, then why would they care?"

"Because they're buying an asset and you're part of that

asset's value." He waved at me with the back of his hand like I was stunad.

My anger amplified. "Who are you to make deals regarding my employment without consulting me? Have you thought that maybe I don't want to work for someone else? Maybe I want to go run PremaPrint and drive *this* business into the ground. It won't be difficult. You're doing it for them already."

"Stop letting your ego get in the way of a good situation. Kane Printing is a great company. I've known Caleb for years. They're taking care of us."

I waved his words away. "They're like all the others. A bunch of chop shops. We might as well move our offices next to the rest of them by Citi Field. I don't want any part of this deal. I'm supposed to be CEO of this company after you, not an employee of Kane Printing."

Pop said, "There is no 'supposed to' in the business world. It changes by the moment."

"And yet we're stuck in the prehistoric town of Bedrock. You're Fred Flintstone and I'm Barney friggin' Rubble. And I hear the five o'clock whistle."

"Huh? It's 9:30."

"I meant, it's quitting time."

"Your responsibility is to this family. Not to yourself."

"Pop, shave your ear hair. I don't think you're hearing me. I'm not doing this."

"You'll do this for the family, because as the head of said family, I'm telling you it's best for us. All of us. End of story. You've never not lived up to the responsibility that I've placed on you. Don't disappoint me now. Capisce?"

I exhaled a shaky breath, my mind racing. *Family first. Always.* I could barely get the words out, "Yes, I understand. What do you need me to do?"

Pop nodded in approval. "I told Rebecca to have Kane's people in by Friday. We came to some high-level agreements in just a week, but you're going to go through the details. I need you to do this for the rest of the family. Show them your value. Make up for the rest of the mamalukes."

"So, what did you already agree to? How much are they paying us?"

"They're paying me four times worst case."

I scoffed. "Four times EBITDA? This is a terrible deal for the family." If you happen to be businessly challenged, EBITDA means earnings before interest, taxes, depreciation, and amortization. And four times was massively under-valuing our company, even with the current stress we were under.

"It could be six if we meet certain hurdles. They have a due diligence process that you'll work with them on."

"Have you looked around here? They're gonna see your brother, your son, your nephew sitting on their asses all day, playing cards, and giving each other wedgies. And don't get me started on the financials…"

"It will work out. Like I said, I've known Caleb for years. It's a good fit. His kid is gonna handle the deal on their end."

"Sometimes, I wish you'd communicate more and then you say stupid shit like this. I like it better when you have nothing to say."

"I always do what's right for this family."

"No. I think you're confusing yourself with me. I'll get the deal done, but it's best *for the family* if you stay out of my way." I stood up and stomped to the door, controlling the urge to punch through the wall.

My father sighed, "Leo…wait."

I didn't.

CHAPTER

Four

THIS DEAL WAS terrible for the family. If my father was intent on getting a deal done, I was equally intent on making sure it wouldn't happen. If I couldn't convince him not to sell, I'd simply convince Kane Printing not to buy. But I had to be smart about it. I'd have to shine the spotlight in a few key directions and they'd get the hint without me being blamed for the doomed deal's downfall. But I'd need some help from some unwitting accomplices.

I walked from my office to the print facility in the back. The floor shook from the hum of the presses in action. I nodded to Jim Garrison as he fixed a paper jam and waved to Carli Bond, our graphic designer, who was not busy designing anything. Where were Benny and Frankie? A print shop is typically pretty loud, but I've found that my brother and cousin are louder and when they're missing, just follow the noise. In this case, that noise emanated from the loading dock. I smelled nothing out of the ordinary, so at least nothing was on fire.

Flacco, Joey Bagels, and Rico, our soon-to-be fired employees, cheered around Benny and Frankie as they sliced, parried, and dodged each other's blows from makeshift swords of heavy cardboard.

I huffed, but wasn't surprised.

Benny unleashed a savage blow at Frankie's head. He ducked and barely replaced his face with his sword, but because the only work Benny does is in the gym, the blow knocked the sword from Frankie's hand. It toppled bottom over top and then rolled under one of our Speedmaster offset printing machines, no doubt never to be retrieved. Benny aimed his sword between Frankie's eyes. "Swear your fealty to me now and you shall live!"

Frankie threw his hands up. "I yield."

The crowd cheered and exchanged dollar bills.

I placed my hands on their shoulders and forced a smile at each of them. "I see you fine gentlemen are working hard, as always. How about you take a well-deserved break and we grab a bite of lunch together?"

"Your terms are acceptable," Frankie said. "I was getting bored with this, anyway. I enjoy jousting better. Swing by tomorrow. We've got a week-long tournament lined up."

"Can't wait." I led them to the front, resisting the urge to pummel them with a cardboard sword.

Benny said, "Let's go to Hooters."

"I second that," Frankie added.

I rolled my eyes. "No."

Benny's face contorted. "You'd rather have flat-chested women serve you mediocre food?"

I laughed. "No. I don't care about the cup size of the woman, or man, for that matter, serving me my food, and I'd also rather eat good food than mediocre. Plus, I don't want to watch you two drool and make fools of yourselves, either. Although you don't seem to limit that behavior only to Hooters." I'd bet serious money that if the two stunads took a DNA test, they'd be more neanderthal than Italian.

Benny nodded. "Yeah, we're pretty much fools all the time."

I rubbed my hands together in my mind and whispered, "And the perfect men for the job."

"What job? We already have jobs we don't do."

Oops. I shook my head, not realizing I'd spoken the words out loud. "Nothing."

Within ten minutes, we were seated at Tonnino's, one of our favorite fast Italian places. Pizza, heros (not subs, grinders, or hoagies), and your standard parmigianas and oreganatas.

Tony Tonnino's daughter, Sophia, gave us menus and freshly baked bread with some olive oil and herbs on a plate.

Benny's eyes followed her as she attended to another table. "I love those brown eyes. I would ask her out, but the food's too good here to mess it up."

"Don't you guys get tired of chasing tail?" I grabbed some bread and dipped it into the oil as I scanned the menu.

"Not particularly, no." Benny turned to Frankie. "Do you?"

"That's a negatory. The question is, why are you tired of it?"

"I have no interest in chasing a woman just for sex. I want to get married. Have a family. I don't care how much she can stuff into a tank top or booty shorts. I want to find the right woman for me and make a commitment to her for life."

Benny cocked his head. "You sound confused."

"How so?"

"I've never heard a dude talk like that."

"Never," Frankie added. "You sound like maybe you want to make that commitment to another man."

I looked at Benny. "Oh, shut up. I'm serious. Building a family. Building a life with the right woman. I take that seriously. Someday, we're gonna be running this family and I plan on doing it right."

Benny's eyes stared down at his pants, admiring the view with a smile. "I'm pitching a serious pants tent."

I rolled my eyes. "Correction: someday, I'm gonna be running this family. And we're not gonna have Sunday dinners at Hooters."

Frankie slammed his menu shut. "That sucks."

Benny shook his head and spoke with his mouth half full, "Whatever. I don't even think they have pasta there."

We ordered chicken, meatball, and eggplant heros, sliced for the three of us to share, and some calamari arabiatta, one of my favorites. The cherry peppers kick it up a notch. Delizioso.

As the food disappeared, with none of us stopping to breathe, I realized it was time to accomplish what I set out to do. I was just gonna dangle the hook and see if I could catch some fish. "Has Mom said anything about the sale? I haven't been able to muster the energy to talk to her about it."

Benny shook his head. "Not much. She's pretty upset. Everyone's really surprised."

I shrugged. "Yeah, well, it was typical Dad. No communication and then, bam!" I mocked him, 'It's best for the family. End of story.' But it's a terrible deal. And it's unnecessary."

Benny said, "Somebody should do something. I don't want to work for someone else."

Hook inserted. "You use the term 'work' very loosely, but neither do I. You know, there's a lot of leverage to be had at a time like this for those who see the opportunity. If only I wasn't management, I would probably strike or something. If they showed up and the team was on strike, game over. But my hands are tied. Dad asked me to get the deal done. I have to do what's right for the family." I rolled my eyes when I said, "End of story."

Benny and Frankie eyed each other and seemingly suppressed smiles.

Benny raised an eyebrow. "When's the meeting?"

I shrugged. "I don't know. Friday morning, I think. 10:00." This time, I was the one suppressing a smile. The funny thing was, they'd probably print picket signs back at the shop, something they don't do even when paid.

Sophia slipped the bill on the table, thanked us quickly, and hustled away, seemingly to avoid the lusty stares and inappropriate comments from Benny and Frankie.

"You ever wonder why she never tells us to come again?" Frankie asked.

Benny smiled. "I would love for her to say that to me."

"Yeah, it's a real conundrum." I picked up the bill and checked the math. "Okay, it's twenty each."

Benny tapped his pockets. "Oh, umm…I'm a little short."

"Me, too," Frankie said, shrugging as if he had no idea what had happened to all his money.

I pulled out my wallet. "No problem. I'll cover lunch if you guys pay your share of the rent this month."

Benny raised a finger. "Wait a second…" He and Frankie pulled out their wallets. "You know what? I won that bet from Joey Bagels." They each tossed twenty-dollar bills onto the table.

I stared at them with an exaggerated smirk. "I thought so. You still owe me the rent. And last month's, too."

Benny laughed. "Good one, bro."

———

I had an early client meeting on Friday morning, so I didn't get to the office until about 9:45. Our office was smack dab in the middle of a grubby industrial area, seemingly inspired by Henry Ford's vomit on his architect's desk, but the scene couldn't have been more beautiful that morning. Benny, Frankie, Uncle Freddy, Flacco, Joey Bagels, Jim, and Rico paraded in front of the building, waving signs and chanting, "What's outrageous? Sweatshop wages!" A ten-foot inflatable rat, typically saved for Manhattan construction union pickets, flapped in the breeze. It was an elegant touch. I wasn't often proud of my brother, but the effort was nice to see.

I approached the stunads, readying myself for a performance. "Oh, no. Don't strike. This is terrible. What're we going to do? And the Kane's will be here within the hour." I ran my fingers through my hair, feigning deep distress, and then nodded to Benny. "Are you behind this?"

"You know it."

I exhaled a long, slow breath. "What are your demands?"

"Demands? Oh, right." Benny eyed Frankie, who shrugged in response.

I groaned inwardly.

Benny surveyed the rest of the crew. "What do we want?"

Joey Bagels yelled, "We want respect!"

Frankie pumped his fist in the air. "When do we want it?"

The crew chanted in unison, "We want it now!"

I nodded. "That's really helpful. Thank you." Before I could ask any clarifying questions, my father burst through the door with Rebecca on his heels.

Pop's voice boomed, "Hey, you mamalukes! Get inside! We got work to do!" It wasn't like one of his forehead vein-popping screams, but it was close.

"We're on strike!" Benny yelled, which was met with cheers from the crowd behind him.

"We're trying to sell the business, you idiot."

Benny threw up his hands, nearly smacking Frankie in the face, which was well deserved. "That's why I'm doing this. We've got leverage."

My father stormed toward Benny. "I'm gonna leverage your face off. Strike's over! End of story!"

Benny shook his head. "We can't do that, Pop."

My father eyed Frankie. "You agree?"

Frankie nodded, but said nothing.

My father twisted his pinky ring, examining the weaved

silver pattern and the black onyx stone as if he hadn't done it a million times. His eyes returned to Benny with a smile. He nodded. "Okay…well played. Or not. You're all fired."

The crowd gasped. Benny's eyes widened. He turned to the employees behind him, clapped his hands together, and said, "Okay, strike's over! This was a wonderful exercise. Back to work. Or just get back inside…"

Everyone stared at Benny, annoyed. He muttered, "They're not happy."

My father shrugged. "I imagine not."

"Can we at least have donuts?" Benny asked.

Pop nodded to me. "Management will buy the staff donuts. Go grab some. Capisce?" And then he addressed the crowd, "And somebody whack this rat."

I scoffed, more disappointed about the rat than the donuts, but unable to say so. "Make him get his own donuts."

"I don't trust him with a company credit card."

"Shocking."

"I'll go," Benny said to me. "Just give me your card. I'll take Becca for company. A little added sugar for the trip." He winked at her, but she recoiled in disgust.

"Everybody inside," I said, grabbing my brother's bulky arm. Only my father stayed behind, pacing off to the side. I whispered to Benny, "Dude, you can't do that. She's an employee."

"So am I."

"No, you're an…owner." It was hard to get the word out. "Act like one. She's not a bag of sugar. She's a woman who deserves your respect."

Benny shook his head. "If I'm an owner, where are my ownerships rights? My sharings."

"Your shares? When you kill your father with your stupidity, you'll inherit your shares."

"That hurts, bro."

"So does your stupidity."

Benny shrugged. "Not me."

I shook my head. "That's always how it works, bro."

"Won't I get paid when this deal is done?"

"You'll be lucky to keep your job when this deal is done."

"Dad said we're all keeping our jobs."

"Nothing's set in stone. Regardless, there's a line, dude. You can't cross it. Leave Rebecca alone. And try to treat all women with a little more respect."

Benny nodded and disappeared into the facility, leaving me alone with my father.

"We dodged a bullet, huh?" he asked.

"Yeah. Great." I forced a smile to conceal my treachery.

"Kane will be here soon. The next chapter of our lives begins!" My father patted me on the shoulder. "Hey, I just wanted to tell you…"

I wasn't ready to accept his apology, but I at least wanted to hear it. "Yeah, Pop?"

"Don't go to Dunkin' Donuts. Go to Bianco's. I want a Bomboloni. It's like a brick in your hand, but so light and fluffy in my belly." He slapped me on the shoulder and headed inside.

Just livin' my best life. I shook my head in annoyance and muttered, "I'm gonna Bomboloni this whole friggin' place."

CHAPTER
Five

THE MEETING GOT PUSHED BACK two hours, which gave me more time to let my agita fester. I had hoped Kane Printing's welcome strike would shut this stunad experiment down before it even started. There were other ways to break the deal, but it was gonna have to be more death by a thousand cuts rather than a killer blow.

I couldn't focus on the business and I had nothing scheduled because of the meeting's delay, so I distracted myself with the dating app Bumble, rejecting more than a few Italians just to stick it to my mother. I know, rule number two. I'll smack myself with a wooden spoon later.

My alarm went off ten minutes before the meeting, which meant it was time for another motivational bathroom session. Sounds weird, I know. I was thinking the same thing. I made a note to buy myself a mirror for my office as I slipped on my blue sport coat.

I stood in front of the bathroom mirror, staring back into my eyes. I took a deep breath, bopping my head to non-existent music. "I got this. This is my town."

Benny's voice yelled back, "This is your town!"

My heart jumped. "Ahhh! Dude!" I shook my head,

breathing deeply. "I gotta check the stalls before I do that. Are you almost done?"

"No. I'm turdsing."

"What the hell is that?"

"Turtle-heading. I made it up. I feel like it's more accurate."

"You're like a prisoner making pickaxes out of plastic forks. Had you put your creativity to good use, you could've been somebody."

"Thanks, bro."

I shook my head and started over, whispering, "This is my town. I'm from Strong Island. No Manhattan douche is gonna come in here and get the better of me." I flexed my bicep, half-hoping I'd tear the sleeve for added confidence, but got nothing. Since I was already there, I gave myself the sniff test and scored it a solid A-minus. It was time to get 'er done.

I stepped out into the hallway to find Joey Bagels, all 6'3" mountain of him, lumbering towards me. "Your mom is in the back and Rebecca said a dude named Ray Kane is here to see you."

"Thanks, Joe."

The bathroom door opened behind me, revealing Benny.

"You're done already?"

"Didn't go. Nonna's right. I need more fiber."

I stared at the ceiling. *Why do I even ask?* You'd think I'd be used to it by now. "Mom's here. I have a meeting with the Kane people, so can you see if she needs help?"

"Yep. I'd help Mussolini if he showed up with Mom's fettuccine."

"That's weird, bro." We made our way to the front. I stopped short. A stunning woman in a blue pants suit and a white blouse with matching pearls stared back at me with big, light brown eyes. Her wavy brown hair fell to her shoulders in sweeping curls.

Damn. Her boss knows how to pick 'em. I shook my head and changed my line of thinking. *I'm sure she's highly qualified.*

Benny leaned in and whispered, "Whoa. She really pushes the boner button, huh?"

"What the hell is that?"

"One look and she makes it go boing." Benny smiled at her and headed out to the parking lot. *Wrong way, idiot.*

Rebecca nodded to the woman and said to me, "Your meeting is here."

"Thanks, Becs," I said, my eyes still on the woman.

I straightened my jacket and approached with a smile and an outstretched hand. With heels, she was only a few inches shorter than me, and more beautiful with each step closer. My stomach roiled. "Hi. I'm, umm, I'm Rocco's son." I looked around. "Do you want to wait out here?"

She peered into the conference room. "For what? Is the room not ready?"

I shook my head. "For your boss. He could just meet us inside, or would that be rude to leave him out here by himself?"

The woman crossed her arms. "It's quite rude, but not why you think. *I'm* the boss. Why do you assume that just because I'm a woman that I can't be the boss?"

I stepped back. My brain overflowed with thoughts. None of them helpful. "Oh, I'm…terrible…terribly sorry. I didn't mean that. Joey Bagels told me I was meeting a guy named Ray. R.A.Y."

"I'm Rae. It's R.A.E."

I threw up my hands, feigning police capture. "Honest mistake. I've never met a woman named Rae before. I have met a woman named Chuck, though, which was very odd, especially since it was in the men's locker room at the gym." I thought for a moment. "Oh, wait. Man boobs." Rae stared back at me, unimpressed. "Sorry. Where were we?"

"Umm, moving on. Please, God."

"Right." I smacked the side of my head, hoping to fix the discombobulated circuits, but I don't think it worked.

Rebecca furrowed her brow in my direction as she asked, "Would you like me to show you to the conference room?"

"No. I got it Becs. Thanks."

She whispered, "What's wrong with your brain?"

I shook my head, not sure myself, and led the way into the conference room. I flipped on the lights and stepped aside to close the door behind Rae after she entered with her long strides, a brown leather bag slung over her shoulder. I'm sure it cost more than a few bucks.

"So, do you have a name, Rocco's son?"

Face palm. But before I could give it to her, there was a knock at the door. I rolled my eyes and as I opened the door a crack, I thought back trying to figure out if I had gotten myself in some sort of *Freaky Friday* mix up and switched brains with Benny or Frankie.

I peeked out the door to find Frankie, who attempted to walk in, but I held the door firm. His face smushed into the door crack. His words distorted, "Clan you open thah daw?"

Nope. No *Freaky Friday* incident with him. Still a stunad. "No. I'm in a meeting." I opened it a smidge, but pushed his forehead back.

Frankie looked past me, eyeing Rae. "Oh, I thought it was with a dude named Ray."

Rae glared at him, arms crossed. I offered her a sheepish smile and then turned back to Frankie. "What do you want?"

"The feed wheel on number three is sticking again. Can we change it out?"

"This is what you had to barge into my meeting for? Have Becs order it. Kindly extract your face from the crack."

He pulled back and laughed. "Ha, ha! That's dirty."

I shut the door and turned to Rae. "Sorry for the interruption." She eyed the oversized portrait of a haloed Jesus on the wall.

I smiled and nodded to The Man. "Don't mind him. He's on our board of directors."

She turned to me, eyebrow raised. "Why do you have a picture of Jesus on the wall?"

"We have to pray to him often after we look at our financials. You don't have one?"

"We're Jewish."

"So was Jesus. Although, I think my mother thinks he's Italian. I mean, he *was* big on bread and we own bread."

I went to grab the chair at the head of the table where my father typically sat, but she beat me to it. I looked around like an idiot, trying to figure out where to go, like I was playing musical chairs or something. I grabbed the seat caddy corner to her, half sat in it, then stood up. *Don't give her the power.* I ran my fingers through my hair nonchalantly. *Real smooth, ace.*

I nodded at the portrait of Jesus. "I'll get you one for your boardroom."

Rae shook her head. "Please...don't." She produced a laptop from her bag and opened it onto the table.

"What are you, an anti-Christite?"

"That's not a thing."

Okay. Stop acting like an idiot. She's hot, but so what? Time to get tough. I channeled my inner Stallone from Rocky IV. Beard stubble grew immediately and my six-pack deepened like a mountain crevasse. This was my Cold War, and I was ready to avenge the loss of my future.

"Something amusing?" Rae asked, eyebrow raised.

"Huh? Oh, I was just thinking of something funny. But playtime is over. Let's get down to business. I have to be honest. We are not just gonna roll over. My dad might be a nice guy. But you don't see him here negotiating, do you? This is my house. This deal comes through me." Was I laying it on too thick? I assessed her, attempting to glean something, anything, but she stared at me with a blank expression. I narrowed my eyes as if that would somehow help me read her better. See into her soul or something. But I'm terrible at poker. Most Italians are. When you grow up in a closely knit Italian community, dating only Italian women, there's just no evolutionary need to figure out what a woman is thinking or feeling. Every ounce of emotion is on display like a blaring neon sign on the darkest night.

Amid this epic stare down, the door creaked open. My mother's voice boomed, "Leo, my darling. You didn't say hello. I, at least, wanted to say goodbye to my handsome boy. There's fettuccine and chicken alfredo in the kitchen."

I huffed. "Ma, I'm in the middle of a meeting."

"Family is more important than business. Give me a kiss."

I could feel my cheeks redden as I sat there and tried to ignore Rae's chuckles. I glared at my mother and nodded to the door, but my telepathy failed me.

Instead, she walked toward me and said firmly, "Give your mother a kiss."

I rolled my eyes, rose from my chair, and gave her a kiss as quickly as I could. "Love you."

My mother grabbed my cheek, pinching down on it like a psychotic lobster.

I swallowed a yelp and pulled away.

"Isn't he so cute?" my mother asked Rae.

Rae suppressed a smile. "So cute."

She pinched my cheek again. "Faccia bella." If you don't know Italian, it's pronounced, 'fahtcha' and means face, and bella means beautiful. She might be embarrassing, but she's not dumb.

My mother continued, speaking to Rae, "These cheeks used to be chubby, but he got tired of being fat and lost the weight." She shook her head, disappointed. "Worst year of my life. Wouldn't touch pasta. Not a spaghetti or a fettuccine. No lasagna. I needed therapy." My mother's diarrhea of the mouth continued, but her focus turned to Rae. "Aren't you beautiful? Stunning, really. Isn't she, darling?"

I didn't know what to say, so I just nodded.

"If only you were Italian. You two would make beautiful babies."

Oh, God. There were crumbs on the floor bigger than my ego. I had to end this. "Mom, get out. I'm begging." She continued to stare at Rae. "Ma! Jesus."

My mother turned to me. "Don't take the Lord's name in vain!"

"I'm sorry, but this is a business meeting."

"Fine."

I whispered, "Mom, please. I will call you later. Thanks for the lunch. You're amazing."

My mother smiled. "Love you, Lee Lee."

I wilted again. My mother turned to Rae and said, "It was a pleasure meeting you."

Rae beamed. "It was an absolute pleasure meeting you, Mrs. Donati. Really. Truly."

I shuffled my mother out the door as my brain attempted to solve my predicament, but even a quantum computer couldn't fix my mess.

I sat down at the head of the table, opposite Rae, barely able to lift my eyes toward her.

She broke the silence. "Bad. Ass." Her lips pressed together, seemingly to hold in laughter.

"Shut up," I chuckled, but more to keep me from crying than because I found it funny.

"No, I can't control it. I am just so turned on by you. You remind me of my brother."

Finally, an opening. "That's really weird."

Rae's face pinkened. "I didn't mean that."

"Is your brother dashingly handsome?"

"No. They were two separate statements, the first being sarcastic about me being turned on by whatever that fabulousness was that just happened after your tough guy act. The second was a factual statement about my brother. He's a mamma's boy who plays in the family business."

"Momma's boy has to go both ways."

She cocked her head at me, seemingly confused.

"No! I mean, not that 'both ways.' I don't accept her coddling. I am very independent. I have my own apartment. I do my own laundry. I'm on track to be CEO of this company." Oh, God. *I'm so pathetic.* I made a mental note to join the witness protection program and disappear forever as soon as the meeting was over.

Rae sat back in her chair, a wide smirk spreading. "No. I think you're on track to be district manager of Kane Printing, working for me, on track for me to be CEO of you."

I crossed my arms and leaned back in my chair. "Sounds kinky. But it would carry more weight if you were wearing black leather instead of a blue pants suit."

She scrunched up her face in anger, seemingly plotting my demise. In case you haven't been counting. The score was Rae- 57, Leo- 2.

I raise an eyebrow. "You look like you're planning my murder."

"Finally, you got something right. I'm just not sure if I should use my bare hands or my three-inch pumps."

I pointed to the empty whiteboard. "You want to write a list of pros and cons for each method?"

"Maybe later," she said, rubbing her chin in thought. "So, I never got your name. Should I call you Lee Lee?"

I shook my head. "My name is Leo." I groaned. "I should've told you I was my brother, gotten facial reconstruction surgery, and then told you I was Leo."

"That probably would've been the better plan, but based on our brief history, I'm not surprised you didn't choose it. I have to say, I'm disappointed. Your father has an excellent reputation. You are *not* living up to it."

"I'm sorry. The black leather comment, while accurate and potentially being stored for later, was inappropriate." I smacked myself on the side of the head, which got a laugh. Not that I was going for it. *What the hell was happening?* I wanted the deal to go poorly, but I didn't want it to be my failure. I wanted her to like and respect me, but also to leave me to run the business, blaming it on somebody else. I took a deep breath to refocus. "I don't know what I did for this karmic load of crap to find its way into my life, but I feel like we either have to start over or I will have to commit hara-kiri."

She chuckled. "I'm not sure even that can save your honor, but I don't really want your blood on my hands. So, how about coffee?"

I smiled, gratitude surging through my pores. "There's a trendy new place that just opened up down the street- they try to hide being a chain by hiring a bunch of hipsters, but they're not fooling me. The coffee is excellent. It's got a unique, nutty flavor."

"So, coffee from hipster douches whose beard oil makes for a unique flavoring? Let's do it."

"Do what?"

"Coffee."

"I thought you were getting kinky again." I looked to Jesus on the wall to see if he had any answers why I was making a complete fool of myself, but he offered nothing. I guess I enjoyed getting under her skin. Maybe it was my way of trying to even the score. I really didn't know.

Rae exhaled a pathetic sigh.

I led her to the door and tried to save face. "You know, most women are much more excited to have coffee with me."

Rae forced a smile. "I'm not most women."

CHAPTER
Six

I HELD the door open for Rae, and then my breath, unsure if I was about to be admonished for my outdated sexism, but she thanked me. The sweet smell of cinnamon rolls and the toasty roast of coffee ensnared me immediately, making the fact that everything at Sugar Cube was annoyingly cubed, less annoying. The backless cushioned chairs, tables, milk dispensers, of course the sugar, and even the mugs. All. Cubed.

Anyway, I offered Rae the lofted (and cubed) menu behind the counter with my hand slowly and dramatically like a game show host. "What would you like from this carte of caffeine? My treat."

Rae reached for the wallet in her bag. "What would *you* like? Acquiring company pays the costs."

Not gonna happen. "How about we go dutch?"

Rae scoffed. "This is NOT a date. This is business. And like I said, acquiring company pays. Gender norms do not apply, so put your man-guilt away."

Two nearby soccer moms gave me the stink eye. The ants were now tossing my crumb-sized ego back and forth to each other like a beach ball. "It was a...umm...figure of speech." *And I don't want your deal.* "I'll pay separately and you can reimburse me if the deal actually goes through."

Rae nodded. "Yeah, I'm having second thoughts, too."

"Nothing would make me happier."

We were about to pace off twenty steps and draw our pistols, but were interrupted by a twenty-something woman behind the counter. "Welcome to Sugar Cube. Can I help you?"

Rae didn't wait for me to pick up the pieces of my once-enjoyable life and stepped up to the counter. She barked her order like a general. "Supreme dark roast. Three clear ice cubes. One teaspoon of sugar. Half inch of steamed soy milk."

"Got it." The woman punched in the order and then her eyes found me. "And you, sir?"

"We're going dutch."

Rae gave me some serious side eye and then paid. The woman's eyes found me again.

"Coffee. Black."

"What size?"

"Large, please."

Like I was a total dumbass, she said, "We don't have large."

"You don't have a large? Okay. Give me a medium."

Hard eye roll. "We don't have medium."

Rae suppressed a smile. I ignored her amusement and asked, "What sizes do you have?"

The woman tapped three cubed display cups that offered different sizes. "Supreme is our large."

"Yeah, so I'll have that."

"A Supreme?"

Someone had to stand up to these people. I summoned my inner Custer. Caffeine was my Little Big Horn. I shook my head. "No. The large that you call Supreme."

The woman huffed, pressed a button, and looked back at me. "Okay. And do you want milk, cream, or sugar?"

"No, thank you."

"Perhaps a pump of caramel?" she asked.

I raised an eyebrow. "Are you flirting with me?"

"No. Umm..."

"Sorry." I eyed Rae. "The last person who offered to give me a pump was definitely flirting with me."

Rae huffed behind me and then interjected, "So very not true."

"What *are* you two?" the woman asked, more confused than anyone I had ever met, except for me, apparently, in the presence of Rae.

"We're going to be business partners," Rae said, apathy seeping from her pores.

The woman chuckled, but then stopped abruptly. "Wait, are you serious?"

Not if I have anything to do with it.

Rae said, "Pray for me."

"Very funny," I said with a smirk.

"Will that be all?"

I nodded. "Thankfully, yes. I'd hate to order an egg sandwich."

"We only have frittatas. Would you like one?"

Here we go. "Only if you have a Supreme frittata."

"They don't come in sizes."

I scrunched up my face with faux angst. "I only eat big-ass frittatas, so I'll pass."

"Okay. Would you like your receipt? We prefer to email it."

"Yes. I'd like it."

"Emailed?"

"No. I don't want it to get lost in the Interwebs. Plus, I work in the printing industry. Gotta keep my people employed, at least until this one fires them all." I nodded to Rae with a smirk.

"So, printed then?"

"Is it recycled paper?"

"Yes. Of course."

Rae cut in, "Oh, my God, you're so annoying."

I shook my head. "She's not annoying. She's just doing her job."

"I was talking to you."

"That makes more sense." Remorse bubbled up inside me.

Rae said, "He'll take the printed receipt." She turned to me and said, "And she'll take an apology."

I felt bad. I was just so riled up. Why did this woman make me act like I was in middle school? Was I trying to impress her? Beat her at her own game? I didn't know. I looked the woman in the eye. "I'm sorry. I'm having a tough day." I blocked my hand so that Rae couldn't see it as I pointed at her exaggeratedly.

Rae reached into her purse, pulled out ten dollars, and slipped it into the tip jar. "For your trouble." She nodded to me, grabbed her coffee, and found a cubed table in the corner.

I paid and then sat across from Rae and watched her as she took a sip. I hadn't noticed her lips before. Full and pink. Supple. Not cubed. Nice. Well, until she opened them to speak.

"This is fantastic," Rae said.

"You like this coffee shop?" I asked, surprised. "They don't even have big-ass frittatas. It's a monstrosity. And don't get me started on the ridiculous sizes."

I couldn't help myself, but to needle her more. "Don't you just hate these mass production businesses? They move in with their big box mentality. Yeah, they put a little lipstick on the pig, pretending they're not a chain, but they don't offer any service. No smile. And they just suck the soul of the local small businesses like vampires of commerce." I feigned surprise. "Oh, what am I describing this for? It's you. That's what Kane Printing does."

Rae gritted her teeth, but then settled down before she spoke. "Had you not been a jackass, perhaps you would've gotten a smile and better service. And I'll have you know that's not what we do. We partner with businesses, share our best practices, leverage our purchasing power, leverage our fixed costs to compete with national players, which little firms like yours *can't do*."

Little firms. I took a deep breath, preparing a response, but she beat me to it.

She took another sip and asked, "Is this how you always behave?"

I'm acting like the company jester, not CEO. I took a deep, relaxing pull from my coffee and refocused. "No. I don't. We were supposed to start over. I'm not sure we won't keep ending up here, but I'd like to try a different track. Maybe we should get to know each other personally." *Maybe if I see you as a person and not a deal-hungry cyborg intent on ruining my life, one of us might not end up in the morgue.* I smiled exaggeratedly. "Why don't you tell me about yourself?"

Rae nodded. "Well, I graduated with a finance degree from Wharton. I love the merger and acquisition side of the business, so my father put me to work there. You get to breathe new life into dying businesses."

I swallowed a rebuttal, intent on keeping the seven seconds of peace we'd had.

Rae continued, "At twenty-five, I'd completed eight deals, all accretive to earnings, and I was promoted to Vice President. I built out our acquisition team and our due diligence framework—"

"I'm sorry. I don't mean to cut you off, but I meant tell me about you. You're not your resume."

She furrowed her brow as if she didn't understand. "The business is what's important to me."

"Maybe you wouldn't be so uptight if you had more of a personal life."

"Well, here's what I think about that." She stuck out her tongue at me. I was so shocked by it, I just broke out into laughter. And then she joined in, huge dimples forming in her cheeks. So big you could hide a cinnamon roll in there. Or cinnamon cubes or whatever they sold at Sugar Cube. Her dimples were adorable. I couldn't stop staring at them.

"Leo?"

I snapped out of my stare with a shake of my head. "Yeah, sorry. I thought you had some cream in your adorab... dimples. In your dimples."

Rae frowned, but continued, "I'm not uptight, by the way. It's called professionalism. You should try it."

Touché. "I typically am. I'm not sure what's going on today. Family stuff, I guess. So, you were going to tell me something personal."

"Like what?"

I shrugged. "What's the craziest thing you've ever done?"

"Skydiving."

"You've gone skydiving? That's actually pretty cool. What made you do it?"

She chuckled. "Mainly because my brother was afraid to."

I nodded in comprehension. "Does sibling rivalry turn you on or just your sibling?"

Rae rolled her eyes. "Those were two separate statements, said one after the other. They were not connected. I am not turned on by my brother." Her words drew a few eyeballs from surrounding tables.

I pointed at her with a smirk. "Oh, right. You did say that."

"Mmm, hmm." She smirked me right back. "How do you get along with your siblings? My father told me you have a brother and a sister."

"Yes. Speaking of sibling rivalry, I wish my siblings were

more of a challenge. Well, they're incredibly challenging, but not from a competitive standpoint."

Rae laughed. "Same for my brother, but he's the first-born son, so he can do no wrong. So, Leo, is that short for Leonardo?"

"Yes."

"Were you named after DaVinci?"

"No. DiCaprio."

She laughed. Dimples again, but gone too fast. "Are you serious?"

"One hundred percent. My Mom was a big fan of *Growing Pains*. I was born just as the homeless teen, Luke Bower, played by Leonardo DiCaprio, was brought into the Seaver family from the mean streets of Huntington, Long Island." I nodded out to the street. "Where we live and breathe."

"You're really serious?"

"Yes. Was she supposed to name me Kirk after Kirk Cameron, as an Italian? How did your parents decide on Rae?"

"My mother named me after Rae Cummings, a character on the soap opera, *One Life to Live*. For most of my life, they told me I was named after my great grandfather, Raymond, but my mother let it slip once. I should've known. She's very shallow."

"Wow. We're both named after TV shows? That's crazy. *Growing Pains* was better, but still. That's pretty cool."

"It was not better."

"I've never even seen *One Life to Live*, so how could it be better than *Growing Pains*? Otherwise, I would've watched it. Plus, *Growing Pains* has the best line in TV history. 'Girl, you've got needs and I've got needs. Why should we be needy on a night such as this?'"

Rae laughed and shook her head. "That's the cheesiest line I've ever heard."

I shrugged. "It worked in high school. Repeatedly."

"Thanks for the info, but your high school conquests will not make my due diligence report. Disappointing for you, as that might be your biggest value add here."

"That's too bad, but understandable."

Rae asked, "Are you married? Kids? In or out-of-wedlock? Given all of your conquests…"

"No, and no. Are you married?"

She shook her head. "No."

"Dating anyone?"

"No."

I feigned confusion. "Just curious…Is that because you praying mantis them after sex and the dating pool is onto you?"

Rae chuckled. "No. Relationships are a distraction to me. I'm more focused on financial transactions." It was one of the saddest things I've ever heard.

"So, you're just going to marry a rich guy? It doesn't matter if you love him or if you're compatible, you just want to make a good business deal?"

"I don't need a man to take care of me. I told you, I just care about the business. Marriage isn't even a thought."

I didn't know what to say. I'd never met a woman so matter-of-fact about anything, and particularly about having no interest in relationships. She was the exact opposite of my mother.

Rae continued, "So, this personal stuff is a lot of fun, but let's get back to business. I'll have to tour all the facilities and do an extensive interview process with your key employees. It's a pretty serious endeavor. I have a sixty-four-point due diligence checklist that we'll have to complete."

I held back a smile. *Sixty-four ways to take down the deal.* I raised an eyebrow. "That's it? Only sixty-four?"

"I know you're messing with me. Our fathers have agreed upon a valuation range, but the actual number will be determined by our assessment." Rae paused for a moment and then said, "I have to tell you. This is not going well."

"Really? It feels like we're only a few questions away from being besties."

She cocked her head and stared at me. "Are you actually trying to tank the deal?"

"Of course not," I scoffed. "Why would you think that?"

"So, this is you trying to make a good impression?"

I thought for a moment, my many flubs flooding my mind. "I admit, my performance has room for improvement."

"I bet you say that often."

"Oh, Ms. Kane. Good one." *I'd like to show you how wrong you are. Ugh. Did I just think that?*

"I'm meeting with the correct Donati, right? I was told you were the smart one."

I laughed nervously. "Well, I am, but in all honesty, that's not saying much. I mean, my sister, Gianna, she could eat a gallon of ice cream- I kid you not- she's done it. No brain freeze. No effect whatsoever. Nothing. Draw your own conclusions."

Rae broke out into laughter.

I shrugged. "It's true. Don't worry. She doesn't work for the business."

"I figured that, given the high bar you've showed so far." Rae downed the rest of her coffee. "Shall we head back and get started on my checklist?"

"Absolutely."

I stood up and met her eyes. It was on. She had skills; I had to give her that. She had bested me so far. I admit, I didn't handle my nerves well, but I chalked it up to a learning experience. And I knew I could win this war. I'd sized up my enemy for a little embarrassment and a few bucks for a poorly marketed but tasty cup of coffee. She was uptight and too rigid with checklists and earnings accretion projections, and probably overconfident. I had my team behind me. I didn't have to see the checklist to know they wouldn't get many check marks. Finally, they would do what I needed them to do. Fail to impress. The strike might have gone awry, but they were still the key to taking the deal down. With enough sustained exposure, they could do so much wrong. I smiled at Rae. "Can't wait."

CHAPTER
Seven

WE MADE it back to HQ without incident. No tripping or fist fights. We didn't skip down the street holding hands, though, either. Oozing with the only success I had experienced that morning, opening a door for Rae, I did so again. She didn't stab me as I turned my back on her, so things were looking up.

As we entered, Rebecca stood up from behind the counter. "Do you want me to bring in some of the lunch your mother made? You can eat and finish your meeting."

I shook my head and turned to Rae. "We are gonna do a quick tour, but I'm happy to feed you. It's in my blood. I can't help it. You hungry?"

"Not really."

"Well, too bad. We're Italian. You will stuff your face or you will be ridiculed."

Rae chuckled. "Can't wait."

Rebecca said, "You want to wait here and I'll let everyone know you're coming?" Her eyes suggested I should really, really do what she had offered.

"No. That's fine, Becs."

"Really? I mean, you sure? It's not a problem. I don't mind at all," she said, opening the door to the facility.

"We're good," I said, leading Rae through the door.

The acidic smell and whir of the machines grew as we entered.

After the door closed, Rae said, "She likes you. Has there ever been an H.R. problem?"

I sighed dramatically. "We get along well. There's no H.R. issue."

"She likes you, likes you."

Jim Garrison nodded as we passed, but otherwise, the room was empty, which meant shenanigans were going on elsewhere. It was the first time I actually looked forward to their idiocy.

I raised an eyebrow mysteriously as we walked. "Is that on your checklist? Employee 'likes' the boss?" I tossed some air quotes out for good measure.

"H.R. risks are on my list, yes."

"Well, in answer to your question, she doesn't. We're like family."

"I still think she likes you," Rae said, matter of fact.

"Better her than you."

Her tone dripped with sarcasm. "That hurts me deeply."

"I think you're jealous."

The sarcasm continued, "Oh, yes. A rude mamma's boy with diarrhea of the mouth. You complete me."

Our witty banter was interrupted by primal screams reverberating off the Speedmaster machines in the back of the facility.

"That didn't sound good," I said, feigning concern. *It sounded fantastic.*

"No. It did not."

I picked up the pace toward the back and said enthusiastically, "I can't wait for you to meet the team. A real group of go-getters. I think you'll be impressed."

"I doubt that."

It was one of the few things we agreed upon.

Our timing was impeccable. Picture this. My brother and Frankie encased in silver-duct-taped cardboard armor from neck to toe, running from opposite ends of the row, long cardboard paper rolls tucked under their arms. Flacco, Rico, and Joey Bagels cheered as each idiot knight jumped onto rolling chairs, knees first. They wheeled toward each other with squeaks and shrieks, ferocity in their eyes.

Frankie's lance connected with Benny's shoulder with a thwack. Benny toppled backward off the chair and crashed onto the floor with a splat and cheers. Frankie popped off his chair and thrust his broken lance into the air with a "Huzzah!"

Joey Bagels held out his hands to each side, a smile across his face, dollars reluctantly slapped into his hands.

I smiled as Rae looked on, horrified. "Work hard. Play hard. Am I right?" She did not appear to agree or perhaps the situation suppressed her ability to form words. I wasn't sure.

Benny stood up and dusted himself off. "You got lucky."

Rae asked, "Aren't you going to do something about this?"

I stepped forward. "Gentlemen! Well, you guys. Great show, but it's over." They all groaned.

Benny clapped his hands together and said, "Okay, guys. Leo's right." I couldn't believe what I was hearing, but Benny continued, "Espresso run! Let's break until 1:30."

The crowd dispersed with excitement, leaving Rae and me alone. I smiled sheepishly. "Sorry you had to see that." I wasn't.

"It's remarkable that the business is as good as it is."

"It's a testament to good management, I guess."

"Seems like you can't manage them at all."

The fun was over. "You know nothing about me or our culture. We have fantastic relationships with our employees and our customers, provide substantial support, and we get things done when we need to get things done. Do we have fun sometimes? Yes. You have to enjoy who you're working with."

"I don't have that luxury."

"What do you mean?"

"Our fathers are forcing us to work together."

I fake laughed. "Agreed. You can buy another company if I am such a horrible person to deal with."

Her only response was a heavy huff.

"Look, things are light at the moment. We just finished up the election season. We've got some temporary pricing pressure from a local competitor. Typical cycle stuff. Am I gonna get crazy for them messing around?"

"Maybe it's not light at the moment or typical cycle stuff. Maybe you can't compete." Rae shrugged and gave a carefree, "No matter. They are easily replaced."

I stepped in front of her, arms crossed and my Sicilian Stare set to stun. "Hold on a sec. These are our people. You can't just start firing them."

"When we own the business, we'll implement a proper review system. If they make the cut, they'll stay. If not, they won't. Nothing personal. Just business."

"It's personal to me," I barked.

"And that's why you've lost control of the business."

I headed toward the front, leaving Rae behind. "This has been a lot of fun, but now that I think about it, I have a lot to get done."

Rae caught up. "You promised me lunch."

"You said you weren't hungry."

"All this talk of firing people has gotten me a little excited."

I huffed and led her to the break room. We were met with the glorious smell of garlic and half-empty trays of shrimp scampi, lasagna, and eggplant parmigiana. I felt slightly better.

"Wow," Rae said, admiring the spread.

"Finally, you're impressed."

"And it had nothing to do with you."

It was gonna be a great lunch. I scooped up some scampi and a square of lasagna, and made my way to the closest table. I pulled a deep breath of garlic in through my nose, attempting to conjure some comfort.

When Rae sat down across from me, I asked, "Now what?"

"Food fight?" she suggested.

I cocked my head in mock consideration. "I *would* like to stuff a square of lasagna up your nose."

She took a bite and said, "Well, it is good enough to inhale, but I'll pass."

I stabbed a shrimp and heard a crack. Only half my plastic fork remained in hand. "I hate that, don't you?" I said, grabbing a replacement.

"Not on the same level as you, but yeah, it's pretty annoying."

I smiled. "You're funny sometimes."

"Who's joking?" she deadpanned.

I let out a faux laugh that sounded more like I was choking. Smooth. "Besides me, what do you hate?"

"Christmas songs before Thanksgiving."

I nodded. "That's the worst. You know what I really hate besides corporate overlords? Unannounced visitors."

"Definitely. When I was a kid, I used to love it when we'd have people stop by. Now, I'm diving behind the couch when the doorman calls."

I scrunched up my nose. "Why wouldn't you just not answer it? They're not outside, looking in the windows."

She rolled her eyes. "What else?"

"When my mother pinches my cheeks in business meetings."

Rae tilted her head and let out a sweet, "Aww, really? That's one of my favorite things." She continued the game, "Clowns."

"You hate my family, too?"

"I was referring to my brother. You're the only one I hate in your family."

"Lucky me. Uber surge pricing."

"That's capitalism. It's what makes the world go 'round. Segway overuse. Again, my brother."

"The sexy one?"

Rae huffed and then took a bite of shrimp. "The only one. When people use delicious for non-food items."

"So annoying. Although, it's okay if you want to use it for me. You wouldn't be the first."

"That's a negative," Rae said, shaking her head.

Benny popped his head into the room, Sugar Cube cup in hand. "Sorry to interrupt, but I have an important question for you."

"Can it wait?"

"No. Can we invite some waitresses from Hooters to our Christmas party?"

"No."

Benny wilted like a child denied ice cream and whined, "But It's such a sausage fest. Except Rebecca, but she doesn't seem to be attracted to me."

I rubbed my chin thoughtfully. "You're so charming. It's a great mystery."

"I know."

I shrugged. "I'll tell you what. If you can get any to actually attend, bring as many as you want."

Rae scoffed.

Benny thrust a fist in the air and said, "Huzzah!" He disappeared and yelled, "Guys, he said yes!"

I answered Rae's glare with a laugh. "Don't worry. He's not gonna get any of them to attend. But did you see how happy he was?"

We finished up lunch without stuffing lasagna squares up each other's noses. #blessed #bffs #besties.

Rae cleared her plate and said, "Well, this has been very...educational."

"I try to create a positive learning environment."

"Mmm, hmm."

"What did you learn?" I asked, pretending to care.

She looked me dead in the eye. "There's a lot of room for improvement. We've turned around worse. And we'll get it on the cheap end of our valuation range. This could be our best deal yet."

"Really?" I suppressed disappointment and more than a fair share of shock.

Rae nodded with a smile. "We'll do whatever it takes to get this done. I'll have my assistant reach out to you."

I nodded. "She can reach out to my assistant."

Rae scrunched up her nose, fists on hips. "Who says my assistant is a woman?"

"Oh geez. I'm sorry. I meant nothing by it."

"Whatever."

I thought for a moment. "You really think this is going to work out between us, Rae with an e?"

Rae scoffed. "There is no *us*. The businesses will fit just fine when I take over and run it the right way."

I took a deep breath. "Purchasing synergies, right? I remember. What's your assistant's name? I'll give Rebecca a heads up."

"Melanie."

I laughed. "Oh, so she *is* a woman? I was right."

"But...your assumption was wrong."

I threw up my hands. "That makes no sense."

Rae revealed her dimples again. "Well, I'm the boss and I make the rules."

I chuckled in annoyance. "You sound like my father. I'm trading one tyrant for another. Except his dimples are on his ass."

Rae laughed. "Valerie in our H.R. department is gonna love you."

I smiled exaggeratedly. "I'm very lovable."

"I've seen no signs of that."

"Well, get your vision checked in those beau—brown eyes of yours. I, umm, am afraid to ask, but what are next steps?"

"We'll set up some appointments with agendas based on the checklist. Financials. We'll tour the other facilities. Go over purchasing and inventory. Oh, and you might want to dust off your resume. Just some friendly advice."

"This business is nothing without me."

"I can't wait to find out." Dimples again, but not that enjoyable.

I followed her as she left the room. "Wait, that's not part of the deal."

"I know, but the look on your face was very amusing."

I smirked and led her to the front. I stuck out my hand for a shake. "It's been such a pleasure."

Rae looked me in the eye, smiled, and shook my hand. "It's all yours. Have a great rest of your day." She turned and walked away.

Benny emerged from the parking lot. We both watched Rae disappear into a row of cars. Benny hung his heavy arm on my shoulder. "Eyeing an afternoon snack?"

"What are you talking about?" I scoffed.

"The forbidden fruit that is Ms. Kane?"

I crossed my arms. "Dude, I friggin' hate her."

"Doesn't mean you can't tap it."

"Shut up."

The truth is, I had never been more confused in my life. I

hated her, but I desperately wanted to kiss her luscious lips. Make her laugh again and again, so I could see those dimples. I also wanted her out of my life and business. The more I thought about it, the more my confusion grew. I only knew one thing for certain. I had to step up my game. I just wasn't sure if it was to win my evil business plan or to win her.

———

Rae's Deal Notes

- Typical family shop, serious room for improvement.
- Employee assessments a must, most won't make the cut, but could be problem from the top...
- Weak management
- Serious H.R. risk
- Needs leadership training
- ~~Friggin' Hot...until he opens his mouth. Strong, wish-he-were-silent type...~~

CHAPTER
Eight

I WAS SO EMOTIONALLY exhausted from the day, the whole week really, that I had considered dunking my head in an ice bath for a few hours to see if my brain would slow down. But it seemed like too much work, and I had already had enough of that. So, I skipped that and my workout, and crashed on the couch, watching the lowly Knicks with Jean-Claude Van Dog curled up in my lap. He was a white, ten-pound Volpino, often confused for an electrocuted cotton ball. I had taken the poor dog under my care because his chooch parents, Benny and Frankie, only need the cute little guy as a wingman in the spring and summer months, and we were heading into winter. Anyway, Jean-Claude was a good pooch. I didn't blame him for his parents or his horrific shedding problem that seemed to follow me everywhere.

I sipped on a creamy Cortigiana beer, enjoying its vanilla and cinnamon flavor, the game barely registering. I pet J.C. behind the ears, questioning my place in the world. "You're the second smartest mammal in our family. Is my career crashing faster than the Knicks' chances to make the play-offs?" He didn't answer. "I don't know, either." My mind turned to Rae. "Who does she think she is? With her feminist outbursts and snooty comebacks, and those dimples," I said, softening. J.C. stared up at me. "I know, bro. She's ruining my life, but I can't stop thinking about her."

The rest of the weekend played out much like that. Me questioning my existence and future, plotting the demise of the deal with Rae and her company, while J.C. proved he was a very distant second-smartest in the family by giving me absolutely zero advice.

On Monday, I sat in my father's office to catch him up on the Kane deal. It wasn't going well. What else was new? Pop leaned back in his chair, a napkin tucked into his shirt collar, while he popped Castelvetrano olives into his mouth. My father loved the sweet green olives from Sicily. My brother, on the other hand, refuses to eat them to this day, because as a kid he thought they looked like Kermit the Frog's head. I know. But remember, he's the meat.

Anyway, I tried to make my case. "Pop, there are so many issues with this deal. I don't even know where to start." I counted them on my fingers. "Poor valuation. Bad cultural fit. People are gonna get fired. If you're still intent on selling the company, at least let me improve the financials and get a better deal. For the family. For all the employees who've become family."

My father popped another olive and said, "We don't have the time."

I threw up my hands in frustration. "Are you dying? What's the big rush?"

He wiped his mouth with the napkin and tossed it onto his desk. "No. The business is dying."

I huffed and shook my head. "Because you won't let me fix it. Won't let me adapt to the changing technology. We need a new strategy, not a new owner."

Pop burped as a response.

"That's the smartest thing you've said in weeks." I stood up. "This is a waste of my time. I should just quit now."

"You're going to do what's right for the family. You want to lead this family someday?"

I gave him my 'are you friggin' stunad?' look. "Have you seen the alternatives? I'm your only choice."

"Well, this is my business. My father built it—"

"And you're running it into the ground."

"Watch your mouth. The industry has changed."

"Exactly! So we need to change."

"You'll do as I say. See this deal to the end."

"The cultures are not a good fit. They're going to slash and burn this business."

"What did I say?"

"Nothing intelligent."

He sighed, but said nothing. His glare said it all. I mean, he from Naples not Sicily, so his glare game wasn't crazy strong, but it made his point.

I stared at the ceiling, hands on hips. With my best drawn-out monotone voice, I said, "See this deal to the end."

"Thank you."

I left in a hurry and a flurry of muttered curses.

As I returned to my office, I had an epiphany. J.C. will probably try to take some credit for it, but it was all my idea. Merge with PremaPrint. Why sell to the first guy or gal through the door? Why not foster a little healthy competition? My father didn't have to know about it until we had an offer on the table. And then he'd be thanking me. He wouldn't have to choose between Boca and Sicily. He could have both.

I picked up the phone and dialed Ted Whittaker, the CEO of PremaPrint. We had met many times at industry conferences and had voodoo dolls of each other.

"Teddy! Leo Donati here from Donati printing."

"Hey, Leo. It's been a while. To what do I owe the pleasure?"

"Well, we've been beating up on each other for so long, I'm wondering if it's not time for a change in tactics."

"Like team up?"

"Yes, team up. You wanna take it to the big boys? Why should two family firms built from the ground up with blood, sweat, and tears duke it out when we can unite against a common enemy?"

"We've got a lot going on right now. Let me talk to my partners and see what they're thinking. I'll have Greg reach out to set up a time to talk."

"See if eleven on Wednesday works."

"Will do."

He called me back within thirty minutes. "Yes, let's meet at eleven on Wednesday."

"Great." We ironed out the details, and I hung up the phone with a smile. But that was only half the plan.

I dialed Rae's office and got Melanie. "Ms. Kane's office," a soft voice answered.

Should I ask for her? No. Absolutely not. "Hi, Melanie. This is Leo Donati from Donati Printing. I was hoping to move my meeting with Rae to first thing in the morning on Wednesday. Can she make the trip out from the city?"

"Yes, that should work. Anything else I can help you with?"

I thought for a moment. "As a matter of fact, there is. What embarrassing thing can you tell me about her? Any damning secrets?"

Melanie laughed. "She said that you were funny."

"She did? I thought she hated me."

Silence. I guess I could be funny and hated.

"So embarrassing moments?"

Melanie said, "I'm sorry. I don't have any. She's wonderful."

"That's disappointing. Thanks for nothing, Melanie," I said, joking.

I hung up the phone and smiled. She thought I was funny. And more importantly, the competition was about to begin.

An evil cackle escaped my mouth, and I didn't even feel bad about it.

———

I got to the office around 7:15 on Wednesday, wearing my finest gray pinstripe suit with a blue button-down shirt, but no tie. Some of my Italian brethren might go with a straight up t-shirt under the suit jacket, but despite my little sting operation, this wasn't *Miami Vice*. Rae was, not surprisingly, early, strutting into the office in a red peplum dress and matching shoes.

I eyed her from head to toe. *Gaddamn.* "Lady Lucifer?"

Rae rolled her eyes.

"Oh, I'm sorry, Rae. I thought you were someone else."

The place was empty except for the two of us. It was too early for Rebecca, so I escorted Rae into the conference room. "Do you want a cup of coffee?"

"Sure."

I scratched my chin, feigning deep thought. "I can't remember your ridiculous order. Was it seven granules of sugar, half an ice cube, and a dash of rat poison?"

Rae smirked. "On second thought, I'll just have a bottle of water. And I'll be the one to open it."

I grabbed one from the mini fridge for her. "Suit yourself."

"And how does one have half an ice cube?" Rae asked and beat me to the head of the table again.

I gritted my teeth and then forced a smile. "Well, it would be full size, just half filled with the poison."

"Just so you know, I've instructed Melanie to alert the police that you are my killer, should something happen to me."

"That's so sweet, but based on the short time I've known you, lengthen that list for greater accuracy."

Rae produced a laptop from beneath the table. "As much

fun as this is, I didn't get up at 5 a.m. and accommodate your schedule only to exchange insults."

I nodded to the laptop. "That was impressive. Do keep that in a thigh holster? So, you can whip out your weaponized due diligence checklist?"

"It's only a tool." Her eyebrows pinched together. She glanced at me and then the laptop. "It's surprising you two don't get along better," Rae said, dimples appearing.

"Hardy har," was the only thing I could come up with to say.

We went through checklist items for over two hours. As much as I enjoyed the relentless questioning about how much we've spent on cyan ink on Tuesdays during Lent since the bicentennial, I was more than relieved when our meeting ended. And excited to unleash the next phase of my plan.

Rae assessed my jacket. "This is the first time I've seen you in a suit."

"Not bad, right? Is sexy motha on your checklist?" I rubbed my nails on my lapel for good measure.

She chuckled and snapped her fingers. "Darn. Just missed the list. Would've been sixty-five."

She nodded to the suit again. "So, to what do I owe the pleasure?"

"Oh, it's not you I'm pleasuring." I smacked myself on the side of the head. "I didn't mean it that way. I have an important meeting following this one."

She raised an eyebrow. "Like what?"

"Oh, that's confidential. Legally, I can't say anything." I forbade myself to smirk, but I may have let one slip.

"What's so funny?"

"Nothing. I was thinking of something…else. Let me walk you out." I opened the door, and we headed into the reception area.

"Who is that?" Rae asked in a whisper, nodding to a lanky man in a blue suit and tortoise-framed glasses.

Rebecca caught my eye and said, "PremaPrint is here for your meeting."

I looked at Rae and then feigned surprise. "Oh, right. That's today. Wow! This is...awkward."

Suddenly, something felt terribly wrong. She was way too relaxed. Confident. Smug.

Rae laughed. "Yes, but not for the reasons you think." She stared at me in amusement but said nothing.

"Care...to...share?" I asked, my brain in overdrive.

"I just bought PremaPrint." Her dimples were not as cute as usual.

Fangool. I looked at Rae and then at Ted from PremaPrint, the gangly, rat bastard that he is, and then back to Rae. I didn't know what to say. Had I known, I'm not sure I could even deliver said words at that moment. After hyperventilating in a paper bag, I was at least able to communicate in cave man. "You...PremaPrint? Discounting?"

"I was playing the game before you knew it started." Rae nodded to Ted and said, "You can head out. I'll talk to you later."

Ted eyed me quickly before obeying. "You got it, boss."

Rae turned back to me. "He called me after you two talked. Tsk." She shrugged. "Since we've got the time blocked off, do you want to still meet? We can talk about trust in relationships."

I didn't answer. Shame coursed through my veins.

Rae pressed on. "I'll take that as a no. I didn't realize you could keep your mouth shut for over six seconds." Her tone turned firm. "I have a business to run. Cute as your little charade was, don't do it again. I'll be in touch." She waved to Rebecca with a smile and disappeared out the door.

Rebecca's bulging eyes locked onto mine. She mouthed, "What did you do?"

I shrugged in flabbergastation. And then realized I needed

to clean my mess up. I hurried after Rae and caught up to her in the parking lot. "Rae, wait! Please."

She stopped and turned to me, arms crossed, her glare level dialed up to military-grade lasers. Nonna would be proud.

I took a step back, out of bag-wielding distance. "I'm sorry. Let me make it up to you. I'm not a bad guy." I took a deep breath and was totally straight with her. "I just don't think this deal is right, and certainly not the right price. I don't know why I'm behaving the way that I am. But you can't blame me for doing what's best for my family."

Rae huffed. "That's what your father said when he agreed to sell to us, so you might want to get on the same page."

"Well, he and I are not on the same page. That's part of the problem." I raised an eyebrow as she continued to glare at me. "You look like you want me to have explosive diarrhea coming on and have to sneeze."

Rae broke out into laughter. "Not currently, no. But only because I'm here with you. Had this been a video chat…"

"I'm sorry. Seriously, let me make it up to you."

"How could you possibly do that?"

I chuckled. "Absolutely no idea." I stood up on my tippy toes, attempting to get a bird's-eye view of her leather bag without getting closer. "Do you have a list of ideas you could share?" I racked my brain for something. Anything. I blurted out, "Come to our holiday party."

She laughed. "Are you serious?"

"I'm…not entirely sure."

She shook her head. "That's not really a good idea."

"You sound like my father. Except he usually insults me with something in Italian. If you're gonna do it, do it right, call me a chooch or stunad."

"I won't do that. I have no idea what they mean. What if it's a trick to compliment you?"

I laughed. "A chooch is an idiot. Some say donkey. Stunad is stupid."

"Oh, so very applicable," Rae said, dimples softening the insult. "I still don't think it's a good idea, ya chooch."

"Much better," I said, laughing.

Rae's face brightened. "That felt really good. Thank you for giving me that pleasure."

My mind drifted to other pleasures she might enjoy giving me.

"Leo?"

I put the black-leather fantasy on hold and said, "Yes?"

"You seem to disappear to Leo Land or something sometimes."

I shrugged. "I have a big brain. It's very imaginative. So, leather? Umm, I mean, it might be cold weather, but the party's a lot of fun."

She shook her head. "It's not a good idea."

I didn't know what I was doing. So, just a regular Wednesday, at least since I had met Rae. "Of course, it is. It'll be the most fun you've ever had. Get to know your soon-to-be employees. See who you're really getting into bed with…business with. Just watch out for my brother and his mistletoe hat."

"Sounds like an H.R. nightmare."

I raised my eyebrows, waiting for an answer.

"We'll see."

"You sound like my parents."

Rae shrugged with a smile. "Well, about to be parent company, but…"

"But what?"

"You ever hear the saying beware Greeks bearing gifts?"

"Trojan horse?"

"Yes."

"I get it, but I'm Italian. And are we really enemies?" We pretty much were, but I honestly didn't have any sinister plan attached to my invitation. I wasn't even sure why I was inviting her.

"Today certainly didn't help. Send me the details. I'll think about it." And with that, she was gone.

I stood there alone, a pit in my stomach and a cacophony of thoughts rattling around inside my brain, as I attempted to figure out how I could possibly have had my ass handed to me that badly, all the while thinking I was getting one up. Rae- 117. Leo- 4. Who am I kidding? It was game, set, match.

I collected myself and returned to the office. My father waited for me. "What did you do?"

"I, umm, invited her to the holiday party."

He shook his head. "You what? I'm talking about PremaPrint."

I glared at Rebecca. She shrugged, unapologetic.

My father continued, "How did we not know they were sold?"

I shrugged. "She's good. Very good." I changed tracks. "I can't believe they did this to us. We should call off the deal. They've been playing us the whole time. This is our partner? More like hostage taker."

"This is business, and you have to do what you have to do. Our competitors don't owe us a phone call after they sell. If anything, I'm impressed. If you can't beat 'em, join 'em. I guess we should be grateful we are."

Agita swirled through my stomach. "Why can't we look for someone else? Consolidated Digital maybe?"

My father shook his head. "They just want the customers. They'll gut the place. Outsource all the print and graphics work to their other facilities. It'll be a nightmare."

It already was.

———

Rae's Deal Notes

- Much-needed smackdown a success!
- Leo threatened to poison me. Feeling is mutual. Have Melanie make actual note of it for police.
- Holiday party, 12/17? Show the rest of them who's the boss lady?
- ~~Leo is sooooo steamy in a suit…~~

CHAPTER

Nine

IT WAS DECEMBER 17TH. It had been a few weeks since I last saw Rae. We emailed some information back and forth a few times, but she hadn't requested to meet since the Prema-Print fiasco, my double cross gone wrong. I was too embarrassed. I sat in my office, staring at the ceiling. Although we closed two hours early to head into the city for our holiday bash and my father would tell me about my bonus payout later that day, I was numb.

A knock at my door jolted me to the present.

"Are you okay?" Benny asked, leaning in.

I shrugged. "Fine." Was I, though?

"You sure you're gonna fly Han Solo to the Christmas party?"

For once, Benny was on point. I was lonely. I nodded.

Benny continued, "Well, it's gonna be a blast. I'm very optimistic there will be four or five of Santa's little helpers attending, courtesy of our local Hooter's. Get a little jollier and one might jingle your bell."

I sighed but didn't answer.

"Toss a few back and you'll be good as new."

I nodded more to get him to leave than anything. "Yep. I'll see you later. I've got to get Pop a report."

"Later." Benny disappeared.

I grabbed a printout of the team's bonus payments, or lack thereof, from the printer out front and brought it to my father. As I entered, he barely looked up from his computer screen.

"Christmas shopping?"

"Yes. I'm going to buy your mother a condo in Florida."

I rolled my eyes, glancing at the screen filled with real estate profiles. "Great," I said, anything but.

"Did you complete the bonus schedule?" he asked.

I handed it to him. He rubbed his balding head as he read through it and then tossed it aside. "Look, I'll skip the fanfare." He pretty much always did, but I kept my mouth shut for once. I didn't have the energy. "You've seen the financials. I've decided that management isn't getting bonuses this year."

I threw up my hands in protest. "I'm like the only one who works around here."

"It will look bad for the family if you take a big bonus and everyone else is squeezed. I know you understand. I'm not taking one, either. It is what it is. Let's put it behind us and have some fun tonight. Celebrate a new chapter, eh?"

The chapter where my life is ruined? Sarcasm seeped through my pores. "Oh, can't wait, Pops. Maybe you should dress up as the grinch?" I walked out and slammed his door, not waiting for his response.

———

I've always loved Little Italy during Christmas. It's fun and festive. The restaurants are louder, more exciting than normal. Sure, black eyes are more common that time of year. It's not from fighting, but from the increased hand gesturing. You have to be quick to duck, but it's still fun. Couples cuddle, arm in arm. Laughter breaking out on every corner, sometimes even into song.

I walked down the street, alone in a crowd, having chosen to take the train by myself. I wore a festive black pants with a matching black button down, and a, you guessed it, black wool coat turned up at the collar to repel the chilly air. At least I had a red scarf on.

Red, white, and green tinsel arched festively across the street from fire escape to fire escape on the side streets. A giant "Welcome to Little Italy" sign lit up Canal Street while giant stars soared across Mulberry Street.

We always celebrated our company party at Gustavo's, a distant relative who operated one of the tastiest hole-in-the-wall Italian restaurants west of the Atlantic. Uncle Gus was a short, stout man with a smile nearly as wide as the rest of him. He grabbed me by both shoulders, pulled me down toward him, man-handling me for kisses to each cheek. He said for all of Mulberry Street to hear, "Leo! Ciao! Come stai?"

"I'm good, Uncle Gus. Great to see you." I forced a smile. "How is Aunt Rose?"

"Drivin' me crazy, you know? But that's-a just how it is with love. It's-a been-a too long, eh?"

I nodded. "Mi dispiace. I'm sorry, Uncle Gus. Been busy with work."

"I was-a hoping it was-a with a lady friend."

"Unfortunately, no."

"Your mother will finda you a nice-a Italian woman. We should-a play some bocce with the boys when it gets-a warmer, no?"

"Sure. My brother plays with his balls enough, but Pop and I will play."

"So funny, eh!" He smacked me on the cheek, laughing. It stung like a bitch.

You ever hear the saying, 'Love hurts'? Of course you have, but what you probably didn't know is that it has nothing to do with emotions. It's physical pain, brought on by Italian family members beating the shit out of you in the supposed name of love.

An older couple entered behind me. Uncle Gus patted me on the shoulder. "I'll be up-a later for a drink, tutto bene?"

"Okay, Uncle Gus." I smiled and headed up the stairs to the private room.

Double wooden doors could barely contain the music and chatter within the room. They opened up into a large L-shaped room, so I couldn't see anything but the coat closet when I entered. But the Sinatra was on full blast and the mood quite festive, unlike my own. I tossed my coat on a hanger and headed around the corner. Cheers broke out. My mother shuffled across the tile floor on her stilts. If she hadn't been smiling, her leopard print jumpsuit would've sent me out the fire escape.

"Leo, my baby. I was so worried." I braced for impact as she kissed my cheek.

"I like your jumpsuit. Festive. If only it was a zoo opening and not Christmas."

She linked her arm in mine. "So funny, my boy. Come on, let's see Aunt Franny."

I made my way around the room, saying my hellos. I forced a few smiles, did a shot with the boys, took some pictures with my mother, and shared a plate of grilled calamari with Rebecca. A squeeze of lime, a dash of olive oil, and a sprinkle of parsley. Bellisimo.

As I sat at the bar, Rebecca asked, "Are you okay, boss?"

"I will be. In my next life." I downed about half a Peroni in one gulp. I nodded at her black dress. "You look nice. I never see your hair down." She tossed it behind her shoulder with a smile.

"Thanks. You know, sometimes, you're so focused on what's wrong, you can't see the good staring right at you."

I raised an eyebrow. Was Rae right? I didn't know why I

should be surprised, but was Rebecca making a move? "What good am I missing?"

Rebecca presented the room with her hand. My sister slow danced with Sal to Sinatra's *My Way*. My mother pinched Joey Bagel's cheek. My niece, Mia, bounced on Pop's knee, a huge grin on her face. A group laughed around Frankie as he entertained them with hip thrusts.

I exhaled, grateful Rebecca didn't appear to mean her. I had enough tension in my life and I didn't have romantic feelings for Rebecca. I took a panoramic view of the room. "Intellectually, I hear what you're saying, but I'm just not feeling it. I'm just so frustrated with the business."

"Things will turn for you. It'll all work out."

"Will it?" My cell rang in my pocket. I pulled it out and stared at it, confused. It was Rae. My heart raced. "Hello?"

"Hi, Leo. Can you come get me?"

I was so confused. "Hi…Rae. Are you in jail?"

She laughed. "No. I'm at the corner of Bowery and Spring. I'm a bit lost. There was too much traffic, so I decided to walk, but none of the streets are numbered."

"Wait, you're downtown?"

"Yeah. I'm coming to the party."

"My party?"

Rae laughed again. I missed her dimples. "Nothing gets by you."

"Yeah, right. I didn't think…I'll be right there."

I hustled back outside and weaved through the crowds en route to Spring Street. My feet stopped when I saw her on the opposite corner. She wore a long, white wool jacket and matching hat with black high heels.

She caught my eye, waved, and walked toward me.

"Hi," I said.

"Hi." She smiled. Almost as cute as her dimples was her peach nose, cold from the crisp air.

"You look…lovely. If not a bit like Cruella de Vil."

She smirked, then looked around, wide eyed. "I've never been to Little Italy before."

"No? The uptown girl is slummin' it with us I-talians? Ms. Sophisticated, who gets lost when the streets aren't numbered? That's okay. I'm glad you made it. It's a lot of fun down here." I described Little Italy as we headed back to Uncle Gus' place. "Spectacular food. Interesting sites. A restaurant around the corner has a giant, light up sausage weenie. It's on this pulley system and when a rowdy waiter pulls the string, the sausage tip rings the bell, and the bulb lights up."

Rae raised an eyebrow. "That's fun?"

"You don't like wieners? It's making more sense why I repel you." I couldn't stop myself from wanting to make her laugh.

"So, you think only lesbians wouldn't find you interesting?"

"Not all of them. I think I could turn a few," I said, suppressing a smile.

She rolled her eyes. "Tell me more."

"There's good history here. Well, not for everybody. Joe Gallo, a gangster in the 70s, was killed in a restaurant across the way over there."

"These are the best points you can make? Light-up wieners and murdered gangsters? It's no wonder no one's ever recommended it before."

I threw up my hands. "Okay. Okay. I'm not going in order of amazingness. Do you want me to prepare a PowerPoint for you for next week after I have time to think?"

"Perhaps."

"The espresso, the cannoli are amazing."

"That I could go for."

My eyebrows shot up. "I'm going to refrain from making a naughty cannoli joke, but just know that I could. I don't want to end up on your checklist."

"You've destroyed the sanctity of my checklist. I don't know what to do with Donati Printing."

"Let's not talk business. It never goes well for us. At least not for me." I returned my thoughts to Little Italy. "During the Feast of San Gennaro in September, it smells glorious. Sausage and peppers. Fried dough." I kissed my fingers with gusto. "Delizioso!"

I opened the door for Rae. Uncle Gus was seating a guest, so we headed straight up, stopping at the coat closet. "Can I take your coat?"

She slipped it off, revealing a white, ribbed cable-knit sweater that hugged every curve with perfection. I nearly walked into the wall after she handed the coat to me.

"Everything okay?"

"Yeah," I said, staring at her bare legs from the mid-thigh down. "I've never seen your...knees before." I looked up at her, feeling my face flush.

Rae laughed. "That's...weird."

I shrugged. "I have a checklist."

"Well, if there are other body parts on it, prepare to be disappointed. Buy me a drink, weirdo."

I introduced Rae around, receiving more than a few curious assessments and a frown or two, mainly from my mother and Aunt Franny. We cozied up to the bar beside Joey Bagels, Flacco, and Rico.

Mario, the bartender, nodded to me. "What can I get you?"

I looked at Rae. "What do you like?"

"Surprise me."

"Do you like bitter or sweet?"

"Sweet."

"Two Bellinis, Mario."

"What's that?"

"It's a peach puree with champagne," I said, pronouncing it with a hard 'g'.

"You're so classy," she said, laughing.

I took the glass, tossed out my most dapper look, and said, "Donati. Leo Donati." And then nearly spilled my peach drink on her white dress, splattering a bunch on the floor.

She jumped back and said, "Smooth. You could be the next Bond."

I looked down at the floor, but my eyes were magnetized to her legs.

"Up here, James," Rae said, lifting my chin until we stared into each other's eyes.

"Sorry. I..umm. Knee caps are my kink. I'm a weirdo."

Rae laughed, shaking her head.

I raised my glass and said, "Merry Christmas." She didn't clink my glass, so I pushed mine to hers. "Salud." Her smiled disappeared. "What's wrong?" I asked.

She glowered at me. "I'm Jewish."

"Happy Hanukkah. I'm sorry. I forgot. I meant nothing by it. Truly. Honestly. I swear."

"But that's the problem, isn't it? You don't think."

"Why do you have such a big chip on your shoulder about being Jewish?"

"Never said I did."

"It's clear as day. The size of Israel itself." I suppressed a smile. "I get it. I mean, we're better than you."

Rae scoffed, hands on hips. "Who, Christians?"

"I can't speak for all Christians, so let's just keep it to Italians."

"You don't have to narrow it down. Eight crazy nights. One day."

"Come on, Rae. Just look at all the stores. How much Hanukkah stuff there is versus Christmas. We have Elf on a Shelf. What do you guys have? A Mohel with a Boil?"

"You are such a...chooch," she said, laughing.

I nodded in agreement. "I am such a chooch. So much that I'm surprised you're here."

"I don't know why I'm here, either," she said with confusion. More firmly, she corrected, "I wanted to mend fences. We didn't end on a good note. We haven't had any good notes."

"They haven't all been bad notes, have they? You're not terrible when you're not trying to crush my soul to feed your capitalist cravings."

A laugh escaped her lips, seemingly against her will. "It's no wonder you're single, if you consider that a compliment."

I shrugged sheepishly. "You want something to eat?"

"Do I have a choice?"

I laughed. "You're learning. No. You do not."

I led her over to the buffet that spread down a long table against the wall. It was a ridiculous offering. I presented it to her down the line. "There's antipasto, tomato and mozzarella, salad, eggplant rollatini, grilled calamari, pasta out the culo. Skirt steak. Shrimp Luciano. Pick-a-protein parmigiana." I used a thick Italian accent, "You-a name it. We-a got it."

"What is pasta al a culo?" Rae asked, brow furrowed.

I laughed. "No. Out the culo. Pasta out the butt. Don't worry. That's not how it's actually made. I was talking more like volume."

"Thanks for the clarification," she said, laughing.

We grabbed some food and a table with a few of the employees from the Riverhead facility. I made some introductions, which promptly scared them off.

I took a bite of meatball parmigiana and stared at Rae. "This is a serious question. I'm not trying to piss you off."

Rae asked, curiously. "What?"

"What do you do on Christmas? I mean, the world kinda shuts down. This has nothing to do with that not happening on Hanukkah."

"Oh, sure," she said, laughing. "And you think I'm the competitive one?"

I continued, "Seriously, do you just sit around eating knishes?"

She rolled her eyes. "We eat Chinese food and go to the movies. It's glorious."

"That's nuts and amazing at the same time."

"What do you do?"

"Eat dinner with twenty cousins at a table for fourteen."

Rae smiled in superiority. "I have six movie seat recliners to myself."

"Really? Hmm, that sounds better than my thing."

"Christmas is better for Jews than Christians? Are you admitting that?"

"Never."

Benny danced over. "Hey, boss!" He shouted, apparently believing Rae's chest was said boss. "Shots at the bar."

"I couldn't tell," I said.

Benny smacked my face. "Come on, big bro. She's here. You're finally smiling. Let's have some fun!" He paused, concern spreading across his face as he studied Rae. "Do you even do shots? You're so sophlista...sophristic...cated."

Rae crossed her arms and leaned back in her chair. "I can do shots just fine, Benny. And you might want to lay off the big words tonight."

"Don't want you to hurt yourself," I added.

He wasn't paying any attention, watching his pecs as he danced. "Meet me there in five. Or ten. Or twenty," he said, laughing as he returned to the bar.

I shrugged, hands in the air. "I have no defense."

"It's the holiday season. Relax."

"You're telling me to relax? Geez. What is wrong with me?"

"I have a whole checklist."

I broke out into laughter as I looked out to the rest of the party, singing, dancing, and stuffing their faces with no coronary concerns, although that was probably shortsighted. "So, what do you think?"

"No sign of any Hooter's girls."

"You sound disappointed. But seriously."

Rae glanced around before concluding, "You guys are really Italian."

I laughed. "How is one *really* Italian?"

"I don't know."

I huffed. "Just say it."

"Say what?"

"You know you want to ask."

Rae shrugged. "Ask what? I have no idea what you're talking about."

"Are we connected? It's okay. You're not the first to ask."

"Well, perhaps I was a little curious and a lot nervous. Before we met."

"Do you think I'd drive a Honda sedan if I were connected?" I used my best Brooklyn accent. "Anyway, the mafia don't exist. If it did, you wouldn't live to talk about it." I pressed my fingers together and held them up to her face. "Capisce?"

"Capisce," she said, smiling.

My sister and her family, parents, aunts, and uncles all left shortly after dessert, leaving me as the only supervision for deviants from seven different printing facilities. I cringed at the thought of the bill, which I realized was basically being supported by my lack of bonus, but then shrugged it off. The alcohol flowed like the Po River through Venice, so I cared a little less than before.

We stood at the bar. Frankie pushed two shots in front of Rae and me that nearly toppled over.

"What's this?" Rae asked, picking it up and sniffing.

"Limoncino," I said, grabbing one.

"What's that?"

"Lemoncello? You ever heard of that? Same thing."

"Yes." She clinked my glass. "Salud, ya chooch."

I laughed, tossed my shot back, and said, "Now, you're just getting carried away. You're a feminist. You should understand my frustration with your cultural appropriation."

"Oh, is that so?" Rae asked, dimples beaming. But then her smile disappeared. "Do you have a problem working underneath a woman?"

"No. I work very well underneath women. I do this amazing nipple twisting thing. Drives them wild."

She smacked my shoulder. "I meant professionally."

I feigned embarrassment. "Oh, I'm terribly sorry. In all seriousness, no. Not at all. As long as she's competent."

Rae cocked her head. "Are you saying women aren't competent in managerial positions?"

"I just don't want a woman to be my boss just because she's a woman. I wouldn't want an incompetent male boss, either." *Like my father.*

"Well, how do you feel about me?"

I had no idea how to answer that. I had no idea what the answer actually was. "I think we should stop drinking."

"Why do you say that? I'm just starting to not wish explosive diarrhea on you."

I slapped my cheeks with both hands in a mock swoon. "Awww. That's the nicest thing you've ever said to me."

A few minutes later, we found ourselves back at our own table, just talking as the crowd grew more raucous by the glass over at the bar.

Rae took a sip of a Bellini and stared me in the eye. "Why are you such an ass half the time?"

"Only half the time?"

"Most of the time. Seriously, though. Why do you have to give me such a hard time?" I was about to apologize, but she cut me off. "You guys are all the same. You think that you're not, but you are."

I didn't know how to defend myself. *You ignite something*

in me...you drive me crazy...I hate you one minute...but can't stop thinking about you the next. "I am different. I promise."

"You're not."

"I am."

"Fine." Rae stood up, grabbed my chair by the side and spun me toward her with a grunt and a squeak of the chair. "You don't see me for me. You just see this." She used her hands to present her body. That dress.

"Well, you do have the sexiest kneecaps I've ever seen," I said, as she stepped closer. *What in the hell is going on?* My heart raced. My words slowed. "If I'm...just another guy... why are you...here?"

Rae sat down on my lap facing me and shook out her hair while maintaining the most intense eye contact I'd ever experienced. The world slowed to a stop. Then she wrapped her arms around my neck and gyrated one revolution around my crotch. Oh. My. God.

I whispered, "This is...a bad..." My eyes closed and I couldn't move. Each heavy breath in my ear was like a bicycle pump to my crotch. I was a metal pipe stuck in putty. A giant, lit-up sausage wiener in the middle of a restaurant. Every fiber of my being was jacked up like an amplifier.

"I have to tell you something," Rae said in a hot whisper.

"What?" I groaned.

"You are...The. Same."

Rae stood up, highlighted my crotch with her eyes, and then covered a laugh.

"That's...so wrong." I stood up and hid my considerable cannoli beneath a napkin. I stepped toward her. "Do I have a biological need to procreate? Yes. Yes, I do. But that doesn't mean we're all the same. You were just able to use science to trick me."

"Right."

Benny wobbled over, interrupting. "Hey, look at me!" A

piece of mistletoe dangled from a string and a stick attached to his belt.

"Oh, God. Dude, what are you doing?" I asked annoyed, but also thankful for the distraction.

"What? You told me I couldn't wear the mistletoe on my hat."

"You can't do that."

Benny nodded to Rae. "Why don't we let the lady decide?"

"She's going to be your…"

Before I could finish, Rae swiped a steak knife from the table and sliced the string like a Marine. Benny and I froze, staring at Rae, mouths agape.

She handed the murdered mistletoe to Benny with a smile. "Here's my decision."

"…boss," I finished.

Benny's mouth hung open as his eyes went back and forth from Rae to his crotch before saying, "That's so wrong."

I patted him on the shoulder. "She's good at that, bro." I nodded to the mistletoe. "Why don't you put that in water and grab a glass for yourself?"

Benny slinked away, well, as much as anyone as muscled as he was could.

My blood had returned to its normal pathways, her Rambo impersonation so terrifying. I tossed the napkin on the table and turned to Rae, who had thankfully returned the steak knife to its rightful place. "That was horrifyingly emasculating and mind-blowingly amazing at the same time."

"Just living my mission statement," she said with a smile. "With that, I should probably go."

I wasn't sure if I was disappointed or not. "Okay. I'll see you to a cab." We headed to the coat closet. I grabbed hers and slipped it onto her from behind, and then she turned to me.

"Why did you really come to the party?" I asked, not sure what I wanted to hear.

Rae studied my face. "I had some news that I wanted to deliver in person."

"That I'm just like all the rest?" I asked, unenthused.

"To the contrary. As much as we've clashed, I've done my homework on you. You have an excellent reputation. We don't have the same style, but that doesn't mean yours is wrong."

"Well...thank you." Even though my blood flow was still normal, I covered my crotch protectively with both hands.

She continued, "And the numbers were good. I won't blame you too much for the PremaPrint squeeze of late." She eyed my hands. "Why are you doing that?"

"I'm waiting for the low blow."

Rae laughed. "There's no low blow coming. I got you a three-year guarantee at your current salary plus cost-of-living adjustments and you will take part in the bonus pool, dependent on how your district performs."

I scratched my head in confusion. "How can you remember all that after all we've had to drink? You're like a cyborg. How do you go from lap dance to contract negotiations?"

She frowned, assessing me. "I thought you'd be happy. I won't be able to fire you."

"What if I plan on quitting because you're blasting a square peg into a round hole, and I don't want to be a part of it?"

"Is that really how you feel? The industry is consolidating. You are either a consolidator or consolidated. You're not gonna find a better fit. And it's a requirement for the deal to go through."

"Great," I said, unenthused.

"You'll be in charge of all Donati, PremaPrint, and a few of the Kane shops in Jersey."

"I should get a raise for that."

"Ted Whitaker at Prema would be happy to oversee you instead."

"Fine," I said, annoyed. "I'll look at the offer. You could have emailed or called."

"True."

"You came for the lap dance," I said, a smile spreading across my face.

"That was not a lap dance," Rae said as she stepped closer. "I came here for this." She pushed me against the wall with considerable force. I groaned in mild pain, but it disappeared as her lips fit to mine. To say I was stunned would be an understatement, but I quickly regrouped, reaching into her unbuttoned coat and pulling her toward me by her perfect hips. Her body melted into mine as the intensity of our kiss grew. Her fingers found the back of my head, massaging my scalp, and driving me wild.

But then she pulled away. Our eyes stayed locked for a moment before she looked away.

"How are those kneecaps now?" I whispered.

"Solid as a rock. Just like you," she said, more confidently than I knew she was.

I looked down and shrugged. "You should've been a scientist."

She smirked. "That's not science. It's art."

"Art is spontaneous. I totally knew that was coming."

Rae laughed and crossed her arms. "You absolutely did not. You looked like Marty McFly in *Back to the Future* when his mother kisses him."

I shook my head. "I kissed you better than you've ever be kissed."

"How could you possibly know that?"

"How many Italians have you kissed in your life?"

"You're the first."

I shrugged, case closed. "Well, there you have it."

"That's it?"

"Italians are rated the top kissers in the world. Google it."

"But you're an Italian-American."

My smile disappeared. "You know, despite your beauty, I find you very annoying."

She laughed. "I'm sorry that you find my superiority annoying."

"Mmm, hmm," I said, not sure of what else to say, well, about anything. "So...now what?"

Rae buttoned up her coat. "I should go. Let me know what you think about the contract by the end of the year. Have a Merry Christmas and a happy New Year. Thanks for having me...to the party. Good night." She turned without making eye contact.

I ran my fingers through my hair, my once-beautifully manicured brain now a war zone of confusion and conflicting thought. "Wait."

She didn't.

I exhaled long and slow. "What. Just. Happened?"

———

Rae's Deal Notes

- ~~No! No! No! No! Can't believe I did that! It was kinda fun and my G_d, that man can kiss. I'm such an idiot...~~
- Refocus on the prize. Get the deal done.
- Apologize. Get contract signed.

CHAPTER
Ten

SHE KISSED ME. She *kissed* me. She kissed *me*. Why? Was it just the booze or was there more to it? Why did she even show up in the first place? I white boarded it. Ran Monte Carlo simulations. Consulted with love expert Jean-Claude Van Dog. It didn't matter what I did; I had no answers. Zero in English. Zero in Italian. The entire week leading up to Christmas was a cloud of confusion. I didn't even sing along to "Dominick the Donkey/The Italian Christmas Donkey" song, my favorite tune. The hee-haw gets me every time. Maybe I do go to Leo Land in my head like Rae said.

We had no direct contact the entire week. And by that, I mean, no phone calls, video chats, or clichéd make-out sessions in oversized coat closets. Rae emailed me the contract on Monday morning with nothing more than 'Let me know what you think about this', but I hadn't thought for one moment about it. I had bigger issues to figure out.

Normally, I plan ahead, but the mess of the week meant I was late on my Christmas shopping, so I found myself with perennial tardy yuletiders, Benny and Frankie, at the mall in my town. We shut down the shop at one on Christmas Eve, grabbed lunch, and then strolled the decked-out halls with the rest of the procrastinators.

We fended off an aggressive kiosk owner, intent on hosing us down with cologne by disappearing into the crowd outside the Apple store, and then out the back of it, continuing down the hallway.

"What are you getting your girl?" Benny asked, straight faced.

I gave him a hefty dose of side eye. "She's not my girl."

Frankie raised an eyebrow. "But you knew exactly who he was talking about."

Benny shook his head. "Man, the look on your face when you came back after she left."

"You guys were drunk. You know nothing. I hate her. I just need her to think that I don't. But make no mistake. She's ruining my life."

"Riiiiight," Benny said.

Frankie said, "You guys should just have hate sex and get it over with."

"Get what over with?"

"The tension." Frankie rolled his eyes. "For such a smart guy…"

Benny took over. "Look, she's Jewish. You're not gonna end up with her. But she's smoking. She's a fling."

"If Pop has his way, she's gonna be my boss."

Benny shrugged as we headed into Coach. "Well, you know what they say: 'Nothing like the boss knowing your wienie size'."

I chuckled, shaking my head. "Nobody has ever said that in the history of corporate America."

Benny shrugged. "Maybe I should be a management guru."

"Yeah, good luck with that," I said.

"You wanna go halfsies on a bag for Mom?" Benny asked, nodding to a selection of Coach bags atop a table.

"Depends. Is that when you get half the credit, but I pay for the whole thing?"

"It could be, if you want it that way."

I laughed, shaking my head. "I'll go halfsies if you pay cash."

Benny looked around. It was nothing but men. "Why is this a total sausage fest? We're shopping."

Frankie rubbed his chin, his few brain cells attempting an intelligent connection. "This doesn't make any sense. This is the Mecca of American women."

We agreed on a white and gold pennie shoulder bag. "Because women actually plan ahead. And we're not here to pick up chicks."

Frankie's confusion grew. "There's never a bad time to pick up chicks. And you never know when one might show up in your life. That wants to do dirty things. It's serendipity."

"Sounds more like serendouchery."

We paid and headed out. Benny said, "I feel like we need to raise our game."

I broke out into laughter. "Ya think? Your game is pitiful. It's based on faux machoism and hair product."

Benny clutched his considerable chest. "That hurts, bro."

"Am I wrong? You remember when we were grabbing lunch at the deli and there was a cute chick in front of us? You called *no one* on the phone to discuss how much you can bench press. And added a hundred pounds."

Benny shrugged. "I don't recall that. No."

Frankie said, "That's a good idea, though."

I groaned. "Don't you want to connect with someone on a deeper level rather than just get in her pants?"

Benny shook his head. "Not particularly, no."

Frankie added, "Yeah, no. That sounds terrible."

Benny said, "And they put you in charge? No wonder Dad's selling the company."

"That's a low blow, bro."

"I could go for one of those," Benny said, waving to a passing woman, who ignored him.

Benny elbowed Frankie and nodded to a small gift shop, Things Remembered. "Let's get each other personalized flasks."

"We did that last year."

"Can you really go wrong with two flasks?"

I rolled my eyes, and we rolled into Things Remembered. There were a bunch of holiday-themed decorations and gift ideas at the front of the shop with vases, champagne glasses, and an array of things to be personalized.

I joked, "Just what I need. Two bulls in a china shop."

"You want one?" Benny asked, heading to the back.

I shook my head. "I'm good."

I browsed the store until Benny and Frankie were done, stopping at a stuffed toy. It was an old man in a blue suit, a shawl, and a yarmulke sitting on a bench. It was named, 'The Mensch on a Bench'.

I picked it up, laughing as I remembered the Mohel with a Boil. "I totally have to get this."

Benny asked, "For her?"

"Yes. Inside joke."

"You have inside jokes, but you hate her?" Benny stared at me, eyebrow raised.

Frankie added, "What the hell is a mensch?"

I shrugged and headed to the counter. "No idea, but I should probably look it up before I give it to her."

Benny nudged Frankie playfully. "Give *what* to her?"

"Shut up."

———

We finished our shopping about an hour later and made it to my parents' house by five, the last to arrive. There were at least thirty people there, overflowing from the kitchen, the den, and living room. Christmas was pretty much the only time anyone was even allowed in the living room, but God forbid a child entered. At least six Italian women would whip wooden spoons from ankle holsters and chase them back to the den or basement. Thankfully, we had moved on from the plastic-covered couch days of old. Not that there was a seat to be had when we arrived.

Laughter and chatter overshadowed Andrea Bocelli singing in the background. He wasn't actually there, just streaming on Pandora. Tall white and red candles flickered around the room while a fire roared in the den. Bombardinos, a fabulous and potent mixture of eggnog and whipped cream topped with cinnamon in an espresso cup, flowed around the house with reckless abandon.

So, Christmas Eve in Italian households is probably a bit different from most. Maybe you've heard of the Feast of the Seven Fishes and already know this, but if you don't, it's an Italian tradition on Christmas Eve. It's pretty simple. Seven courses. Seven fishes. I'd be cool if it was only four or five because once we get to the smelt and eel, things go downhill for all but the most diehards. There's no set lineup, but bacala, scungili, spaghetti with clam sauce, fried smelt, and calamari (often pronounced galamad by the old timers) were some of the traditional ones. My mother and Nonna typically whipped up some shrimp scampi and lobster fra diavalo as well. It was a legit feast and a nice impromptu leg workout. Seven courses, up and down...

When you host thirty people, you have to get creative. Tables were arranged from the dining room into the kitchen a bit like Tetris. Kids and their parents were banished from the dining room and the rest were based on family tenure. I was the oldest of my siblings and cousins, so I had been at the adult table since my grandfather passed a decade ago. Nonna still wore black every day, but that's a story for another time.

My cousin Anthony was twenty-five and six-foot-four and still sat at one of the fold-up kid tables, his knees nearly toppling the table with every shift. If you wanted to move up, somebody had to kick the bucket, or get banished. Sometimes, it took decades. We loved each other, but nobody was willing to giving up their spot, even temporarily.

Anyway, we sat around the table awaiting another round of fish. My mother had a system to maximize culinary pleasure. She would start with a crowd pleaser or two, say a shrimp scampi, and then mix in the questionable ones once the Bombardinos kicked in, then go strong again to finish off. We were in the lull in the middle.

I sat in a non-cornered seat as usual, next to Uncle Freddy, with Benny and Frankie across from me. My sister insisted on sitting two inches on the other side of the threshold, having earned a spot after me, but reluctantly relinquished it to Benny once my niece was born.

My Uncle Freddy took a bite of Capitone, which is fried eel, and asked, "So, Leo, what's new with the business?"

"I don't really know what to say. I still don't think it's the right move, but I'm doing what was asked of me. We've been discussing the future of the employees. We're going to lose people."

Pop interrupted, "Anyone who doesn't stick will be better off."

"Why is that?" I asked, annoyed.

"Because you're the only one who actually wants to work there."

"You want Benny and Frankie to lose their jobs?"

Benny looked at Frankie and said, "I'm cool with that. You?"

"I'm hoping for it."

Benny added, "We don't pay you rent anyway and eat most of your food, so nothing would really change for us."

"We'd have a lot more free time," Frankie said excitedly.

My father took a sip of wine to wash down the eel. "Have you talked to Rae lately?"

I shook my head. "No. Haven't heard from her since the party. They want me to sign an agreement to stay on for three years, be district manager."

"Great. It's moving in the right direction." Pop raised his wineglass. "To Leo. District manager."

I popped a piece of eel into my mouth and muttered, "I was supposed to be CEO of this family's firm, not the district manager for some soulless corporate entity."

"This is what's best for the family," Pop said.

Beating him to it, I mocked, "End of story."

My mother turned the charm up a notch, forcing a smile. "It's Christmas Eve. Enough of this business talk. I care much more about what everyone thinks of the Capitone."

"What's Capitone?" Viola asked from the other room.

Sal said, "It's eel."

"This is friggin' eel?" Gia shrieked, dropping her fork with a clank. "I thought it was Capitone?"

Laughter broke out at the adult table.

"This is the adult table. Please keep conversations limited to your own room," I said to Gia's glare.

"What's the deal with the eel again?" Frankie asked.

Nonna answered, "It-a symbolizes the victory over Satan. It's-a the snake of Original Sin."

Benny turned up his nose at the rest of what was on his plate. "That's disgusting."

"Nonna, is it true that you used to keep the eel in the bathtub before cooking it when you were back in Brooklyn?" I asked.

Pop interjected, "No. That was my mother. It was more of a Neapolitan thing."

My mother added, "Mama taught me the recipe. We added it to our celebration as we merged our families together."

"That was the best tradition you could come up with? It couldn't be Neapolitan ice cream for dinner?"

My mother said lovingly, "Shut your mouths and eat up."

Benny nodded, forked a piece of eel, and said, "How the hell am I supposed to do that?"

We all laughed. I mouthed to Benny, "Ask Nonna about the seven fishes again."

A smile curled up on Benny's face. "Hey, Nonna. Speaking of traditions, where does the feast come from again?"

My mother quickly spit out the words, "There are seven sacraments, seven deadly sins."

"Nonna has a different story," Frankie said. "Don't you, Nonna?"

My mother cut in. "It originated in southern Italy. My family has been celebrating it for decades. As Roman Catholics, we used to fast before communion. Seven sacraments. Seven deadly sins. Seven fishes. Eat up. The Capitone is best when it's hot."

"So, we fasted, but we ate fish? That doesn't make any sense," I said.

"No, that's-a not it," Nonna said. "St. Thomas Aquinas said it's-a because meat-a makes-a people horny and fish-a do not."

"Why do you encourage her, boys?" Pop asked, all of us holding in laughter.

"What does horny mean?" Mia asked from the other room.

The laughter could be held in no more as both rooms broke out into hysterics.

"What I really want to know is why the table looks like Santa crashed his sleigh into a tree," Benny said, brow furrowed.

"What are you talking about?" I asked, as Benny pointed to a cornucopia of pinecones and red Christmas balls scattered between candles, wine bottles, and serving dishes.

"The pinecones. Rudolph's nuts rolling across the table."

My mother signed the cross. "Honestly, Benito. It's Christmas and there are children."

"Way to ruin it, bro," I said, smirking.

He mouthed, "Wait until you see the nativity set."

As if stuffing ourselves with seven courses of fish and pasta wasn't enough, there was still dessert.

I stood with Benny, Frankie, and Anthony shooting the shit while sipping on a digestivo, a drink meant to aid in digestion, but to be honest, I'm pretty certain it's just an excuse to keep drinking. Mine was sambuca, which tasted like licorice.

My mother interrupted with a tap on my shoulder. "Can you help me with the dessert?"

I furrowed my brow. "Of course." It was odd that she was asking, but I downed my sambuca and followed her to the kitchen.

"You need me to reach something?"

She shook her head. "Sit down. I want to talk to you about something."

I plopped into a chair next to the table, overflowing with desserts. Italian cheesecake. Cannoli. Four panettones, which was like the love child of a fruitcake and bread. Italian butter cookies. Lemon ricotta cake. I wasn't sure whether to chow down or vomit. We used to have a huge medley of nuts as well, but the jokes got to be too much as the boys and me hit our teenage years. "What's up, Ma?"

She stared at me for a moment, just the two of us in a quiet room in a raucous house, and then said, "It makes me sad that you're alone during the holidays. You're thirty years old. And look at those two." She nodded to Benny and Frankie through the doorway into the den. "You're our only hope."

"So, you're saying I'm Obi Wan Kenobi?"

"What? Stop messing around. I'm serious."

I huffed. "What do you want me to do? I haven't found the right person."

"Natalia is a sweet girl. Beautiful. From a wonderful Italian family. Remember the summers we spent up at Villa Roma? Didn't you like her? What's changed?"

"Ma, come on. We were teenagers back then. Yeah, we liked each other. But I also liked velvet track suits and high-top sneakers. We have nothing in common. We tried as adults, too. It didn't work."

Her voice firmed. "It's about the family. And why do you think Italian wines are so good?"

I laughed unexpectedly. "Look, I love our culture, but if you're trying to tell me that Italian wine is more powerful than love, I'm just gonna lose it, Ma."

My mother's attention shifted to the countertop of the hutch. I did a double take.

She said, "Oh, mother of God. Those two mamalukes. Every Christmas." She signed the cross.

The nativity scene. I stood up and rearranged the animals, so the ox was not mounting the donkey from behind.

"You should worry about those two. Not me. People my age don't get married in their early twenties like you did. Give me some time. I've got enough to worry about with the business." I needed to change the subject. "Pop is getting you a pretty nice gift."

She smiled, but it quickly faded.

"What's wrong?" I asked, stepping closer to her.

"I'm not saying I'm not excited about Florida."

"You know?"

My mother chuckled. "Of course, I know. He told Uncle Freddy. Uncle Freddy told Aunt Franny. It's easy peasy."

I huffed. "Pop doesn't tell me anything."

My mother shook her head and caressed my face. "I don't care about the gift. The only thing I want is for my boy to get married and become a man."

I stepped back and laughed. "Ma, I'm thirty years old!"

She said, "You'll become a man on your wedding night."

I threw up my hands. "Ma, I'm sorry to have to tell you this—"

She turned away, giving me the hand. "Ah, ah, ah! You're a boy until your wedding night."

"Okay. Fine. You can have that one."

My mother grabbed my chin and looked into my eyes. I could see the sadness growing. "Can you make your mother happy and give Natalia another try? I really think you two can make it work."

I took a deep breath and exhaled slowly. "Okay. I'll call Natalia."

She pinched my cheek and then slapped it. "Good boy. I knew you'd come around. Mothers know best."

"Really? You married dad."

My mother winked at me. "I wasn't a mother then."

"What about Nonna?"

"Why do you ask so many questions? Just listen to your mama. Love is a verb. An action. Don't worry about the feelings. You'll find common ground. And make beautiful Italian babies."

I shrugged, smiling sheepishly. "I'm happy to try."

My mother's tone turned firm. "On your wedding night."

"Right. I can't wait to become a man."

My mother wrapped me in a hug. "I love you, Leo. Don't make me give you the spoon."

CHAPTER
Eleven

IT WAS a light week at work between Christmas and New Year's. Normally, I'd plan for the following year, set my goals, clean up and reorganize my office, have a few lunches with the crew, but not only was my future up in the air making planning moot, but nobody was overly enthused with their bonus number, including me. So, I lay low in my office, attempting to figure out how to get myself out of my current predicament.

But I was interrupted. A FaceTime call popped up onto my laptop. It was Rae. My heart rate went full Ferrari. I fixed my hair, made sure my eyebrows were firmly attached, used the screen's reflection to check up my nose for any olives in the jar, and then answered with a smile.

Rae's beautiful face filled my screen. Her mauve gloss sparkled as she smiled. Yes, some dudes know what the color mauve is. We're a rare breed.

I smiled and gave a goofy wave. "Ms. Kane. To what do I owe the honor?"

"I wanted to say thank you for the mensch. I cracked up."

"No problem. They were out of the Mohel with a Boil. Apparently, huge seller."

She laughed, giving me a closeup of her dimples. I regret not having snapped a screenshot of it, creepy as it might sound. Rae said, "So, Hanukkah isn't as lame as you thought, huh?"

"I never said it was lame. I'm just not convinced it's as good as Christmas, eight nights or not. It's not eight presents to one. Stockings are, well, stocked, and we had to put the tree on a platform last year to make more room for all the gifts."

"Sounds like gluttonous consumerism to me."

I chuckled. "I can't win with you."

"I feel the same way about you." Rae looked down at her desk for a moment, her voice fading, "Speaking of feelings, some of them quite awkward, should we talk about what happened at the party?"

I feigned confusion. "What happened at the party?"

Rae sighed. "Much to my everlasting shame, we kissed."

I scrunched up my face with exaggeration, as if deep in thought. "I distinctly remember *you* kissing *me*."

Rae crossed her arms. "Fine. It was my fault." Her tone morphed serious. "It was totally unprofessional. I'm sorry. You can submit a formal complaint if you feel like it was unwanted." Her face reddened.

I feigned deep thought. "Unwanted? Who's to say? It *was* unexpected, and you were reasonably decent at it, so...don't worry about any formal complaints being filed."

"Reasonably decent?" Rae asked, eyebrows shooting off the screen.

"Yeah. Not bad. Solid, for a non-Italian." I suppressed a smile, but couldn't hold it. "It's not a big deal. Don't worry about it." I checked over my shoulder directly behind me to make sure I'd erased my whiteboarding session about what her kiss meant. I exhaled upon positive confirmation.

"I have been worrying about it. I had too much to drink."

Why was she making excuses? Did she regret it professionally and personally? I didn't know, but the more she protested, the more my mood slipped.

Rae's brow furrowed. "What are you thinking about?"

I answered without thinking, "Benny and Frankie think we should have hate sex and get it out of our systems."

Rae nearly fell out of her seat. "What?"

I don't know why, but I felt the need to defend their stunadity. "I mean, we're both attractive people—"

"That is absurd."

My flustering snowballed. "I'm not saying I agree with it. It's not the worst idea, though. We take care of business. Cut the tension. Move on. That's their thinking, anyway?" Had I committed a crime at that moment, I absolutely would've pled temporary insanity.

Rae scoffed. "I have nothing in my system that would require that. And I don't hate you. You're an annoying and often sexist jerk, but hate is a strong word."

"You said sexist, not sexy, right?"

She ignored me, which was probably the correct strategy. "So, we agree, it wasn't terrible, but it was a mistake."

I couldn't let her have the last dig. "Yeah, it was a mistake. It could never work."

She apparently felt the same way. "Agreed. You're going to be my subordinate. Personality mismatch. Different religions. The list is long."

I waved her concern away with exaggeration. "It's fine. It's in the past. I get it. I'm attractive. Your alcohol consumption lowered your guard, and you followed your instinct. I respect your professionalism, but nobody's perfect."

"Can we move on?"

"Of course. As long as you agree to never maul me again."

"Maul?" she growled.

Despite the computer screens between us, I covered my face in defense. "Just kidding! Geez. I'm with you. Let's move on. We've covered the mensch and the make-out session. Anything else?"

"Have you looked at the contract?"

"Yes," I lied. Truth is, I hadn't looked at it. I still couldn't accept that path as my own. "But it's early goings and my lawyer is on vacation until January 3rd. You know what would help me decide on this whole thing?"

"What's that?" Rae asked, tentatively.

"A tour of PremaPrint." I wasn't anywhere close to sure that this deal would close, but before it went bad, I figured I should gather some competitive intelligence.

"Why?"

"You want me to run it, right? Before I sign this contract, I want to know what it's all about."

"Fine. We'll set it up. Let me just check my calendar….late morning on January 6th at their facility in Queens?"

"It's a date," I said with a smirk. Her screen went blank. "Aaaand she hung up on me."

Rae's Deal Notes

- Crisis averted! The anxiety was killing me.
- ~~The mensch was a thoughtful gift. He must've had a brain aneurism…who even knew there was a brain behind all that talking? Hate sex? I mean, honestly…~~
- Set up PremaPrint tour.

CHAPTER
Twelve

NEW YEAR'S came and went. I party-hopped with Benny and Frankie, starting at my parents' place, then heading into town to hit the bars on Main Street. We ended at a Hawaiian restaurant that turns into a dance club after eleven. It's typically a lot of fun once you look past the strangeness of it all. While many people got leid, nobody in my crew got laid. Not that I was looking for it. All I wanted was somebody to kiss at midnight, but I didn't find that, either.

That being said, I did wake up to licks to my face on New Year's Day. I sat up to avoid the onslaught of slobber. Jean-Claude Van Dog popped onto my lap and climbed up, front paws on my chest, continuing his attack. "Easy boy. You need to meet someone worse than I do."

In the den, Frankie lay seemingly half dead on the couch in nothing but heart-strewn boxers and blue running shoes he did not wear out the night before. I held Jean-Claude over Frankie's face to check his vitals. J.C. lapped up Frankie's ear lobe like it was coated in beef.

Frankie giggled playfully. "Oooh, that tickles," he muttered. "More, baby."

"Oh, God," I said, pulling Jean-Claude away, suddenly realizing why we went through so much peanut butter.

I bundled up in my black Eddie Bauer parka and headed outside to walk Jean-Claude. As the puffed-out pooch did his business on his favorite oak tree behind our complex, I replayed the events of the past few weeks in my mind. My father's desire to sell the business. Meeting Rae. Hating Rae. Kissing Rae. A boring, lonely New Year's. The promise to my mother that I'd call Natalia. What struck me most was how quickly things could shift. CEO-in-waiting to pissant. Hate to confusion. Not gonna happen to gonna make it happen. Much as I wasn't excited about it, I intended to keep the promise to my mother, as I always did. Family first. It's a rule.

I strolled around the complex so that Jean-Claude could strut his ten-pound stuff and mark his territory. That bastard beagle, Maurice, needed to know who was in charge in our hood. I did a double take and chuckled at the sight above me. Frankie's jeans hung from a bare dogwood tree below our apartment window.

I headed inside and decided not to ask any questions, but the boys rehashed the supposed epic night through lunch, after which I excused myself. After the craziness of the past few weeks, I needed to make the start of the new year better than how it ended.

I stared at Natalia's phone number in my contact list for a moment before dialing.

Natalia answered with a curious tone, "Hello?"

"Hey. Happy New Year," I said, doing my best to pretend it wasn't weird that I was calling so out-of-the-blue. My heart raced. I was a lot more nervous to talk to a woman I dumped than I'd expected.

"Hi, Leo. Happy New Year. I was surprised to see your number pop up."

"Yeah, well. It's been too long," I said, suddenly wishing I had game-planned or at least slapped myself across the face in the bathroom a few times before making the call.

"We broke up."

"Yeah, there is that. Listen, I've been thinking about some things…"

"Like what?"

"You. Me. I've…missed you. I was hoping I could buy you a meal and catch up."

"Yeah. I'd like that. Emilio's?"

I exhaled. "That's our place. Seven on Friday?"

"It's a date," she said, sweetly. "I'm glad you called."

"Me, too."

———

Emilio's was a cozy, rustic Italian restaurant. A long, dark wood bar oversaw the main dining room with its matching wood beams. Green vines outlined white brick and arched windows. I sat at the corner of the bar, my back to the wall. I fended off the inviting eyes of two gaudy cougars while keeping my own eyes out for Natalia. The door opened, and she entered. My breath was sucked from my chest.

It had only been a few months since I had ended things, and I had known Natalia for most of my life, but she was more beautiful than I remembered. I didn't know where to look first. Her jet black hair shined from the soft sconce lighting beside her. The cherry red lipstick. The shoe straps wrapping her taut calves. A tuxedoed maître d' slipped the coat from her shoulders, revealing a powder blue cutout dress that exposed slim sides. I would've dropped a few ice cubes down my pants to cool things off a bit had it been socially acceptable.

I waved, catching her eye, and headed toward her, thankful to make it past the cougars without one of them slashing my nice blue sport coat. Natalia smiled, her blue eyes sparkling deeper with each step. I kissed her on each tan cheek, our lips nearly brushing in between. I held her shoulders, arms extended, taking her all in. I stared down at her, almost a foot shorter than me. "Wow. Just...wow."

She relished the attention, smiling brightly. "Thank you. Sorry, I'm a bit late."

"Worth the wait."

The maître d' smiled and said with a modest Italian accent, "Pardon-a the interruption, but may I show you to your table, Mr. Donati?"

My hand found the bare small of Natalia's back, soft and smooth. I fought the urge to caress her. My hands missed her, too. The maître d' led us to a table tucked in the corner beside a potted dracaena tree, brown with long and thin green leaves. He left us with the menus and a smile.

"So, how was your Christmas?" I asked, noticing her out-of-season tan. "Did you go away?"

"Christmas was great. I needed a break from school, so Marie and I visited her grandparents in Fort Lauderdale for a few days. You?"

"It was fine." I wasn't about to go into all the family business details, although I was sure she knew some of it through the Italian grapevine, surprisingly not an Italian saying, despite our love of both grapes and gossip.

Speaking of grapes, we ordered a Soave Classico, a light white wine with hints of citrus and honeydew, that pairs well with a good parmigiana. It was a must at Emilio's and one of Natalia's favorites.

"Salud," I said. We clinked glasses, and I took a sip. "I haven't had this in a while. I know you love it."

"I'm surprised you remembered," Natalia said.

"Why wouldn't I?"

Natalia's typical confidence disappeared, her eyes finding a crusty loaf of basketed bread between us. "You never seemed all that interested in me. Or at least after a while."

The words hit hard, but it was a lot more accurate than Nonna's spaghetti slinging. "I'm sorry I made you feel that way. It wasn't you. It was us. I wanted to settle down, live life a little slower. I was working all summer while you were off from school, going to the beach all day and out all night with Marie and Gina." Even though it was only a few months ago, it seemed less important at that moment. I grabbed her hand. "You were never not important to me."

"I'm glad you called. Have you...dated at all?"

"Not really. No." The most action I had in the past few months was with Rae, followed by Jean-Claude. She appeared satisfied by my answer, but I wasn't sure I wanted to know hers. I asked anyway. "You?"

"Yeah, I have. A lot."

Not the answer I was hoping for. "Uhh, okay."

She apparently picked up on my discomfort. "I'm here, aren't I?" Thankfully, she changed the subject. "I don't know why, but after you called, I thought about that kiss when we bumped into each other after the pub crawl. My sophomore year."

"I remember. Barely. It wasn't your fault, though. It was the booze. It was outside the old Book Revue?"

Natalia laughed and grabbed my hand. "Yes. Benny was eating a slice from Little Vincent's, but he topped it with rice and beans from Pancho's. Wanted to make a Mexican pizza."

"I rarely make excuses for Benny, but that place makes a good margarita. It dulls your wits, and he's already operating from a low level."

Natalia laughed then continued, "Frankie was throwing handfuls of rice in the air as we kissed, yelling that we were gonna get married." She smiled. "I had wanted to do that for a long, long time. I had such a huge crush on you growing up. I couldn't wait for every summer to go upstate with you."

"Crazy day." A nervous chuckle escaped my mouth. "Even back then, you were a pretty good kisser."

"I'm Italian."

"That's what I said."

Natalia's brow furrowed. "To who?"

I shook my head to shake Rae from it. "I just kiss random people and when they regain form from the puddle I left them in, they ask how I could possibly be so good at it. I smile and say, 'I'm Italian.'"

Natalia laughed, but then her face morphed serious. "Can I ask you something?"

"Anything."

"What made you call?"

I scraped at the small stain on the tablecloth as I spoke. "I was thinking about you after New Years. There was just something missing in my life. You popped into my head. I took it as a sign." I shrugged. "What made you agree?"

"Well, as I said, I've been on lots of dates—"

I interrupted, "We don't really have to go into that."

"I was having trouble moving on. I think there's a reason for that."

Our eyes connected for a long moment before she looked away, smiling. In case you were wondering, she was referring to me and all my fabulousness. I'm hard to get over.

We continued to reminisce over dinner. The lady had a pesto and olive crusted cod while I had the chicken a la Emilio, which is the love child of parmigiana and a la vodka. Try it some time. You're welcome.

"Do you remember that lake we used to swim in on the way home from the Catskills?" Natalia asked.

I laughed. "How could I forget? It's the site of the infamous disappearing bikini top. It was the first time I saw naked boobs. How is your mom, by the way?"

Natalia cocked her head with a smirk, her blue eyes boring into me, but then smiled. "She's fine, but I remember it as the first time we held hands. You jumped off that cliff with me into the lake."

"Oh, yeah. That, too." I smiled sheepishly.

Natalia continued, "It wasn't romantic or even a big deal to you, because I was only thirteen, but it was for me. Major crush."

"You never told me that," I said, willing Mrs. Romano's boobs from my mind, amazing as they once were.

"Did you know that Anthony Russo and Michelle Alberto are getting married?"

"No. I'm surprised my mother hasn't held that over my head."

Natalia continued, "Supposedly, he cheated on her with some Irish girl who worked at Flannagan's, but they're going to move past it."

"The beer specials *are* dangerous there. Speaking of the need to drink, how is your kindergarten class this year?"

Natalia's face brightened. "They're amazing. I just love them. I mean, it's tough to have twenty-three of them running around a classroom all day, but to play a part in raising them. It's a blessing."

I smiled, happy she was passionate about her career. At least one of us was. "It was always fun to see you with kids. Mia and Viola always loved you. Even Matteo and he only likes spaghetti. Or just throwing it against the wall. I've never seen him actually eat any of it." As you know, most kids grow out of throwing their food at the wall by kindergarten, but Italians don't. I'm afraid Nonna might need Tommy John surgery soon, typically reserved only for baseball pitchers. "You really have a way with kids, though."

"So do you. I always thought you'd be a great father. Husband, too. You're smart, you have a big future with your family business."

I held in the vomit. Not because of the mention of marriage, but the family business. "I get a lot of hands-on experience now that I'm Benny and Frankie's guardian. They live with me. Rent free."

"Really? Oh, that's…interesting."

I laughed, more than a reaction to her than because it was actually funny. "You have no idea. They have a love child. Jean-Claude Van Dog. I've grown quite fond of the bastard. He's a Volpino."

I showed her a picture. She craned her neck to see. "So, cute."

"He was supposed to be a chick magnet." I threw up my hands. "Not for me. For the stunads, but J.C. is more house-keeper, cleaning up all the snacks and crumbs they leave behind."

Emilio, a tall, lean Italian man with thinning, slicked back hair, approached in a tux and a smile.

"Ciao, Leo, Natalia. Welcome back! I haven't seen you two here for a while."

I smiled. "Well, we haven't been."

"How was the food, amazing right?"

"Absolutely."

"Spectacular. Dessert on me. How does that sound?"

I cocked my head, assessing Natalia's desire.

Emilio said, "The Italian cheesecake. To die for. The gelato. Oh, is it amazing. It comes with two canestrelli cookies. So light. So flavorful. We've got tiramisu. And of course, we've got the cannoli. When the cream hits your mouth…"

I suppressed a smile. "Natalia?"

Her eyes bore into mine as her foot found my crotch beneath the table. "I'll have the cannoli."

I gulped and jolted back, then attempted to play it smooth, turning to Emilio and leaning my arm atop the back of my chair. "Same," I whispered. I wanted the cheesecake, but 'same' was the only word I could muster.

"Excellent. Wonderful to see you again. You both look amazing." With that, he disappeared.

"You do look amazing," Natalia said, leaning in with a smile. "I can tell you've been working out."

"Thanks. You as well. Like I said, I haven't been dating much. I have a lot of sexual energy to work off, I guess."

"Well, you can still make an ovary quiver from fifty yards." She nodded to the bar. "Those cougars can't keep their eyes off you, claws at the ready." She paused for dramatic effect. "And I'm only a text away."

I swallowed hard. She stared back at me with a look I had always found hard to say no to. Natalia stood up. "I'll be right back."

"You're just gonna leave me here, cougar prey?"

Natalia leaned down and tilted my chin up, her lips only inches from mine. She turned to the cougars and smiled, then pressed her lips to mine for a brief but explosive kiss.

"If I'm not back in five minutes, it's because I'm going Brooklyn street fight on those cougars," Natalia said, smiling.

"Hurry back, slugger," I said, laughing.

While Natalia escaped for a ladies' room break, I wondered if I should see her again, while refusing to make eye contact with the salivating, martini-sipping beasts as they licked their chops. Natalia was young and still a little immature. Shallow even. But at her core, nice and sweet, and hotter than the volcanic lava in Mount Vesuvius. Random Italian fact while we're discussing volcanoes. Did you know Italy has the only active volcanoes in continental Europe and one of them is called Stromboli?

Anyway, by the time Natalia returned, I realized she might be a little immature now, but if you're looking to grow old with someone, how they are at twenty-six matters a lot less than every year after that. And why waste the energy of youth? She seemed to want to consume me with it. Who was I to deny her that pleasure? And like my mother said, she was a good woman from a good Italian family. I could do a lot worse. I mean, I already had. I was waking up to a half-naked Frankie on most mornings.

Our dessert arrived shortly after Natalia settled in. The

cannoli was just as Emilio so eloquently explained and more. Crisp with a touch of sweetness, the shell tasted like an unglazed donut. The filling was light and creamy, a perfect mix of ricotta and mascarpone with a smattering of chocolate chips scattered throughout. It was a fabulous end to a better-than-expected date.

I turned down a digestivo, having already had two glasses of wine, and walked Natalia to her red Alfa Romeo Giulia. I opened the door for her. She tossed her bag inside, then turned to me and pulled me toward her by my lapels. I was six feet tall and in the best shape of my life, at nearly two hundred pounds of Italian beef cake, but I was getting tossed around by tiny women like a rag doll lately. One pushing. One pulling. But that's not the important part. The kiss. Had she always kissed with such energy? Such passion?

I peeled myself away, trying to avoid going to Bonerville, and said, "I'd love to see you again."

"Me, too." She smiled and kissed me again.

"Maybe next time we could go somewhere different," I said.

Natalia's brow furrowed in confusion. "Like what?"

I shrugged. "Don't know. American. Mexican. Maybe one of those hibachi restaurants where they burn your eyebrows off as entertainment?"

"But we're Italian. This is our place."

"I know, but there are other cultures out there. Other good food."

"Not as good as our food."

I shrugged. "Maybe not. But still good. Here's what we'll do. Why don't we stay in the neighborhood and stick to Mediterranean? I'll take you to Zorba's. We'll have Greek. You'll love it."

"Okay," she said. "I'm open to new things." Her hand found its way to my crotch and squeezed. "And familiar."

Welcome to Bonerville. Population one.

CHAPTER
Thirteen

THE PREMAPRINT TOUR accomplished two things: I got over the awkwardness of seeing Rae in person since we kissed and decided it was a drunken mistake, and it added fuel to my fire to run my own company. I didn't want to partner with them. Their culture was way too stuffy.

Rae and I said our goodbyes to Ted and headed for the exit. I stepped to the side of the door and pushed it open for her. "Ladies first."

"You sexist bastard," she said, smirking.

"You see me," I deadpanned. "I know you're joking, but I think it's just nice." I followed her outside, stopping next to the PremaPrint sign in front of the parking lot. "Would you prefer, 'Can I get the door for you, my gender-neutral acquaintance'?"

"Now you're just being a jerk."

"I can't win," I said, shaking my head with a smirk.

"Because I'm better. What did you think of PremaPrint?"

"Impressive. Efficient and well run. The culture could use some improvement. It doesn't have the camaraderie of my place."

Rae nodded. "You're right. It's hard to achieve that frat

house feel that fuels massive outsized profits. Wharton, Stanford, Harvard...Donati printing has succeeded where the Ivy Leaguers have failed."

I was about to respond with something eloquent and witty, but my stomach grumbled like a Jets fan in the fourth quarter.

Rae nearly cowered behind the sign in shock. "What the hell was that? Do you need medical attention?"

I stepped back, defensively. "Not mouth to mouth, if that's what you're thinking."

Rae crossed her arms. "Hilarious."

"I'm starving. I didn't eat breakfast. Gotta keep the six-pack tight with a little intermittent fasting. Are you hungry?"

"I could eat. But what?"

"Buns."

"Huh?"

"Not my buns. Do you really want to bite into rock?"

"Not particularly, no."

"I'm talking about buns quite possibly better than my own."

"So, all of them?"

I feigned a phone call, "Yes, H.R.? Ms. Kane has been staring at my ass. And needs an upgrade to her vision plan."

"I've never stared at your ass," Rae said defensively.

"Right. Too professional? I've noticed some serious slippage lately, Ms. Kane."

She shook her head. "We are heavily influenced by the company we keep."

I feigned emotional anguish. "Ouch. But I have the remedy. Bao buns."

"What the heck is that?"

"It's lunch. I know a place not far from here." I waved her on. "Come on. We'll go dutch." She huffed, but followed along. "I know it's not a date," I said in a mocking tone. "For the record, I went on a date the other night." I studied her face for a reaction, but got none.

"Did it involve hand lotion and the Internet?"

I stopped and said, "You think I can't get a date?"

"I think you could get almost any woman you wanted."

My body reacted with shock. Until she added, "If you were a mute."

I smiled. "That means you think I'm hot."

Rae shrugged. "You're easy on the eyes...but tough on the stomach."

"That hurts," I said, disappearing into my car.

Rae followed me as we weaved through the streets of East Flushing en route to Main Street. We parked and met up on the corner of Main and 37th and walked down Main to a hole-in-the wall restaurant that you would probably walk right by without a second thought if not for the sweet aroma of seared bacon.

I pointed to a small sign in the window that read simply, 'Dumplings' and said, "I give you Shangri-La Garden!"

"This is it?" Rae asked, unimpressed.

"Do not be fooled by its commonplace appearance. As the Buddha said, 'True beauty is in the buns.'"

"Did he now?"

"He also said, 'May I meet the suffering and ignorance of others with compassion.'" I scratched my chin in faux thought and then said excitedly, "I've unlocked the secret of the universe! He was referring to you."

"One hundred thousand dollars."

"What's that?"

"How much I just knocked off the buyout price." Rae smiled. And while I was lost in her dimples, she patted me on the shoulder triumphantly and headed inside, leaving the door to slam in my face. Ladies first. Men? Broken face.

"That's not right! And now, you're definitely buying me lunch," I called to her through the door. I headed inside the small eatery. Bamboo walls and green plants spread throughout. We were seated tightly at a table for two. Rae inhaled with curiosity.

"Fried pork and hints of?"

"Spectacularness," I suggested. "Or maybe it's the bamboo you smell. I think they bake the buns in some sort of bamboo container. This is Shanghainese food, by the way."

"That's not a thing."

"Well, prepare to eat your words and some amazing food. I have three words for you. Chicken. Soup. Dumplings."

"What?" she said, excitedly.

"I should've asked this before, but you eat pork, right?"

"I don't keep kosher."

"So, yes? You eat pork? I don't really know the kosher rules."

"Yes."

"Good. I don't trust people who have something against bacon."

Rae raised an eyebrow. "Even religious somethings?"

"Even worse," I said.

"Stop joking."

"I'm sorry. If you want, I can make fun of my own religion. We have many ridiculous things to discuss."

Rae assessed the menu and said snootily, "That's okay. I prefer not to make fun of people."

"Aww," I whined like a toddler. "That's one of my favorite things to do. And you're increasingly becoming my favorite subject."

"Lucky me." Rae examined the place. "How did you ever find this place? I'm surprised you eat food other than Italian."

I scoffed. "That's horrifically stereotypical and offensive. Do you only eat matzah and drink Manschewitz wine?" I held in laughter.

"I'm sorry. That was terribly—"

I laughed. "I'm just kidding. I do branch out from time to time."

We ordered and were quickly served chicken soup dumplings in a covered bamboo dish and pork bao buns on an open bamboo tray.

Rae poked the white bao bun with her finger. "I've never seen anything like that."

I grabbed one, holding it like a taco, took a bite, and sighed with satisfaction. The crisp pork burst with juice and flavors and then the pickled onions and creamy sauce kicked in. I groaned with pleasure.

"Easy now," Rae said.

"Sorry. You know how easy it is to get me excited," I said, remembering the unforgettable lap dance.

Rae took a bite and her eyes bulged.

"Amazeballs, right? So light and fluffy, and then the flavors kick in like Bruce Lee."

Rae shook the sticky bun from her finger and said, "Wow. These are so good."

"Thank you," I said.

Rae frowned. "For what?"

"The compliment."

"You didn't make them."

It was time to lay down something very important that we Italians don't like to brag about, but is a pretty well-known thing. "It's the bread that makes the bao bun special. The Italians, we own bread."

"That's not a thing."

"It most certainly is. Everything with bread is a little Italian."

Rae shook her head and took another bite. "You own *a* bread. Italian bread. It's good, but it's not *the* bread."

"You don't have your own bread," I said with faux accusation.

"We do. It's called challah."

I sat back in my chair and crossed my arms to consider this. "Touché." I merged the braided bread with a rap 'Holla' and let out a throaty, "Challah!"

The dimples came out again. I looked away, fearing I might lose control of all senses. "What is that?" Rae asked, laughing.

"That's how they say it here. It's a very rap heavy community- LL Cool J, Run DMC, Public Enemy, Fitty Cent, Nikki Minaj. This is Queens, baby."

"Don't forget A Tribe Called Quest," Rae added.

I leaned forward on my elbows in amazement. "Who are you? You like old school rap?"

"I do. My brother was in a terrible rap group in middle school. The Yarmulkids." She rapped a few lines from "Bonita Apple Bum" as I nodded along until she ended with arms crossed and a hard look on her face.

"Not bad for a Manhattan Jew," I said, chuckling.

"Yeah, I know. We're not exactly known for our rapping capabilities. Can we talk business for a bit?"

I shrugged. "Sure."

"I feel like we're making progress, but I really need to lock down that contract."

The dreaded contract. Seemingly, my only leverage. "I got pulled in a lot of directions during the holidays. Mainly by my relatives, clamping onto my cheeks with a vice grip. I will look soon. I promise."

"Good. This is going to work. I know we have our differences, but it's the right fit."

I chuckled pathetically. "It doesn't feel that way sometimes. I feel like I'm getting my ass kicked. Like I'm the ultimate underdog, like Rocky Balboa. I might have to watch it to get my spirits up."

"That movie sucks," Rae said, simply.

"What?" My eyebrows shot to the nail salon upstairs.

"What in God's name is wrong with you?" I shrieked, attracting stares from surrounding tables.

"He loses!"

I whisper-yelled at her, "What did you say, you blasphemer? That's not the point. He knows he's gonna lose to the best ever, so he sets out to go the distance. He achieved his definition of success."

Rae crossed her arms. "Sounds a lot like what a loser would do. He should've just been the best ever and won."

I threw my hands up, nearly dislocating both shoulders. "He does! In the second movie!"

With zero emotion, she said, "Didn't see it." My eyes bulged in astonishment. Rae added, "Why would I, after the first?"

My eyes instinctively searched for and found the defib machine on the wall behind the hostess stand, my body teetering ridiculously close to non-perfusing ventricular tachycardia, or at least it felt that way. "Oh, my God. You are one of a kind."

"That's the nicest thing you've ever said to me."

"Don't celebrate just yet. I haven't decided if it's a compliment or not. I'm still in shock here. So, what's your favorite movie?"

"*Erin Brockovich*, or if I'm feeling sappy, *Titanic*."

"Really? You watch a story about thousands of people drowning in the arctic as a pick-me-up?"

Rae explained, "The love story is amazing."

I stared up at the ceiling in disbelief before my eyes found hers again. "You're loony. It's a story of evil and betrayal. Rose is a horrible person. True, you don't ultimately find that out until she's an old bag, but still. Who just drops millions of dollars into the ocean? Poor Bill Paxton is searching the depths of the Arctic Ocean, putting her up at his expense. She doesn't say a word. Not a friggin' word that she knows where it is. I mean, that's psycho. And let's not forget, poor Jack. He's freezing his ass off and there's room on that floating door. You know there was room. And she just lets him drown. Is that love? I would let you on my door and I don't even like you half the time."

"I'm just racking up the compliments over here. You really know how to make a colleague feel special. And just for the record, your statement suggests you do like me half the time."

I grabbed the bill from the waitress and said, "Can you strike my comments from the record?"

She frowned while Rae rolled her eyes. "Please ignore him. I find it's the best way to deal with him." Rae handed her a credit card and continued our conversation. "It's about his love for her. His sacrifice."

I sighed. "I just don't know about you, Rae Kane."

"Right back atcha, Leonardo. So, what's the time frame on the contract and getting this deal done?" Rae asked.

I groaned inwardly. I didn't want deadlines. I wanted ambiguity to string things along until I could somehow get myself out of the familial mess I was in. "No word from my lawyer, who is notoriously slow. I'm sure there will be some issues. Then we'll negotiate."

"Oh, no. The bad ass is coming out to play?"

I chuckled. "Shut up. That was one of the worst days of my life. How about February 15th?"

Rae's tone turned serious. "How about this? January 31st. Any delay beyond that and the entire deal is subject to financial adjustments as your business continues to deteriorate. PremaPrint is feeling like their prices are way too high to start the year."

What a great way to ruin a nice day. "You're going to drop this bomb on me when I introduced you to bao buns?"

Rae stood up and slung her bag over her shoulder. "This doesn't have to be a competition, but if you insist on it being such, you should know that I'm going to win." She scooted between two tables and strutted to the door.

I followed her with frustration. "You think I'm the competitive one? You're the most competitive person I've ever met."

She just stared at me.

"No answer?"

"This deal is extremely important to me, Leo. My career."

"Not more than mine," I argued.

Our argument spilled onto the sidewalk, the frigid air no match for her tone. "Whose fault is that?"

I counted on my fingers. "Yours? My father's?"

"It's your own. Your lack of assertiveness."

"Is that one of your checklist items?"

"Wouldn't you like to know?"

"Thanks for lunch and then ruining it," I said.

"Yeah, this was fun," her tone indicating anything but. She looked to the heavens, seemingly for answers, and then left me alone in my frustration.

The thing is, it actually was fun. Until she ruined it. I was not ready for this deal to close. Ever. I headed to my car, no idea about what to do as her words dug into my pride and festered. *This was my fault? Not assertive enough?* And then it hit me. *I'll show her assertive.* I was going to buy the business myself.

———

Rae's Deal Notes

- Contract deadline: January 31st.
- Submit expense check. Ask for hazard pay.
- Speak to H.R. about banning all rap from future business meetings. ~~What an idiot I am!~~

CHAPTER
Fourteen

I ROLLED into work just after eight, Rebecca already at her desk, organizing files. She looked up with a smile. "Hey, boss."

"What up, Becs?"

"Hey, are you still going to that conference in the city in a few weeks?"

"Yeah. I go every year. I don't know if Pop is going, but I plan to. Maybe I should bring my resume," I joked, and then tossed my credit card on the desk in front of Rebecca. Her eyes lit up like I had just offered a Rodeo Drive shopping spree. "Shoes?"

I laughed. "Invest now, so I don't need to bring my resume. Shoes later." She frowned in confusion. "Add that to the Facebook account for ads. And research landing pages, please. Looking for something I can A/B test but won't break the bank. Oh, and look up all the Long Island zip codes that are heavy into office and industrial space."

"What is it for?" Rebecca asked, her brow pinching together.

"Investing for the future. If my father won't give me the money to save this place, Visa will."

Rebecca said, "I'm not sure it works that way."

"I have a budget. But I'm not against maxing it out to make this all work. I refuse to go down without a fight. If I have to fund my plan personally, then that's what I'll do."

Within two days, we had built three different landing pages outlining our value proposition, displaying design examples, and providing reviews from our Facebook page and Google, while avoiding all discussion of family disfunction.

I stared at and proofread the landing page one last time, pressed 'Publish', and then prayed to the Patron Saint of Printing, Saint Augustine. Yes, that's a thing. And then to the Patron Saint of Entrepreneurial Profits, Sir Richard Branson. Not yet a thing. The Vatican has not officially recognized Sir Richard with that title, but I, for one, believe he's earned it, and I figured it couldn't hurt.

The day after that, we had Facebook ads running in more than a dozen local business areas. I sat in front of the computer in my office, willing online business to Donati Printing. I wiggled my fingers at the monitor as if conjuring magic. "Come to me, Internet Dollars. May my words reach the wise creator of the Internet, Al Gore. It is me, Leo Donati, your humble servant. Send me your leads."

Rebecca leaned on the door frame of my office. "What the hell is going on in here? Who are you talking to?"

"Al Gore," I said, like she was the new model for stunad in the dictionary, replacing a long-standing picture of Benny.

She scoffed. "Do you have his direct line?"

I mustered as much confidence as I could and said, "As far as you know."

"Yeah, right."

"So, I wasn't talking to Al directly, but to his greatest invention, the worldwide interwebs."

Rebecca furrowed her brow, deep in thought. "They've finally done it. They've broken you."

"Who?"

"Your family."

I shrugged in partial acknowledgement, but then a strange ding popped from my speakers, pulling my attention. "What have we here?" Staring back at me from the landing page dashboard was a name, phone number, and an email address of an interested printing party. I thrust my arms in the air like Rocky atop the stairs of the Philadelphia Museum of Art. "We have a lead!" I refreshed my Facebook ads dashboard. "Twelve bucks. We've only spent twelve bucks on ads today! We could make hundreds or a thousand on a good project. I am a god of Printing! I am the Federal Reserve. I print money!"

"You're losing it, Leo," Rebecca said.

Perhaps I overreacted, given that I hadn't even talked to the lead, let alone closed or delivered any business, but it was a win, and more important, a lifeline. My career was mimicking the Titanic, and I was gonna have to find my own door to stay afloat.

"That's a strong possibility, but I need results. I want to meet with Sal at Citizens. Can you update our financial PowerPoint, send it to me, and set up a meeting for next week with Sal to talk about financing?"

"Last I checked, we don't need any equipment, nor can we afford it."

"I'm not buying new equipment. I'm looking for a partner. How much do you think people would pay me for my body?"

"Huh?"

"Forget it. We're not there yet."

"What are you doing?"

"Brainstorming."

"It sounds more like losing your mind."

———

I wouldn't say that leads from my new effort were piling up at Donati Printing, but it was a solid trickle. We even landed two minor projects for some point-of-purchase displays. Proof of concept was proving itself. At least a little.

It was lunchtime on Wednesday. I was en route to Rodrigo's, a Brazilian steakhouse, wearing a blue suit, no tie. Single-breasted, of course, if that's a thing. Whatever it was, it was not double-breasted. I never understood why my dad was so big on his double-breasted suits when he plays cards in an undersized tank top, but whatever. I didn't like the feeling of being constrained by a tie. And even though we weren't eating at an Italian place, the less clothing an Italian wears to a meal is usually better with sauce and oil flying everywhere. My Papa used to eat every Sunday dinner in his boxers and tank top. Somehow, we all still had an appetite.

I found my way into the restaurant and was seated with Sal. He was a squat Italian banker with a receding hairline and a strong Roman nose. The lunch hour was bustling with an endless stream of waiters carving and serving steak, sausage, and chicken from large skewers.

In his raspy voice, Sal said, "I love this place. Rodizio style. All you can eat meat. Am I right?"

"You're not wrong, bro."

Sal looked around as we settled in. "Two Italians in a Brazilian steakhouse. It ought to be illegal. By the way, was she hitting on you?" He nodded to the hostess in the midst of seating a couple nearby.

I waved him away. "Nah. She's just nice."

"I wish she were that nice to me. She's looking at you. You should ask her out."

I scanned the drink menu. "It's just not how it works in my family."

Sal raised an eyebrow. "You have an arranged marriage situation?"

I laughed, sitting back, arms crossed. "No. Of course not."

"Then what's the big deal?"

I leaned in toward Sal. "What nationality is your wife?"

"Italian."

"Your brother's wife?"

"Italian."

"Your sister's fiancé?"

"Italian." Sal's face conveyed understanding. "Oh, I guess I see your point. But it wasn't forced on us. That's just our community. You swim in the same pond, you're more likely to end up together."

We ordered our drinks and then continued our conversation. I said, "My uncle is excommunicated. He married a Jewish woman."

"Well, that's not Italian and certainly out of the religion. Most of Brazil is Roman Catholic. And I think half of them are models."

I shrugged. "If you say so."

"Can't you just date her a few times and tell me what the sex is like?"

"No. Sal. I can't," I said, laughing.

He said, annoyed, "You can't, or you won't?"

"Can we get serious? I've got important things to discuss. I want to take our business to the next level." I tossed him a copy of my financial presentation, perfectly bound at Donati Printing.

Sal licked a fat finger and opened the report. "You looking to buy new digital equipment?"

"No. I'm looking to buy our existing digital equipment. And everything else."

Sal stopped and eyed me for more information. "Huh?"

"I want to buy the business from my father, but I don't have the capital."

"Really? Well, that's interesting." He sat back and surveyed me. "How much do you need and with what collateral?"

"How much will you give me if I use the business as my collateral? And my Honda Civic," I threw in for good measure. "It's got 50,000 miles and runs like a dream."

Sal thought for a moment. "We just completed a leveraged buyout for a construction firm. Not a whole lot of collateral and we made it work, but they were highly profitable." His tone brightened. "It could work. Let me dig into the numbers here."

Excitement brewed in my chest. Sal could be the answer to all my problems.

Sal studied the numbers for a moment. "Is this for last month?" His eyes bulged, finding the answer himself. "It's for last quarter? What? The business has deteriorated this much?" I hid my grimace as he continued, "What are you buying? He might just give it to you if you ask nicely."

I chuckled pathetically. That would never happen. "He has a mediocre deal from Kane Printing. If I can match it, I can't see why I can't buy it myself. I just need the financing."

Sal tossed the presentation to the side as a waiter arrived with an inviting skewer of steak, who carved two platefuls and moved on to the next table.

As Sal stuffed his face, I said, "You've always been there for each stage of our development. This is our next one. We've always met our obligations. Always pay our debts. We're the Lannisters without the incest and backstabbing."

Sal nearly choked on a bite of steak. "Despite the *Game of Thrones* reference, I just don't know what I can do here. The business is deteriorating. There's no way they'll let me give you the whole thing. I'll get smacked upside the head if I even try."

"You can take a punch, just as long as they don't break out the wooden spoon."

"Anything but that," Sal said, a touch of fear registering on his face.

We continued to talk and brainstorm as we ate.

Sal asked, "What's the valuation?"

"Four times last year with some minor adjustments."

Sal made some calculations on the presentation and studied them. I did the same to his meat sweats. I wasn't sure who was more disgusted. "I just don't see how this can work. The ratios will get rejected without a second look. You'd over lever and not be able to pay it back unless you really grow the business. Like double it."

"Is that all? Easy," I said with false confidence. Even with my new online venture, I'd be lucky to grow by ten percent to start. Maybe within a year, if I kept rolling the profit into the ad budget, we could get thirty or forty percent, but double? It was impossible. I stared at my plate, defeated by both the amount of meat still on it and my takeover attempt.

Sal must've noticed my dampened mood. "You know how I feel about you. It's not as strong as I feel about the hostess. You still sure about her?"

"Yes."

"Where was I? I will help you as much as I can. I will always be there to support you, but the numbers are the numbers. It's a business. They won't approve it."

"I get it. It's not your fault." *It's Rae's and my father's.*

"Dessert?" Sal asked, excited.

"No. Sorry, bud. I gotta be getting back." I couldn't sit there in shame just for a piece of New York cheesecake. Life was dipping low, but not that low.

"I'm gonna get some to go then," Sal said, catching the waiter's attention.

An idea popped into my head. "What about fifty percent financing and I'll see if my dad will finance the rest. He would get a sizeable chunk up front, buy Casa de Boca, and then I could make payments to him."

Sal nodded in thought. "I could probably make that work if our debt was senior to his. If you couldn't pay, it would be him. Let me talk to my boss."

I slapped the table and it shook with the clashing of silver-ware. "That's what I'm talkin' about, Sally boy!"

I grabbed Sal in an enormous bear hug and then we parted ways, optimism brewing.

I headed back to the office right after lunch, singing and playing the drums on the steering wheel all the way there. I hit all the high notes like a champ.

I bumped into Benny and Frankie in the parking lot.

"Where were you?" Benny asked.

"Lunch with Sal. Keep this between us, but I'm gonna try to buy the business myself."

"They're gonna give you all that money?" Benny asked, eyebrows raised.

"No. Maybe half. I have to ask Dad to finance the rest."

"I can't even get Dad to lend me a hundred bucks."

Frankie offered, "Borrow money from Fat Tony instead."

I laughed at the stunad. "You want me to borrow a few mil from a loan shark? It's like five percent interest a week or he breaks your kneecaps. Fat Tony will be running the shop in six months and you'll be pushing me around in a wheelchair. Do you want that?"

Benny shrugged. "I'm sure we'd get donuts every day. Fat Tony loves his donuts."

"He'd definitely be a better boss than you," Frankie added unhelpfully. "And with your broken legs, you'd be the ulti-mate chick magnet. I like my idea more and more each minute."

I shook my head. Just livin' my best life. "Being an adult is possibly the dumbest decision I ever made."

Benny nodded thoughtfully and rubbed my shoulder. "And that's why I don't do it."

CHAPTER

Fifteen

I OFFERED to pick Natalia up at her house for our dinner at Zorba's, but she met me at the restaurant instead. It was a simple place known more for its food than its decor. All you need to know is that everything was blue and white, including the oversized wooden bar. Natalia looked stunning as usual with skin-tight jeans that hopefully came off easier than they looked to put on and an off-the-shoulder black sweater.

As we sat at our table for two, she stared down at the menu, which highlighted her smokey gold eye shadow. It was a new look for her, and I liked it. "I don't know what to get. I don't know what any of this is," she said.

"You've literally never had Greek food?"

"Never. We didn't eat out much when I was a kid. My mom cooks what she knows."

I looked around at the crowd. "Well, Greeks are like our next-door neighbors."

A group of two forty-something couples at the bar yelled in unison, "Opa!" And then downed a shot. Half the restaurant cheered.

I nodded to them with a smile. "See, they're crazy like us.

One time I was here, and the owner had just found out his daughter was engaged. Every time they did a shot, somebody threw a plate against the wall. Thankfully, Nonna's always throwing spaghetti at me, so my cat-like reflexes kept me alive."

"I'm glad," she said, laughing. "The pastichio looks good."

I scoffed. "It's ziti with meat sauce. Try something new. Expand."

"I'm not that adventurous."

I whispered naughtily. "That's not what I remember."

Natalia chuckled. "That's a different activity."

"Okay. We won't get crazy. At least not at dinner." I gave her my best smolder, known in six states to turn a woman's clothes to ash. I was a little out of practice, so fortunately for Natalia, she remained fully clothed. For the time being. I'm hoping you've already realized I'm not the typical guy. I'm not just looking for sex and I don't have a timetable for it, but we'd dated for months and known each other our whole lives, so there wasn't a get-to-know-you-before-we-get-naked phase to get through.

Natalia asked, "What should I get?"

I scanned the menu. "Let's stick with foods you're familiar with but prepared in a new way. You know eggplant, so let's have some babaganoosh."

"God bless you," Natalia said without looking up from the menu.

I laughed. "No. It's a food dish."

"Oh. I hope it tastes better than it sounds."

"It does, but I think it sounds fun. You gotta say it with gusto." I went heavy on the hand gesture and boomed, "Babaganoooosh!"

Half the restaurant stared at us. Natalia buried her face in the menu. "Stop it," she said, whisper-laughing.

"Sorry. If that's too embarrassing for you, spanakopita is

basically just spinach, feta, and dough, and delicious. And for an entrée, how about some gyro meat? It's like rotisserie beef. Have it in a pita. You're Italian. You eat bread, right? Or you could have it over a salad. You got this, Nat."

"Okay. If you say so."

"I do," I said, smiling.

"'I do'? This is only our second date."

"I didn't mean that kind of 'I do' but...I do feel like this differs from last time in some ways."

"How so?"

"You seem more confident. Know more of what you want, besides food."

She scrunched up her nose. "You said 'different in some ways.' Are there some ways it hasn't changed?"

"Well, we haven't even ordered on our second date, but we never used to do anything together besides eat or drink."

Natalia argued, "There was other stuff. Granted, it was all R-rated."

I nodded, smiling. "I remember it well. I'd like to make fresh memories in that department, too. But I'd like to do couples' activities with you. What do we both like that we can do together?"

"I don't know."

"You want to go to an Islanders game?" I asked.

"I don't like hockey."

I raised an eyebrow. "Knicks?"

"I don't like basketball."

I shook my head in agreement. "Yeah, they stink, anyway. Baseball's not for a few months. You want to watch a rom com at my place?" I make no apologies. I enjoy a good rom com. But apparently, she doesn't.

"I don't like rom coms. Do you like horror movies? I haven't seen that new Steven King one."

"I can't do it. I get too grossed out. And you're a kindergarten teacher. How could you be that cute and like horror?"

"You haven't been to kindergarten lately. I couldn't keep showing up if I didn't enjoy being horrified. You have no idea what goes down in that bathroom."

"Huh. I did not know that. Nor do I want to continue thinking about it while eating. What about skiing?"

"Too cold. Do you want to go to the meatpacking district? There's a new club, Velvet, that I've been dying to go to."

"You know I hate clubbing. Arcade?"

"I don't really like video games."

I thought for a moment, disappointed. "So, dinner then?"

"Or we could just order in and be each other's desserts."

I nodded in agreement, a smile curling on my lips. "I think that's something we could agree on."

We both ordered gyro salad, which arrived on the quick. We talked about old times. When Benny put ketchup on my pasta when I was ten. Then there was the time Frankie buried his report card, so he could avoid summer school. Aunt Franny found out on vacation, exploded, and then refused to talk to anyone, earning the nickname 'Italian Ice Storm.' Another time, Benny ran away and pretended to have been abducted by aliens. It would've explained a lot of things, but I'm pretty certain he was lying. Good times.

I tossed the last bite of pita onto my plate, nearly disgusted with myself. "Do you want dessert?"

"It doesn't look like you do," she said, laughing.

"I have a dessert stomach," I countered.

"You sound like my kids."

My eyes bulged jokingly. "When were you gonna tell me you had kids?"

"Not that kind. I'm not ready for kids. I was talking about my students." Natalia stared at the dessert menu. "Do you have the apartment to yourself tonight?"

I tried to suppress my excitement. I shrugged. "The boys will be out in town until one or two, I'm sure. And somebody's pants might end up in the tree, but—"

Natalia eyed me seductively. "I'll toss mine if you toss yours."

With way too much enthusiasm, I called out to the waiter across the restaurant, "We're gonna skip dessert!" So much for suppressing my excitement.

Just because she wasn't ready to have kids, and I wasn't either, didn't mean we couldn't practice, right? I mean, how could you be ready for the real thing if you don't prepare? We were adulting.

The waiter arrived with the bill and the maitre d' with a shot of ouzo in a small, chilled glass. It was a cloudy white, partially crystallized, with a wedge of lemon.

"Just a little parting gift." The maitre d' took a heavy swig with us and then made three stops at different tables, handing out shot glasses.

I whispered to Natalia, "I don't know how this guy doesn't fall over by the end of the night. Let's get out of here before everyone gets shitcanned on ouzo."

We stood up and waded through the tables, heading for the door. "The saucers are about to fly like the discus on Mount Olympus." I grabbed her shoulders and said, "Duck!"

Natalie cowered and then smacked me with the back of her hand and a smile across her face. "Jerk."

"I gotta keep you on your toes."

She stood on her tippy toes and whispered into my ear. "I prefer my back."

My eyes bulged, and they weren't the only body parts to do so. She was a lot more aggressive than just a few short months ago. And I liked it.

We didn't even make it into the apartment. Our hands and lips were all over each other as we navigated the hallway, eyes closed. It was a tad bumpy, and we almost kicked down Mrs. Albrecht's door when the key didn't work, but we eventually made it to my apartment.

I keyed in and opened the door, immediately met by Jean-

Claude Van Dog, who would just have to understand. I needed this. He'd have to take one for the team. We pushed past him, lips locked, but he followed us into the bedroom. I disengaged from Natalia, scooted J.C. out the door with a not-so-sorry grin, and then let the adulting begin.

———

I woke up the next morning, a naked Natalia snuggled into my chest. My eyes bulged for a moment and then all the amazing memories of the night before rushed back to me. I closed my eyes in satisfaction, letting the visions replay.

Natalia stirred and whispered, "Good morning."

"A delightful morning. I guess we figured out one way we fit very well together."

She looked up at me. "You look happy."

"I am. And my parents will be thrilled, too."

Natalia shrieked, "You're gonna tell your parents we had sex?"

I sat up in the bed, exposing my bare chest. "No. I just meant that things are…back on track."

"On track for what?"

"Relationship adulting. Your parents aren't on your ass to marry a handsome Italian stallion?"

Natalia suppressed a smile. "I don't know any."

"Good one. I didn't know you had jokes, Nat."

Natalia said, "Yeah, my mother is all up in my biz, but…" I lost track of her words as she stood up totally naked, and strapped on her bra. Women are sorcerers. They can stop time.

"Leo, are you listening to anything I'm saying?"

"I'm listening to your body talk."

Natalia laughed. "Men."

"Where are you going? Why do you have to do that?" I asked, more confused than I had ever been in my life.

"Get dressed? It's socially required in public. Especially where I'm going. I have to meet my parents at church."

I chuckled. "You might want to swing by confession. You are a very naughty kindergarten teacher."

"You're not exactly an altar boy, either."

I shrugged with a smile. "Do you really have to go?"

"Yes. I'm sorry."

"Fine. Tell your parents I said 'hi'. Maybe one day you'll let me pick you up and I can do it myself."

"I haven't told them about you."

"Oh." I frowned, staring at her. "Why not?"

She climbed onto the bed and kissed me. "I'd rather keep you all to myself."

I wrapped my arm around her, pulling her onto me as she shrieked. We kissed again. "Where do they think you are now?"

"With Marie." She pushed herself off me. "I'm gonna be late for church. My parents will kill me."

"I think they'll understand. You communicated enough with God last night. You called out for him quite a few times."

"Shut up," she said, laughing.

I wrapped her in my arms one last time. "When can I see you again? And what are we going to do?"

"Let's just do everything we did last night. It was perfect."

It was.

CHAPTER
Sixteen

I GOT to the office early on Monday morning. I only had a few hours there before I had to head into the city for a conference. Rebecca was already in, checking emails. She looked up at me, a huge smile on her face.

"We got a big order from Dynamix!"

"Yeah? The one in Rockville Centre?" They were one of our leads generated online.

"Yep. We sent them that proposal last week."

I smacked the counter with both hands. "Boom, baby! Internet sale. Cha cha ching!" I strummed more air guitar than was professionally acceptable and sang in my deepest voice, "Mojo rising."

She eyed me suspiciously.

I stopped mid-strum. "What? You never heard that song? They used to play it at the Mets games when a rally was heating up."

"And the air guitar?"

"Impromptu magic. I'm one of the best air guitarists around."

Rebecca cleaned her red glasses with her shirt. "I don't

want to be around any guy when his mojo is rising. Even you."

"Are you asexual now? Seems like my air guitar steamed up those frames."

Rebecca smirked. "Not steamy. Just dirty. And if I have to see that air guitar again, I'll regret cleaning them."

I leaned my elbows on the counter. "Things are looking up, my friend. Maybe my father will listen to me now."

She laughed. "Good luck with that. How are you going to broach that subject?"

I shrugged, not really sure. "Straight up, like Paula Abdul. We're Italian. We just get right into it. I'm taking the train into the conference and then I'll catch a ride with him on the way home. I'll bring it up then."

"If you say so. How was the weekend?"

My smile widened. "I had a good second date." And great after hours. "My parents like her. Oh, well, you know her. I'm back with Natalia."

"Oh. I thought you had nothing in common?"

I shrugged. "There are a few things. Plus, my mother is thrilled."

"I bet."

I continued, "I had dinner with the family yesterday. We didn't talk about the business at all, which was a solid positive. I was the big winner at cards, Night Baseball, while my father was the biggest loser, which felt good after the bonus situation, and the shrimp scampi was out of this world. Nonna must've made a deal with the devil."

"Wow. Things are looking up for you."

I drummed the countertop with gusto. "Even the sun shines on a dog's ass once in a while," I said with a shrug. It would probably all come crashing down sooner rather than later, but I was going to enjoy it while it lasted.

"What time are you going to the city?"

"Tennish. Hopefully, mend some fences with Pop. It's

been long enough. We don't normally go this long with tension. We yell. We scream. We kiss and make up."

"But this was a big one."

"The biggest." I headed to my office. "Buy everybody lunch. I gotta get a few things done before I head into the city and hobnob with my soon-to-be fellow CEOs. Leo Donati is on the rise." I turned back to her and drew my finger guns and then spun back to my office with a smile.

———

Margins in the printing industry were tight with paper and ink costs rising, so we had to hike downtown to cheaper hotel convention space, but the hotel was nice enough. There were probably a hundred people at or around the check-in and breakfast buffet just outside the meeting rooms. My guess was there would be four or even five hundred guests, peaking into the happy hour later in the day.

I hadn't confirmed with Rae that she'd be at the conference, but I was pretty certain she would be. I checked my coat and her kiss popped into my mind, but I pushed it away. I got my badge, and scanned the agenda in the main hallway.

"Welcome to PrintCon," Rae said, stopping in front of me.

"Why does everything have to be a con?"

"It's short for convention, ya schmuck."

I frowned and put my schedule away. "That's uncalled for. Your old man coming?"

"Yep. He'll waltz in for the cocktails. You?"

"Yep. God forbid they try to learn anything, right?" I turned, stared nervously at the coat closet, and then turned back to Rae.

"What are you doing?"

"Just checking my distance to see how far away I am from the coat check. You're a strong one." I nearly choked on my laugh.

Rae's face reddened. "I don't recall you resisting." She huffed. "Well, I just wanted to say hi. We should probably avoid each other to not give anything away about our deal."

I fought disappointment. "Right. I was going to avoid you, anyway."

She shrugged. "It's hard to be overshadowed by superior talent. I get it."

I laid the sarcasm on heavy. "I'll miss you. The joy of your company."

"Well, look forward to the joy of my company later. My father wants to meet you."

"Looking forward to it." I almost was.

I made my way from meeting to meeting, learning about new print technology and innovations in ink. I was starving by the time lunch rolled around. I hit the buffet hard and grabbed a seat at an empty circular table. A seasoned exec quickly joined me. Tall and thin with short gray hair, he extended his hand to me with a smile. "Sam Bennington from Impact Ink."

"Leo Donati. Donati Printing." We exchanged a handshake and business cards. "How's the conference treating you so far? What did you come for?"

"So far, so good. I'm here same as everybody. To learn. Network. Kiss up to David Rosenblum since we're all going to work for him some day. And if you don't work for David, you'll work for Caleb Kane."

"Tell me about it," I muttered, before regrouping. "Are you guys on the sales block?"

"Nah. We're solid for now, but as you know, it's grow, die, or merge in this biz."

I knew it well, but kept my mouth shut. Most conversations throughout the day were like that. Basically, a bunch of people bemoaning the few winners while acknowledging that the rest of us were screwed. It was highly motivational.

The table filled up, so our merger talk died down and

shifted to the usuals: passing of the bread, the breaking of physics laws in hotel poultry preparation, and despite 2,500 years of use, why no one has figured out how to make low-priced ink. It was riveting stuff.

My eyes found Rae as I battled with a seemingly impervious piece of chicken that had no desire to break down despite repeated chewing. I watched her across the room, holding court with a bunch of old men, putty in her hands, regardless of how much Viagra they had in their pockets. They certainly were itching to use it. She couldn't see me smile at her, but I did so anyway, confident the tide was turning in my direction. I had Sal on my side and was going to pitch my father on selling the business to me. How could he say no?

After lunch, I saw Rae in the afternoon here and there. My father arrived by midafternoon following a lunch with industry friends. I don't think he attended one meeting. This was more of a social event for him. Perhaps his last hurrah before retiring to Florida. He and I grabbed a drink at the happy hour, standing at a high-top table just off the bar. I sipped on a Negroni, scanning the bustling room.

"There's your girl," Pop said, staring behind me.

"Huh?" I said stunadishly. I turned to see Rae toward us, red wine in hand. And then my eyes found the impeccably dressed man in his early fifties beside her. Custom gray pinstripe suit. Diamond cufflinks. Monogrammed shirt. Whitened teeth. "Is that her father? The CEO of Kane Printing?"

Pop stepped forward, all smiles. "Caleb! I was hoping you'd make it."

"Wouldn't miss it."

Rae laughed. "You missed the whole thing."

Caleb waved her words away and raised a mixed drink. "Not the important stuff."

Pop stepped to my side and patted my shoulder. "May I introduce my eldest son, Leo?"

I offered an extra firm grip as he studied me. "A pleasure, Leo," he said in a measured tone. "I've heard good things."

I looked at Rae. "Really? You haven't found her with a voodoo doll of me?"

Caleb laughed. "No. Not yet, anyway. If I find it, I'll let you know, if you promise to do the same for me. If I don't give her a promotion soon, I think she's going to deny me grandchildren forever."

Rae inhaled sharply, but said nothing.

I forced a smile. "Will do."

Caleb leaned in and whispered, "So, when are we going to get this deal done?"

I shrugged. "We're still going through Rae's six-thousand-point checklist."

"And you're sitting on the employment contract," Rae added firmly.

Caleb scanned the room. "I'd hate to look at other options."

I whispered to Rae, "No. Please don't."

She rolled her eyes at me.

Pop said, "I want this deal done as soon as possible. But, I have to admit, I wasn't happy about the squeeze you put on us from PremaPrint. You had to be doing business at a loss and it was just to hurt us."

A smile broke out across Caleb's face. "I can't take credit for that. It was Rae's idea."

Pop shook his head. "We did not find it as enjoyable. Not exactly how partners should behave."

Caleb clapped Pop on the shoulder. "Rocco, we'll be superb partners. But we aren't yet. It's just business. Nothing personal."

I whispered to Rae again, "Learn that from Daddy? Where's your brother, by the way?"

"Probably doing donuts on his Segway in the ballroom."

A waiter strolled through, the most important man in the room, stocked with chicken and beef skewers. We encircled him and quickly relieved him of half his inventory.

Rae dug in, devouring a chicken skewer with almost more fire than she burned with in the coat closet back before Christmas.

"Those seem as tasty as me," I said without thinking. Rae's eyes bulged. "I mean, my buns." Pop and Caleb stared at me, confused. "No. The bao buns." I explained to the fathers, "We stopped for Shanghainese food in Queens when we went to PremaPrint." Exhale.

Rae's cheeks pinkened. "These are pretty good, but not as good as the buns. The bao buns. I love a good pork...in buns."

I nearly choked on a piece of beef. My father clapped me on the back, my near physical death saving Rae and me both from psychological death.

"You okay?" Pop asked.

"Never better," I said in a raspy voice. I downed half my Negroni, reasons split equally between a dry throat and a need for more alcohol.

Caleb smiled and said, "Will you excuse us? We have another merger to work on." He nodded to David Rosenblum. "Printing's golden boy. And an upstanding Jew."

It was an odd thing to say, but I smiled anyway. I shook Caleb's hand and said, "It was a pleasure meeting you. Your secret is safe with us, but you might want to watch the merger talk in front of some of these gossip hounds. David's company is public."

Caleb squeezed my shoulder. "Oh, it's not a business proposal. At least not yet. It's for marriage."

"Oh." My eyes found Rae's, but they didn't tell me anything before she looked away. My lungs hardened.

"Great news. Well, good luck," Pop said. "Leo's back with his old flame, so we're hopeful on the marriage front as well."

"Mazel tov."

"Bless you," Pop said.

Caleb laughed. "It means congrats." His eyes found me. "He's a handsome lad with a brilliant future ahead of him at our firm. Be well. Let's celebrate when this deal is all finished, huh? Maybe we'll celebrate an engagement or two." His smiled nearly sparkled in the fluorescent lighting.

Rae and I stared at each other, neither of us sure of what to say.

My father said, "David Rosenblum is the belle of the ball. It's amazing what he's done. They'll be a handsome couple." It was amazing how much my father could talk when he wanted to.

Caleb tossed an arm around Rae and said, "Better be on our way."

"Good luck," I said, forcing a smile. *I hope he chokes on a chicken skewer.*

Rae offered a quick, sheepish smile, and then disappeared into the crowd beside Caleb.

"That's one hell of a merger," Pop said. "David is actually a pretty good guy. Very smart. I mean, look at what he's done."

I ignored Pop as he blathered on, downed the rest of my Negroni, and slammed it onto the table. "I need another fucking drink."

"What's wrong with you?"

I shook it off. "Nothing. Just a long day."

"You ready to head home soon? The apps are dwindling. I'm sure your mother has something good waiting for me."

"I'm ready when you are."

We were in the car within twenty minutes, which in Manhattan parking garage terms is like winning the World Cup. The stress of navigating the traffic-heavy city kept us from much conversation until we found more open road in Nassau County, open road being a very relative term. We drove through the darkness in the latter part of rush hour. Despite my bitterness, my father was apparently in better spirits. Perhaps the prospect of some parmigiana and a lack of confusion over feelings for Rae had him in a better mood than me.

I took a few moments to control my emotions and plan my words carefully. "Listen, Pop. I know we haven't been on the same page lately. I'm sorry I've been so angry. Our numbers are turning around. I've been personally funding online advertisements. We've landed more than a few minor projects and a big one this morning. Everything I said I could do, I've done. I'm still learning and tweaking, but my return on investment is like forty percent. I have proof of concept. It's working, Pop."

My father said nothing for a moment. He just stared into the night as we drove down the expressway. "You've been spending your own money on this?"

"Yes. I believe in it. And you should, too. It's working."

"Well, that's good."

I pumped my inner fist.

But Pop continued, "We can sell to the Kane's at a higher price then."

"What—" I rubbed my face with my hands, attempting to gain control of my anger. "How could that possibly be your response? We don't have to sell."

"But I want to."

"Why? What are you so worried about?"

He didn't answer.

It was the perfect time to go for it. "What if I could pay you half now and half over time?"

"You don't want to own this business."

I huffed. "I do. I've made it very clear. I met with Sal from Citizens. He thinks they'll finance half."

"Kane wants you to run the ops still, right?"

"Who cares about that? We don't need them. I deserve this, Pop. Your father gave you the business. Why are you taking this from me? It's the family business. You've said it a thousand times. Or was that just because you wanted to break child labor laws and have us slave as printer's devils as twelve-year-olds?"

"You got paid."

"In Marino's Italian ices."

"It's strong currency. Stronger than the Lira these days."

I smacked the console between us. "I'm being serious. Stop being a mamaluke. This is my life. My future."

"That's what I'm looking out for."

I turned in the passenger seat to face him. "How are you looking out for me by taking away my future?" I didn't wait for an answer. "Will you sell me the business or not?"

"No."

I surged with anger. "Pull the car over."

"We're on the Expressway, Leo."

Anger surged through me. "Let me out or I'll jump out."

"You'll kill yourself."

"You're already killing me, Pop. Don't make me pull the emergency brake."

"Fine." My father pulled over across two lanes, took the next exit, and turned into a Shell station. "Just let me drive you home. We don't have to say a word."

I laughed, annoyed. "Oh, I'm done talking to you. That's not the problem. I don't even want to look at you. Your presence makes me sick."

"Your mother's gonna kill me."

"Mother knows best."

"Leo—"

I unlocked the door, stepped out, and slammed the door. I muttered curses, stewing in angry regret, as my father pulled away.

Admittedly, my timing could've been better. I was still about six exits from home, which would be a few hours walk if I didn't get run over or fall into a world-famous Long Island Expressway pothole, which I'm certain was the basis for Star Wars' Sarlacc's Pit. In said pit lived a beast that digested its tragic guests over a thousand years. Wanting to avoid that cheery end, I called an Uber instead, and stewed all the way home, bantering back and forth about whether to apologize for wishing him dead or to yell some more.

———

Rae's Conference Notes

- Informative and well organized.
- Meeting with David a success. Dad was happy.
- Explore on-demand printing and customization.
- Can we use smart printers? ~~Leo's definitely not one...lol.~~

CHAPTER
Seventeen

WORK the rest of that week was tense. My father and I didn't speak at all. It was all grunts and groans. I know, hard to distinguish from my father's normal communication, but I said nothing to him, either. He was winning the stink eye competition, but I had him on door slams. Surprisingly, it didn't seem to relieve any tension. Natalia was my release. She stayed over Tuesday and Wednesday night. On Thursday morning, the sun peeked in from the side of the blinds, waking me. I spooned Natalia while rubbing her bare thigh beneath the covers.

"How 'bout a morning workout?" I whispered, the workout muscle in mind already getting its pump on.

She didn't answer.

I shook her shoulder. "Rae?"

Natalia turned to me, eyes wide and brow furrowed. "Who?"

I tried to hide my slip up. "Bae. I meant Bae. It's too early for my lips to work properly. You think I'd call you Ray, like a dude?" I forced a laugh.

Natalia sat up and slipped out of bed. "I can't. I have to go. I gotta get to work."

"We have time. Certainly, you have two minutes. This is exactly why the quickie exists."

She slipped on the previous day's clothes. "That's not a good idea. I have something to say." Natalia sat on the bed beside me.

"This is getting serious," I joked.

She didn't crack a smile. "It is. I made a decision."

I sat up, my heart pounding in expectation.

Natalia looked away and said softly, "I don't think we should see each other anymore."

I didn't know what to expect, but not that. My head jolted back, smacking the headboard. "What are you talking about? Why? Were you faking it?"

"No. It has nothing to do with that. Well…"

I ran my fingers through my hair. "I don't understand. You slept with me last night. Didn't fake any of it. Now, you're dumping me this morning? What could possibly have happened between now and then?"

She exhaled, staring at the bedside clock. "I needed to get you out of my system."

I scoffed. "That's not a thing." Was it? Could Benny have actually been right about something? Impossible.

"It is. I was having trouble moving on. I told you that. We had such a history together. You were my first love. I know we don't have a lot in common besides our past, but I needed to be sure."

"You told me you were having trouble moving on, implying that you wanted to be with me. Not use me for therapy to then move on."

"I'm sorry. It wasn't some sinister plan. When you called, I had been thinking about you. Wanting to be with you. But I've realized, this just won't last. You know it. It's why we broke up in the first place."

"I know. But you're different now." Even as I said it, I knew it was the right call.

Natalia shook her head and finally looked at me. "We're just not right for each other. I thought we could make it work, but relationships shouldn't be forced. There was a reason we drifted apart. We want different things. We like different things."

Was it really happening? She was dumping me? My emotions teeter tottered between anger, confusion, mild amusement, and agreement.

Natalia walked around to my side of the bed, kissed me on the cheek, and said, "Goodbye, Leo."

I didn't say anything. Didn't do anything. I just watched her leave. As much as I didn't like getting dumped, there was a reason I didn't follow. Didn't really protest. She was right. There was a reason we broke up the first time. While we might've gotten a second sexual wind, there was nothing to sustain us. As beautiful and sweet as she was, I wanted more.

Still somewhat confused, I made my way out to the den, took Jean-Claude for a walk, and fed him breakfast upon our return. As Jean-Claude went to town on his breakfast chow, Benny stumbled shirtless into the kitchen, his hair jutting in every direction, the result of a night of sleep and entirely too much hair product the previous day.

He rubbed his face. "Did he go out twice this morning? I thought I heard the door a few times."

"No. Natalia was here."

"Two nights in a row?" he asked excitedly. He raised his hand for a high five, but I didn't complete it.

"It won't be three. We're done. Finito."

"Mom's not gonna be happy you dumped her again."

"I didn't dump her."

"She dumped you? She's been in love with you since we were kids. You must've really screwed the pooch." He turned to the dog. "Just an expression, J.C."

I fired up the stove, intent on making myself a fat omelet with bacon, heavy on the cheese.

Benny plopped into a chair. "I'll have five eggs."

"Does this look like Leo's Diner to you?"

He shrugged. "What happened?"

I replayed the morning in my mind. "I called her Rae."

"You told Natalia about her?"

"No. I just don't know why. We broke up because we shouldn't have been together in the first place."

"You gonna hit that?"

"I just told you we broke up. And please fix your hair. You look like one of those annoying trolls."

Benny shook his head. "I was talking about Rae."

"No. But I'd like to hit you."

Benny shrugged, unfettered. "Mom's not gonna be happy either way."

I flipped the omelet and said, "What does she want from me? And Pop, for that matter? I've been doing it their way and my life sucks."

"You can't give up."

"Coming from the guy who has never actually tried."

Benny scoffed, offended. "Not true. It's all about self-care these days. You gotta take care of number one."

"That sounds like a whole lotta number two."

"We should go out tonight. Shake this off. Frankie's in."

"No. I just want to hang with Jean-Claude Van Dog. He's the only one who understands me."

"Dude. You'll figure it out. If anybody's got this, you've got this."

I shook my head in confusion. "What am I doing with my life? I feel like none of it's mine."

Benny said, "Welcome to the Donatis."

CHAPTER
Eighteen

I HADN'T SEEN Rae since the conference. As unforgettable as she was, I had barely thought about her or the deal for days. I had other females ruining my life to worry about. Not that there was anything to do but stew about it. At Natalia. My mother. On Friday morning, I lay back in my chair, hands behind my head as I stared at my office ceiling. The front bell dinged, announcing a visitor. I groaned. It was Rae. I didn't want to do this.

But when I saw her, I smiled. An absolute smile. She wore a slate grey skirt and matching blazer, a white silk blouse beneath it. She was already making herself comfortable at the head of the table when I arrived in the conference room.

I reached out to shake her hand. "Good morning, Ms. Kane." *Ms. Kane.* The thought of her becoming Mrs. Rosenblum hit me like a kick to the pistachios.

She stared at my hand and then looked up at me. "Really?"

"What? That's not professional?" I pointed to the lobby. "Would you rather head back out to the coat closet?"

Rae rolled her eyes. "I just feel like we're past handshakes."

"There's nothing professional past handshakes. Whip it out."

She scoffed. "Whip what out?"

"The professional etiquette guide you keep on your person at all times."

"I don't have a personal etiquette guide."

"Well, that explains the coat closet incident." I held out my hand again. "So, will you shake my hand already?"

"I guess, but I feel like it's too formal, like we've almost..."

"Almost what?" I had to know.

She raised an eyebrow. "Become friends. Or friendly... ish." Rae took my hand and shook it firmly. The touch of her soft skin was gone too quickly.

I shrugged, attempting to play it cool. "I don't know about friends, but I don't throw up in my mouth anymore when I see you. But I thought that was more related to you leaving your hair down lately."

"Could be," she said, revealing those dimples. "Many people think I have a very nice neck, although you probably prefer the back of my head while I'm walking away."

Without thinking, I blurted, "I'm not looking at the back of your head when you're walking away."

Rae chuckled. "So much for your professionalism."

My face flushed. I looked away for a moment. "Touché, or should I say, tush-ay?"

She frowned, seemingly holding in a smile. "No. You shouldn't."

I plopped into my seat and smacked the table. "Since we're friendsish, let's catch up. How was your weekend, your evening with David, the Prince of Print?"

"It was fine."

"Just fine? I thought you guys were gonna 3-D print little babies together?" If it was gonna happen, I'd hope that would be the way.

"Please stop."

I shrugged. "Okay, friend. What do you want to talk about?"

She leaned in and said, "I want to talk about getting this deal done."

I got serious. "That's business. Not friend chit chat. But okay. I need you to stop squeezing my business from Prema-Print so we can work on the deal in good faith."

Rae's eyebrows rose in disbelief. "You give up? Sign the deal."

I shook my head. "I'm not sure the deal works for me. I'm going from the CEO-in-waiting to the district manager."

Rae added, "Of a company ten times your size. And might I add, not my problem. Your boss is selling the company."

She wasn't wrong, but I still had no interest in making it happen. "I see how it's good for everyone but me and, as you've said, I'm very important to this deal. I'm not trying to be a jerk. If you want this deal to happen, it goes through me. My father and I aren't on speaking terms. I'm starting to not care what he wants."

"Maybe I should talk to him then."

I laughed pathetically. "Good luck with that. He's stunad and near impossible to deal with."

Rae huffed in frustration. "I've been gaining some wonderful experience in that department lately. Although it's not just you."

I thought needling her would make me feel better. It usually did, but not then. "What's the matter?"

Rae jolted back in her chair. "You actually sound concerned. I didn't think you cared at all."

"What makes you say that?"

"Your perpetual jerkiness." She cocked her head in confusion. "Is that a word?"

"No. But since we're on the subject, Italians have the best words. So much better than your words."

Rae gave a deep, but fake, belly laugh. "Oh, you most certainly do not. You got bupkis on us, you schmuck."

I chuckled. "That's actually not bad, but we got gabagool, you stunad."

"You got a lot of chutzpah, I'll give you that. But you're meshuggeneh."

"I'm not your sugar."

Rae laughed and corrected me. "It means crazy. You make me want to kick you in the tuches."

"Oh, you wanna fight?"

She threw up her hands in an exaggerated shrug. "Why not? We have Krav Maga."

I scoffed. "We got street fighting from Brooklyn."

"You think a bunch of schmedricks from Brooklyn can take on Israeli special forces training?"

"I think it would be a fair fight. If we exclude the metrosexuals and hipsters. Unless hipsters are allowed to use their flip flops as a weapon?"

"Oy vey." Dimples. "You're an eyngeshparter. A very stubborn person."

I shrugged, uncaring. "It's part of the Sicilian way. You give me agita," I said with a solid hand gesture.

"What is agita?"

"Anxiety."

"We have that. It's dayge."

I laughed. "Agita is absolutely more powerful than dayge."

Rae shook her head. "It *might* be a better word, but Jewish anxiety is the most powerful force in the universe."

I frowned in confusion. "I thought that was love."

"You don't know too many Jewish mothers, do you?"

I shook my head, thinking. "No. I don't know a lot of Jewish people, to be honest. At least not well. I have one that I'm friendly...ish with. Teach me."

She sat back, seemingly surprised. "Like what? There are a

lot of types of Jews- Sephardic and Ashkenazic are two here in the U.S."

"I never noticed."

"You wouldn't know them by looking at them. The ones that stand out the most are the Hasidic. They have the enormous hats and the curly sideburns."

I scratched my head. "I thought those were pilgrims."

Rae sighed. "Oh, Jesus."

"I thought you don't believe in Jesus?"

"I don't. It's just an expression."

"To you, maybe. When will I meet your mother, by the way?"

"Soon. At my funeral. I think you're going to kill me."

That's not at all what I wanted to do to her. "We're friend-sish. I should meet your mother." Most guys don't want to meet a woman's family because it makes the relationship real, and it's a step towards more commitment, but I've always wanted commitment. And I wondered if I wanted it with Rae. I was starting to think I did. Could that be true?

Rae said, "Can we get back to business?"

"Nah," I said, scrunching up my nose. "I kind of like hassling you."

She turned the sarcasm faucet on high. "Oh, you don't say? Thank you for pointing that out to me. I was completely unaware."

I feigned surprise. "You don't like our banter? Does the Prince of Print give you this?" I gestured to the invisible connection between us.

"Verbally abuse me? No. He treats me with respect."

I studied her eyes. "But does he treat you like an equal? I think you like our banter. The challenge of it all."

She laughed. "You really don't know how to read women."

"Sorry. I'm Italian. You don't have to read Italian women. If you don't like it, don't engage."

"Gladly." She seemingly gathered some patience with a deep beath. "Look, we need to work together. Not against each other. Kane Printing prides itself on collaboration."

My eyes found her chest. "How should we collaborate?"

"Up here," Rae said, pointing to her eyes.

I rubbed the back of my neck. "Sorry, I, umm, slept funny. Big crick in my neck."

"Right," Rae said, seeping with sarcasm. She continued rambling on and on about teamwork and communication, but my eyes were glued to her supple lips. Oh, how I wanted to kiss them again.

She continued, "We've got a few more facilities tours to schedule. And if we could actually get something done today, preferably look at the depreciation schedules of all the equipment, I'd appreciate it."

"Depreciation schedules? And I thought conversing with you couldn't get any worse."

"You love conversing with me. You wouldn't give me so much trouble if you didn't. I think it's you who loves the challenge of it all." She shrugged. "Or you're just bitter about me taking over your business."

She was right. About both. It was at that moment I knew I was totally crazy about her. Nobody challenged me like she did. All the joking and teasing were just an effort to get one up on this incredible woman that was always one step ahead of me.

———

Rae's Deal Notes

- ~~Almost enjoyable. And those eyes! I think he wanted to kiss me again. I have to admit, I've thought about it more than a few times.~~

- Professional relationship improving with Leo, finding common ground. Barely. Perhaps I slightly misjudged him.
- Do I make him nervous? Intimidate him? ~~What does he think about me? Is he engaging in some sort of immature, playground tactics?~~

It was Fat Friday. My mother texted me, so I met her out front. Rae had been gone for an hour, but she was still deeply entrenched in my mind.

My mother's fingers chomped down on my cheek like a starving pit bull, while she kissed my other cheek. "I've got eggplant rollatini, chicken saltimbocca, and acqua pazza." She pulled back and studied me with suspicion. "What are you smiling about? You're glowing."

I grabbed the tin trays from the trunk. "I'm not glowing. Men don't glow."

Her face broke out into a wide smile. "Is it Natalia? It's Natalia, isn't it?"

I shook my head and chuckled pathetically. "Not at all. We broke up."

Her voice broke Mariah Carey's Guinness world record for the highest whistle register. "What happened?"

"She dumped me."

"Impossible," she said, opening the door for me and then again en route to the break room.

I laid the trays on the kitchen countertop and turned to her. "Very possible. In fact, a certainty. My ego can attest."

"The Romanos- a bunch of neanderthals, anyway." She scoffed and waved them away.

I threw up my hands, anger rising. "You said they were a great Italian family."

She snapped, "Things change."

I rolled my eyes and opened the eggplant. "Quickly, apparently."

My mother's tone softened. "You'll find a nice Italian girl. Not one who doesn't know the worth of gold."

Without looking up, I asked, "What if I didn't want to date and marry an Italian?"

"Stop kidding," she ordered.

"I'm serious." My mother glared at me. I felt my life force drain. "Okay, okay. Fine. But hypothetically speaking, what if I found someone who wasn't Italian, and I was totally in love?"

"Does she look Italian?"

I shrugged. "I don't have anyone in mind. What if she was Hindu or Jewish? Or an atheist?"

"God forbid. Uncle Michael can build an extension on his house for you."

I laughed. "I have my own apartment. But it's nice to know how conditional your love is."

She smiled and gave me a firm love tap on my cheek. "I love you no matter what. I will just disown you if you go outside the family."

"Now we're talking incest? I draw the line."

She rolled her eyes. "You know what I mean. It could never work otherwise." Her eyes morphed to daggers as she stared up at me. "Is there something going on?"

I threw up my hands. "No. Ma." She raised an eyebrow. "I swear. No."

"Just trying to kill me with agita?"

I forced a smile. "Yep. Like any Italian son."

"The good ones aren't supposed to give their mothers agita. Benny gives me enough for both of you."

"I can't argue with you there," I said, as the crew filled the room. I filled my plate. I shook my head and chuckled to myself. *What an idiot I am. It could never work.* How could I have been so stupid to think it could?

CHAPTER
Nineteen

I WOKE up thinking about Rae. I grabbed a quick protein shake and plopped onto the couch. Jean-Claude snuggled next to my thigh.

"It could never work. Am I wrong, Jean-Claude? No. No. I am not. Or could it? My mother talks tough, but I'm her favorite."

Jean-Claude cocked his head and stared at me.

"You make a good point. Uncle Michael was her favorite. But I've tried it their way. It hasn't worked. It's my life. I should have some say in it. What do you say to that?"

Jean-Claude lay his head in my lap. "I knew it. You got nothin'. I got nothin'. I'm losing my mind." I lay back, emotionally exhausted, but bounced right back up. "I don't have to tell them. I didn't tell them when…"

I pointed to Jean-Claude and emphasized, "…*she* kissed *me*. Why can't it be a secret?" I fell back into the couch, jolting J.C. again. "She feels the same way. But she'll never say anything. She's too professional. I'm totally dragging her down. But she'll never be the one to take the first step."

I popped from the couch, nearly launching Jean-Claude to

the ceiling. "Sorry, J.C. But I'm gonna tell her. I'm gonna tell her right now. You can't stop me. Try it, bro." He didn't.

I found Rae's number in my phone and FaceTimed her. I wanted to see her. I needed to see those dimples when I told her how I felt.

Rae answered with a raised eyebrow. "It's Sunday."

"I was thinking you missed me."

She unleashed her dimples. "As per usual, your thinking is inaccurate. Seriously, though, what do you need? Did you finish looking at the contract?"

"Almost," I said, my confidence faltering. "I was, umm, just checking the weather for next week. It looks like it might snow or even sleet for our visit out east next week."

"I saw it was supposed to stay west and hit more upstate than eastern Long Island, but we'll monitor it."

"Okay. Let's do it…The plant tour, I mean."

Rae huffed. "So immature."

"How am I being immature? I clarified for you."

"Unsolicited. You are definitely the most immature person I know besides my brother."

I shrugged. "We can't all be as mature as the Prince."

"Whatever. Is this the only reason you called?"

"Yes. No."

Rae furrowed her brow in confusion.

"I've never seen you without makeup. You're…beautiful." I couldn't believe what I was saying.

She attempted to finish my sentence, "But then I open my mouth…"

I smiled, but then feigned seriousness. "As Socrates said, 'To know thyself is the beginning of wisdom.'"

"Oh, shut up." Dimples. Sigh.

"You said it, not me."

Rae's tone turned serious. "Can I ask you a question?"

"Umm, sure. I don't put out on the first date, but with a

nice steak and chianti, I would reward your patience on the second date."

"That was not my question. At all."

I shrugged. "I'm sorry. I just get the question a lot."

"Sure you do."

"I am in demand." *Yeah, right.* I had to hold back laughter.

Rae nodded, unconvinced. "Yeah. It surprised me to hear you have a girlfriend. I feel bad for women with self-esteem issues."

I shook my head. "I don't have a girlfriend."

"Your father doesn't strike me as a guy to make stuff up."

"He didn't. We just broke up. I don't really want to talk about it. Anyway, shoot. What's the question?"

"Do you take me seriously?"

I frowned. "Why would you think otherwise?"

"You haven't looked at the contract. You're always messing with me. If my brother was sitting here, would you treat him the same?"

"I probably wouldn't have told him he was beautiful, and not that there's anything wrong with it, but I may have reacted differently in the coat closet. But, yes. Well, maybe yes and no. I mean, I do think your being a woman adds to the tension a bit....being we're both attractive."

"Oh, are we?"

"Why are you asking? Why do you care what I think?"

"Sometimes, most of the time, I think guys see only skin deep."

"Does this have to do with Prince David?"

"Don't call him that. I'm in line to be CEO of my father's considerable enterprise, if I can get a deal done with this annoying guy I've been working on. I feel like people treat me like my only role in this world is to be someone else's wife. Arm candy. Or baby-making machine. Sometimes, even my father does it."

I had to know. "Are you really gonna be with David?"

"Why not? Yeah, I mean, he's practically perfect in every way."

"He's a Jewish Mary Poppins? Is that what you're looking for?"

"I crush him in squash, but—"

I laughed. "I don't want to make excuses for the guy because I hope he gets leprosy and gets sent to a colony far, far away, but I feel like nobody is good at squash. I mean, what is it, anyway? I thought it was a vegetable."

"It's a sport."

"Is it, though? Since we're discussing sports, if squash *is* more than just a vegetable, I have to say, we Italians crush you in sports. I mean, it's not even close."

"That's not true."

"You have one athlete- Hank Greenberg. He's like 200 years old. We got Piazza. Andretti. DiMaggio. Rocky Marciano. Rocky Graziano."

Rae interjected, "We have Goldberg."

I waved away her response. "Wrestling isn't real."

"He was a professional football player, too." Rae thought for a moment, which gave way to those dimples I so loved. "Sandy Koufax."

My chest constricted. I gasped for air that wasn't there. I nearly dropped my phone as my lungs finally found the fuel of life. I whispered, "Draw. I was hoping you didn't know that." I raised my finger, confidence returning. "But then, the great Brooklyn Dodger is also Baseball's Leonardo, which makes him part Italian, no?"

"No," Rae said, firmly.

I shrugged. "Whatevs."

"Can you just be serious for a minute?"

"Labs have tested that, but all have come back inconclusive."

Rae's eyes bore into me. "You never answered my question."

"Okay. I'm sorry." Why did she care what I thought? Because she was into me. I had to stop dicking around and talk to her about why I was calling. "It's complicated. I respect you as a businesswoman. I think you handle yourself very well. And you have kicked my ass quite handily if I'm being honest. I have nothing but respect for you. And you are a gorgeous woman, which must appeal to me in some unconscious, biological way."

"Right."

"Why are you asking me this?"

She shrugged. "You're kind of my only guy friend. Much as I hate you." Dimples.

"Look, Rae. Can I give you some advice?"

Rae stared back at me in confusion.

"Why are you looking at me like that?"

"Most men I've been around don't ask. They just start mansplaining."

I shrugged. "I guess you need to be around better men."

"Like you?"

"You said it."

"I didn't. It was a question."

"That's not how I remember it."

"It just happened!"

"So, you admit it?"

"Admit what?"

"That you need to be around me more." Maybe I could Jedi mind trick her into us being together without me even asking...

Rae shook her head in disagreement. "We were discussing better men, and it has yet to be confirmed whether you fall into that category."

"I think it's obvious. But you never answered my question."

She nodded. "Yes. I would appreciate your advice."

I turned up the serious dial. It creaked from under-use.

"Look, we may have started off on the wrong foot. And I blame that on me. I was unhappy with the situation. So, I'm sorry about that. We are kind of friends…ish. So, my friend-lyish advice is, I think you need to loosen up a bit. Live a little."

"I'm happy with my life. I'm accomplishing what I set out to do. You're the only one keeping me from what I want."

"Are you asking me out?" I knew she wasn't, but I couldn't help myself.

"You think that's what I meant?"

"I *am* the Italian Mary Poppins."

Rae shook her head, laughing.

I continued, "I need to tell you something. I don't really know how to say it. I don't know if I even should say it. The personal and professional lines have been blurred ever since that lap dance you gave me. So, really, this is your fault…I think what I'm trying to say is…I don't want to be your friend."

Rae's brow furrowed. "What? I'm so confused."

"I'm sorry that I gave you trouble. I didn't want our deal to close from the beginning and I still don't. Even more so now."

"Why not?"

"I want to run my company. And I want to date you. To banter with you. To touch you. To kiss you."

"What?" Rae shrieked.

I nodded, sheepishly. "Yeah. I'm kinda crazy about you."

"Yeah, you are definitely meshuggeneh."

"What? Remind me- is that a jerk or crazy?"

"Crazy."

I nodded with satisfaction. "Okay. I feel like that's progress, no?"

She laughed, but her smile faded quickly. "Leo…" She shook her head and continued, "Leo, we can never be together. There are too many reasons to list. My phone battery will die before I'm done listing them all. Work. Religious. Family. The three most important to me and you."

I nodded, willing the pain away. "I...understand. I've considered all those, but I still had to try. But you wouldn't be asking me these questions if you weren't looking for more than you have, Prince of Printing or not." I stared at her for a moment, waiting for a response, but received none. "Am I wrong? He doesn't see you."

Rae's voice rose a decibel. "It doesn't matter!"

"It does! It's your life. It certainly matters. If I traded in my baseball hat for a beanie?"

"A yarmulke?"

"Right. And if we didn't work together, would you want to be with me?"

"I admit you're different. But it doesn't matter. Your family is die-hard Italian. And you don't meet my family's expectations."

I guess I expected that, but it still hurt.

"Leo, let's just get this deal done so we can move on. We can restructure things if you don't want to report to me. I don't know. I'm sorry, but this is just how it has to be."

I stared at the ceiling. "I'll email you. I can't look at you right now. And just be forewarned, I'll be wearing a paper bag on my head for the plant tour."

"I think everyone would prefer that, Mary."

Those dimples caught the corner of my eye. That joy was now pain. "Yes. Please add fuel to the fire. As if my life doesn't suck enough. Losing my business. Got dumped. Got rejected. Insulting nickname. Just livin' my best life." I sighed.

"You're not a schlimazel."

"Is that good? It doesn't sound good."

"A schlimazel is a person cursed with constant bad luck."

"No. That sounds exactly like me." I hung up. Suddenly, my plan to join the witness protection program wasn't looking like such a bad idea. I'd just have to figure out how to get my mother's chicken parm. FedEx?

Rae's Deal Notes

- ~~WTF? Date me? Is he crazy? Sex me, maybe...OMG brain!~~
- Stay on top of weather for Long Island tour.
- Research Jewish athletes.
- Add meditation to morning routine.
- ~~Discuss with decorator- adding padded walls to apartment. He's driving me crazy! In multiple ways...~~

CHAPTER
Twenty

RAE INSISTED on picking me up. Vehicularly speaking, that is. She's a strong woman, but she had emasculated me enough. The last thing I needed was for her to sling me over her shoulder and toss me into the car en route to our plant tour. To be honest, even having her drive me out to the facility was difficult to swallow. It had nothing to do with her gender and everything to do with her rejection and my fractured ego. I had to pretend she was my chauffeur when the blue Genesis SUV rolled to a stop in front of my apartment building. The service was terrible as she didn't even open my door, but I convinced myself it was true by slipping into the back seat.

Rae turned around with a frown. "What are you doing?"

"Bad back. Need to stretch out my leg," I lied.

"Okay," she said, unsure, and then threw the car into gear. "How are you?"

I still was a little bent out of shape, and a lot embarrassed by our last encounter. I said stiffly, "Fine. You?"

"Great. Seatbelt please."

"Of course. You don't strike me as a Genesis girl," I said, admiring the leather seats.

She glanced back at me in the mirror. "How does a

Genesis girl strike you? Karate chop to the jugular? I could make it work."

"Hardy har."

"Seriously, it's well-made, luxurious, a good value for its offering."

I shrugged. "I don't know. I guess it's fine for a non-Italian car."

"Oh, here we go," Rae muttered. "You drive a Honda!"

"Well, Italian cars are expensive. That's because they're the best. Do you guys even have cars? I mean, you're definitely behind. We've got Ferrari, Lamborghini. You guys should get cars. That way, you don't have to walk everywhere."

Her eyes rolled so hard I thought she might lose sight of the road. "We have cars. You're in mine. Some Jews choose not to use technology on certain days. It's not because we don't have them."

"That sounds kinda Amish." I continued through a suppressed smile. "I mean, we don't even have to go Lambo on you, though. We got you with Vespas." I ignored the glare reflecting back at me. "You would look good on a Vespa," I said encouragingly.

"I thought you were gonna wear a paper bag?"

"It's at the cleaners."

"Can you just stuff your sock in your mouth?"

"That hurts."

"It'll hurt less when I sock *you* in the mouth."

I stared out the window. "You did that the last time we spoke."

Silence. Rain pelted the windshield. Despite the winter weather, with the heat on full blast, I was growing significantly concerned about a breakout of swamp ass. "Can you turn off the flamethrowers back here? My crotch is on fire."

Rae chuckled. "That might not be the heat, Mr. Crabs."

"Don't call me that. Mary was bad enough."

"How about Mary Crabs?" she asked cheerily.

"No."

"Mary Grumpy Crabs," she said, somber. And then laughed at me in the mirror. "This is fun. Now I know why you're always on my case."

I crossed my arms and stared out onto the Long Island Expressway through the frosty glass as we headed east against the rush-hour traffic. "It's raining. You sure you still want to head out there?" I wasn't overly concerned about the weather, but my enthusiasm for the trip had evaporated. "The rain could turn to sleet."

"The weather services are always wrong. I want to get this done. What do I need to know about the Riverhead facility?"

"It handles all our East End business. Sometimes we can hop on the ferry and deliver some jobs to Rhode Island and lower Mass. We've done a lot of work for the water park out there. Hamptons magazines. Some wineries. Paffuto runs the place."

"Paffuto?" she asked, unsure.

"That's his name. Well, nickname. It means 'Chubby' in Italian."

"That's so wrong."

"He likes it. He lost the weight. It's not like he's fat now."

By the time we had reached the Donati facility in Riverhead, the temperature had dropped at least two or three degrees and the rain intensified.

Rae failed to open my door upon arrival, so I stepped out of the car on my own, a chilly wind gusting in my face. On the plus side, cold air is a swamp ass suppressant.

"Wow. It's cold," Rae said, wrapping her white coat with faux fur tighter around her body.

I led Rae to the front door. "Yeah. If things don't work out in printing, my backup plan is glass cutting."

"Huh?"

"My nipples can cut glass right now."

Rae sighed. "You're just devolving."

I opened the door and stepped aside with a shrug. "When no one wants you, it's hard to pull yourself up by your bootstraps."

Rae's smile disappeared. "I'm sorry. I didn't mean to joke."

I smiled pathetically. "My life's a joke, so have at it. If I deserve it from anyone, I deserve it from you."

"I won't pile it on if you can't take it. I won't stoop to your level."

"I take offense to that." I thought about it for a quick second. "No. Actually, I deserve it."

We were interrupted by the svelte Paffuto, his green beady eyes locked on Rae and an oversized sport coat from his paffuto days hanging from his body.

"Yo, Paffoots! Give me a hug, ya sexy bastard." I pulled him into a hug. "This is Rae Kane."

Rae forced a smile from her stunned face. "It's nice to meet you, umm…"

"Anthony, but you can call me 'Paffuto' if you'd like."

"Okay, Anthony."

Paffuto waved us forward. "Come on. Let me give you the tour."

The tour, along with Rae's inquisition of the staff, which fell just short of C.I.A. waterboarding torture, took over three hours. I bought the employees off with lunch from The Smoke Pit, a local BBQ joint with some of the best ribs around. By the time we were done with her insane checklist, it was pushing 2:00.

We said our goodbyes and headed out to the parking lot. An onslaught of wind, frozen rain, and a ground of ice and slush met us harshly.

"Oh, boy. This isn't good," I said, walking beside Rae.

"I'm sure the Expressway is clear. Whoa!" Rae wobbled

and then tumbled back, her feet slipping out from beneath her.

I wrapped my arms around her waist, catching her with a groan. I held her hovering over the ground for a moment, losing myself in her baby brown eyes again, before hoisting her up to her feet again.

"Thank you," she said.

"No problem."

Rae stared at me, but said nothing.

"What?"

"No snippy comment? Something about me falling for you? Or 'usually that happens after I kiss a woman'?"

I chuckled pathetically. "As much as I'd like to see you kiss a woman, I can't joke about that right now."

She rolled her eyes. "Guys are so gross."

I shrugged and exhaled a long, slow breath. I reluctantly offered my arm. "Do you want to hold on? I can deliver you to your door. This parking lot is a sheet of ice." She frowned with reluctance, but took my arm.

I escorted Rae to her door and got in beside her.

"No back seat?"

"I just watched you eat ribs. I can barely look at you, let alone hook up with you in the back seat."

"Oh, now you can joke?"

"Who's joking? I thought I was watching a lioness on Discovery Channel."

"Shut up," she laughed. "I didn't eat breakfast, okay?"

"Well, now you should be good for the week."

Rae blew raspberries at me and started the car. We waited for the windows to defrost and then headed out onto the winding road that led back to the Long Island Expressway and home.

There weren't any cars on the slick roads. We trudged through the slushy puddles at barely thirty miles an hour, the windshield wipers on full blast. We had barely made it a mile when the car slid into the empty lane opposite us. Rae turned the wheel into the slide, but the car didn't respond, instead spinning 270 degrees and headed straight toward a line of thick trees just off the shoulder.

"Holy mother of fuckness!" Rae shrieked as she attempted to regain control of the car, which sputtered as the anti-lock brakes kicked in. I extended my arm to the dashboard to brace myself, but no impact occurred as we jerked to a stop just inches before a 'caution- winding road' sign.

Rae unleashed a plethora of curses, her white-knuckled hands pulverizing the steering wheel while my hearted pounded out of my chest.

I put my hand on Rae's and took a few deep breaths. "It's okay. We're okay."

She let go of the steering wheel and collapsed back into the headrest, her chest heaving. "Oh, my God. That was not good."

"No. No, it was not. As much as my life is already firmly headed toward a fiery death, I'd like to avoid it for the time being, if possible. We should go back to the facility and wait it out."

Rae glanced at the weather app on her phone. "Wait it out how? The sleet is not going to let up into the morning. And the temperature is going to drop even more."

"Now you listen to the weather app?"

She gave me some serious side eye. "If we go back to the facility, we'll have to sleep there. We can go to my house."

I raised an eyebrow. "You have a house in Riverhead?"

"Westhampton. We can take Old Riverhead Road south into town. It's a lot quicker than going home and we won't have to sleep on an offset printer."

"It's a reasonable plan. Just go slow. Holy mother of whatness?"

"Yeah, that's what I said."

"Sounded like something else."

"I curse when I get nervous. Can't help it."

"That's good to know," I said, smiling.

She smirked, but said nothing.

We made it into Westhampton and across the bridge to Dune Road. Oversized beach houses lined the bay and beach as long as the eye could see.

"You live on Dune Road?" I asked, surprised.

"Yeah. We've had it since I was a kid," Rae said, like it was totally normal to have a ten-million-dollar summer home.

We pulled into the driveway of a white three-story beach house with a four-car garage.

"Geez," I said, admiring the house as I exited the car. "Do you have a key?"

"No. We'll have to break in."

I did a double take to find her dimples.

"I have the garage code."

We were inside the den of the ginormous house within a minute. It was like Martha Stewart designed it on steroids.

I took in the beauty of the place. "This place is amazing. But damn. It's like forty degrees in here. It's gonna take forever to heat this place up."

She nodded to a pile of wood next to an oversized brick fireplace. "We should build a fire."

"We as in me?"

"I know how to build a fire," Rae said.

"It's fine. I'll do it. I was a Cub Scout. Do you want me to take my shirt off or do you want a literal flame?"

Rae rolled her eyes. "Literal flame."

I shrugged. "Fine."

"I'll go turn on the burner and the water in the garage. Be back in a few minutes."

I had some old newspaper and the Duraflame lit by the time she got back. She knelt next to me.

"Need me to blow on it?"

I eyed her curiously.

"Ugh. The fire."

I nodded thoughtfully. "For someone so articulate, you could do a much better job choosing your words."

She shrugged and fanned the flame with a magazine.

"That ought to do it," I said, standing up. "The house will be forty-eight degrees by morning. You should tell someone we're here so they can recover our frozen corpses."

Rae laughed. "The heat is working. It'll just take a while." She stood up and looked toward the kitchen. "I'm hungry."

"How the frig is that possible?"

"Never comment on a woman's food intake."

I scoffed. "I'm not sure you're a woman. I'm pretty certain you're the love child of Joey Chestnut and a cyborg terminator."

"Who the heck is Joey Chestnut?"

"Umm, only the seemingly fifty-time Nathan's Hot Dog Eating champ, held at Coney Island on July 4th every year. One time he ate like seventy hotdogs and took out a protester that crashed the contest with a devastating choke hold. In the middle of the competition and still won."

"Never heard of him. And never been to Coney Island. And I'm not a terminator."

"That's not possible."

She frowned at me.

"I mean that you've never been to Coney Island."

"Never been," Rae said, leading me into the kitchen. "Can I ask you a question?"

"You just did without asking."

Rae flipped on the light, revealing an oversized kitchen of black and white with seating for six at the island and at least a dozen at the dinner table. "Seriously, how do you generate such a great rapport with people?"

I shrugged as I took in the scene. "Respect, kindness, fun in the moment."

"Respect? Kindness? I'll give you fun in the moment."

"Oh, really?"

Rae's shoulders slumped. "I mean, you can be fun from time to time. I'm always so afraid I'm going to mess up."

I turned to look at her and said firmly, "You mess nothing up. You've completely been a step ahead of me this whole time."

"But I'm not good with people."

"Well, that's your cyborg half. It's not your fault."

A pointy elbow found my ribs.

"Oww. What do you have, elbow daggers?" I checked my side for puncture wounds.

"Leave my elbows alone. They're my worst feature."

"That's debatable."

She aimed an elbow at me until I recoiled, but then her ocular scanner locked onto the fridge. She opened and scanned it, and then the freezer. "Oops."

"Oops? The golden girl made a mistake?"

"No. We have water bottles and some frozen matzah ball soup."

I spotted a half-full wine rack. "I've got some kosher wine over here."

"We can order something in."

I waved her words away. "I don't want anyone risking themselves for us."

"It's not enough."

"We can make do. You want to heartlessly order some poor delivery boy or girl here, that's on you, but I'd love to try some matzah ball soup."

Within ten minutes, we sat in front of a roaring fire, sipping soup and wine while encased in blankets.

"God, it's cold in here," Rae said, shivering.

"You want to go equal partnership on my glass cutting business?"

"I just might."

"Let me see." I reached for her blanket.

Rae pulled away, shrieking.

"What? You think I'm just gonna give you half my business without seeing your equipment?"

Rae laughed. "I'll show you mine if you show me yours."

My eyes bulged. "You really want to go down that path?"

"No. No, I don't."

I scanned the room, admiring the white and aqua mix, a plaster conch statue, and a family picture of the four Kanes that must've been twenty years old, Rae's dimples the highlight.

My soup bowl suddenly felt lighter. I glanced down to see a piece of bobbing celery and a missing matzah ball. I stared at Rae, mouth open.

"What?" she mumbled and then swallowed what was left in her mouth.

I pointed my spoon at her. "You stole my matzah ball and you know it."

"What proof do you have?"

"I have no proof, but do you realize the jokes I could make right now?"

"Probably, but you should focus on something else."

"I'm trying not to think of your perky nipples."

Rae shrieked and then broke out into laughter. "That's not what I was talking about!"

I smiled sheepishly. "My bad. Forget I said anything—"

She interrupted, "I often do."

I pursed my lips together in mock anger. "What is it?"

In a somber tone, Rae said, "I hate to burst your bubble, but—"

"But what?"

Her face morphed through a range of emotions, from sadness to amusement, and ended on confident. "We have better soup. You cannot beat this chicken and matzah ball."

I scrunched up my face. "Look, I don't want to speak ill of your religion and culture, but yeah, we do...It's called pasta."

"That's not soup." She broke out into laughter. "No. You're not doing this. You're not winning this on some inane technicality."

I scoffed. "Why eat soup when you can have pasta?"

She reached for my bowl. "Okay, so give it back. Where's your precious pasta?"

"Wah," I said like a baby.

"Wah?"

I laughed. "Yes. I'm sad because I'm hungry now and you don't even like me enough to feed me."

"No. You mock my meal when you have no other. Beggars can't be choosers."

"So, you admit this isn't the finest of cuisines?"

"It's an expression. The soup is amazing. My Bubbe makes it."

I stared at her, confused. "What the heck is a Bubbe?"

"My grandma?"

"Oh, Bubbe Kane. I can't wait to meet her." I slurped a sip of soup. "Bubbe's soup is amazing."

"When it's my soup, it's not the finest of cuisines. When an old grandma makes it, it's amazing?"

"I love grandmas. Mine's the best."

"We're gonna argue about that, too?"

"No. I draw the line there. Your Bubbe is great. My Nonna is great. She does hold a mean grudge, but..." I thought of Uncle Michael and then changed the subject. "I do like your soup."

"Is it the best soup?"

I nodded. "It is the best soup. But pasta is better than soup."

She grit her teeth at me playfully.

"What? You want me to lie?"

"No. Just stop trying to one up me."

"I'm constantly underneath you. I'd like to be on top."

"Now who needs to choose their words more carefully?"

Rae placed her bowl on the stone in front of the fire. "I'm still hungry."

I chuckled. "Unreal. I don't think we have any dessert."

"We have the best desserts."

"You just said we didn't have any."

"I meant, the Jews."

"Okay. Tell me. I want to learn."

Rae thought for a moment. "We have chocolate babka."

I countered, "We have tartufo."

"Lekach," Rae said, simply.

"Bless you."

Rae laughed. "I didn't sneeze. It's a cinnamon gingerbread honey cake."

"Don't call me honey cake."

"Rugelach."

"Cannoli."

"Sufganiyah."

I feigned annoyance. "Now you're just making stuff up."

"I am not. It's a jelly donut served on Hanukkah."

"You can't just take other people's stuff, rename it, and say it's yours." I shook my head and huffed. "But I'm no longer interested in conversing about desserts. I think we should have some dessert."

"I told you, we don't have any. The place is bare."

I inched closer to her. "I'm still hungry. I need to taste something." She stared into my eyes, perhaps even moving closer. "I just can't stop thinking about you. Craving your eyes on me. Your lips. Your hands."

She moved closer again, whispering, "This is a bad idea."

"This is the best idea I've ever had," I whispered, inching so close I could feel her breath on me.

She closed her eyes as I leaned in, pressing my lips to hers.

The wind howled, rattling the French doors. I pulled back, my hand still on her face. I looked deep into her eyes and whispered, "You're right. That was a bad idea."

She smacked me playfully. "Take that back."

"Fine. That was definitely the best idea I ever had."

"I agree."

I kissed her again, looked at her with the light of the crackling flames, and then delivered the famed *Growing Pains* line, "Girl, you've got needs and I've got needs. Why should we be needy on a night such as this?"

Rae laughed. "Still the worst line ever."

"You want me to leave?"

"No. Take me, you cheese ball."

"I told you it works," I said, leaning into kiss her.

Before long and despite the cold, clothes flew in every direction but the fire. I had only had a few sips of wine, but I was drunk on Rae. And the dessert was indescribable.

I WOKE up the next morning, a surreal feeling as Rae and I stared at each other, neither of us knowing what to say.

"Good morning," I whispered.

"You don't have to whisper," she whispered.

"Well, we were loud enough last night. The neighbors should get a little sleep."

Rae laughed, but her dimples quickly disappeared. "Now what?"

I knew what she was thinking, but I said, "Well, I need to wipe the drool off my shoulder. For the record, I prefer the other methods we used to exchange bodily fluids."

"So gross."

"I know. It's fine. But don't worry. You're the sexiest slobberist I know."

She pushed my shoulder playfully. "That's not a thing. Don't make that a thing."

I didn't listen. "You should put that on your resume."

"I'm not looking for a job."

"Maybe I'll get a t-shirt made then."

"I won't be wearing that."

"That's fine. I quite enjoy it when you don't wear things."

I pulled her in toward me, kissed her neck, and then worked my way down.

Rae moaned and then grabbed my ears. "Wait. Come up here. We have to talk."

"We *were* talking. The international language of love. And easy on the ears. You're like Sister Ethel from my high school. She ruled the school by the ear."

Rae looked away and whispered, "We don't love each other."

I didn't know if she was right or wrong, but it stung given how easily and forcefully she said it. I scooted up and propped my head up on my hand, staring at her while on my side.

She added, "This changes nothing."

"What about when I did that thing with my tongue? You said it was life changing."

"I'm serious. Okay, it changes things. But it doesn't change the most important thing. We can have this, but we can't be together *together*. Ever."

"Why not?"

"For the same reasons as before. And nobody can ever know about this. You know I'm right."

I didn't, but I nodded reluctantly.

"We take this to the grave. Or I'll dig yours."

I chuckled. "That's kinda hot. It takes my dominatrix fantasy of you to a whole new level."

"You have a dominatrix fantasy about me?"

"Maybe."

Rae gritted her teeth and said with force, "Tell me."

"Yes, mistress," I joked.

She broke out into laughter. I kissed her again.

Rae was totally going to ruin me, but I had never been happier.

———

Rae's Deal Notes

- ~~"Tour" was mind-blowing! I have never, ever, ever…the things he did. The way I felt. The way we connected. Finally, he figured out how to use his tongue properly…lol. Talk about needing padded walls…But it can't be. Why can't I have a guilty pleasure? A fling? Because it's not professional. Because it could never, ever work.~~
- Set professional boundaries.
- Reread The Power of Discipline.

CHAPTER
Twenty-Two

I'D SAY the ride home was quieter than a funeral, but Italian funerals can get pretty rowdy. Maybe it was more like a library. With no Italians. I mean, if we don't respect the dead, you think we're gonna respect a bunch of paper and ink, my career aside?

It's hard to explain how I felt after. Contented awkwardness? Rae had given herself to me and me to her in a way that I had never experienced with anyone. The energy. The passion. The connection. But then she rejected me again and had barely said a word since. Where did we go from here? Neither of us seemed to know.

She dropped me off at my apartment just before lunch. I leaned in to kiss her cheek, but stopped and pulled back. She reached out her hand for a shake, but then tried to meet my kiss. We both chuckled nervously.

"We should probably just high five," Rae said.

"Meet you at fist bump?" I said, holding my fist out for a pound.

She pulled her hand away. "No. Can't do it. I'll text you."

"How about this?" I used my best English accent, "Until we meet again, my Juliet."

Rae laughed. "Too dramatic and morbid."

I huffed. "Whatevs." I got out of the car. "I will await your text." I watched her drive away until she disappeared down the street. She was out of sight, but not out of mind.

I replayed my night and morning with her repeatedly, not sure when I even fell asleep. I felt like I was up all night, my mind reeling.

My phone dinged with a text, waking me up. I reached for it with a groan, sat up, and read it. It was from Rae.

'So, we're making progress.'

'I'd like to think so. Are you against ice cubes next time? It was a little too cold for them the other night, but I've got some creative ideas that I think you'll like.'

'I was referring to our deal.'

'Whatever deal we make should include my frozen water idea. It's mutually beneficial.'

'I'm serious. This is important to me. We have to complete the valuation in the coming few weeks or month.'

'Fine.'

I tossed down my phone with a huff. She had gone straight to business, not even acknowledging where we had left off. Could she ever loosen up and be who I wanted her to be? Or at least acknowledge that there was something between us?

Jean-Claude scooted into my room and yipped until I picked him up. I scratched his ears as I held him in my arms. "How the hell am I going to get out of this mess, little man? I don't want this deal to happen. But I don't want my relationship with Rae, whatever the hell it is, to end. But if I work for her, she'll no doubt cut us off. This is already a stretch for her, no matter how much I stretch for her." I laughed to myself and plopped Jean-Claude on the floor. "I wish you could understand that. Not the stretching part, even though it's pretty funny."

I dug out Sam Bennington's card, the guy I met from

Impact Ink at the conference. Could he be looking for more? Professionally, I mean. I wanted Rae, and I knew it would never work if I worked for her. Sam was the perfect target for me. Strong family values. Cares about his firm's legacy and didn't have a successor. Maybe he would pay up for one.

CHAPTER
Twenty~Three

ON MONDAY MORNING, I was sitting across from Sam in a high-back leather chair, his mahogany desk between us. He seemed to be successful enough. Maybe we could make a deal.

I leaned forward and looked Sam in the eye. "Look. I'll be completely honest. We have a deal on the table. It's not a good deal for my family or for me. My dad wants out for whatever reason, and he accepted the first deal that came our way. I was supposed to run the business once he retired. I still want to. I'm looking for a better fit, valuation-wise, and from a career standpoint. I enjoyed our conversation at the conference, and I wanted to continue the dialogue."

Sam thought for a moment, his eyes brightening. "We have been looking for a stronger footing on Long Island. What kind of valuation are you looking for?"

I shrugged. "I mean, five times is not out of the question in this market. And a succession agreement for me."

"Why not a merger of somewhat equals?"

"My dad wants to cash out. Lounge around in Sicily or Boca. Don't ask."

Sam nodded. "I'm sixty-two. I'd like to work another

three, maybe five years. I could sell out to one of the heavy hitters, but I just don't know if I could stomach that. My kids didn't join the business. I'd love a young buck to come on, work with me until I retire, and then take over."

"I think you're looking at him."

"Tell me about your business philosophy."

I thought for a moment. "We need to take our relationship business and add twenty-first century tools. The landscape is changing. We have to change with it. Let me tell you how I've been winning new business." I explained how I built landing pages, social media ads, and used our email lists to capture leads and new clients.

My phone rang in my pocket. "Oops. Sorry." I pulled it out. It was Rae. I shut it off and slipped it back into my pocket.

"You need to take that?"

I shook my head. "No. It's fine. I'll deal with it later. My focus is on what's important. And that's here."

"What about culture?" Sam asked.

"It's really important. It's one of our advantages. We work hard," I said, trying not to laugh, and then continued, "We're professional, but we also like to have fun."

"Same here."

"You guys ever do chair jousting?"

"No, but that sounds amazing."

"Well, my guys will teach you." I threw my hands in the air. "See, we're already finding synergies." I sat back and studied Sam's face. "What do you think?"

"I'm interested. I like you. I could see you running this place one day."

I nodded, holding in a fist pump. "As I said, we're farther along with someone else, but I'd rather do a deal with you. We'd have to move relatively fast, and you'd have to beat their price to change my father's mind."

"Understood. Let me crunch some numbers, talk to my bank, and I'll call you later in the week."

I stood up and held out my hand. "Deal."

Sam laughed. "Not yet, but I'm hopeful."

I nearly cartwheeled out to my car. I may have busted out the moonwalk as I maneuvered between my car and another one, but nobody saw, so you'll never know for sure. I hopped in and headed home. I tapped the steering wheel to the beat, cruising down the Saw Mill River Parkway north of Manhattan, when my phone rang. It was Rae. I popped the call onto Bluetooth. "Talk to me, girlie."

"You sound happy."

"Why wouldn't I be hearing from you?"

"Are you in the car?"

"Yep. What's going on?"

"I…want to see you."

"Personally or professionally?"

"Personally."

"Hmmm. Interesting. I think I could arrange that. How about forty-five minutes at your place?"

"You can get here by then?"

"I'm in Westchester."

"What for?"

"Umm, lunch with a friend." I couldn't tell her just yet. I'd have to see how things played out a bit more. She certainly wouldn't tell me if we were in opposite positions.

"Where are you? I've never been to your place."

"Oh, yeah. Right. Park on 68th between Broadway and Amsterdam. I'll meet you outside the garage. Who did you have lunch with?"

"Jealous?"

She scoffed. "No. Just curious."

"My buddy Ron from college." I felt bad lying, but like she said, it was just a fling. And she had more than worked the deal for herself. "Don't worry. He does not look anywhere close to as good as you naked."

"That's not comforting at all."

I chuckled. "To each his own. I'll see you soon." I drummed the steering wheel and said more to myself, "This is crazy."

"What is?"

"You like me."

Rae laughed. "Is this grade school? Yes. We like each other."

"Based on what I have planned, this is not grade—" The phone cut out. Apparently, she hung up on me.

———

Rae's Deal Notes

- Lift professional boundaries temporarily ~~for personal pleasure...~~ for camaraderie and team-building potential. Colleagues work better together when familiar in each other's company.

CHAPTER
Twenty~Four

THREE DAYS LATER, I found myself back at Rae's apartment, having spent the night. A lovely night, and morning, if you know what I mean. I stood in front of her, holding out a cup of coffee as she pulled her hair back into a ponytail.

"Tell me again why we're wearing jeans and sweatshirts to a business meeting?" Rae asked, concerned.

I smiled and handed her the cup. "Because I'm the only person you're meeting with and I've seen you in a lot less, so consider this dressing up."

She smirked and then asked, "But what are we doing?"

"You don't trust me? Have I had any bad ideas?"

"Not that I can recall."

I shrugged. "Well, just think of it as we have some due diligence to do."

"For what?"

"I want to check out a property."

"Where?"

"This isn't twenty questions. Brooklyn."

Rae scrunched up her nose. "You don't own anything in Brooklyn."

"Fair point, but I'm in pursuit of a new opportunity," I

said enthusiastically. "Let's go, Sunshine. Traffic should be dying down."

"From Manhattan to Brooklyn?"

"Fair point. I *could* leave my car here for the day and maybe night, if you wanted to hop on the train."

She kissed me, but then pushed me away. "Good try, but I have something tonight."

"What?"

"Family stuff."

Was it David? "Are you...seeing him?"

"Family stuff," she repeated, and then smiled. "So, let's go. Due diligence waits for no one."

"You're such a weirdo that I have to motivate you with the prospect of due diligence."

"I'm motivated by other...stuff," Rae said with a love tap to my crotch.

I shrieked and crumpled in overreaction, prompting those dimples I love. I stood up straight, tossing my shoulders back in an attempt to regain lost self-esteem. "Is that where the saying about the carrot and the stick comes from?"

Rae laughed, shook her head, and led me to the door.

It took us forty-five minutes to drive seventeen miles, but we finally made it. We drove past the Brooklyn Cyclones minor league baseball stadium, barely noticeable if not for the towering lights spread out in the distance. We parked on 115th street and made our way to the boardwalk and the inviting scent of Nathan's hotdogs and fries. I had to force myself to look away from Nathan's yellow and red sign, my brain questioning 'why?' I then found the white roller coaster in the distance with the words 'Cyclone' written in red, an early spring blue sky stretching behind it.

"We're going to Coney Island? How is this a new opportunity? And in the middle of the workday?" Rae asked, confused.

"Are you suggesting a nooner?" I asked, eyebrow raised.

"God no!"

"That's a little hurtful," I said, pushing out a quivering lower lip.

She kissed it and then nibbled on it.

"Oww," I pulled back, more dramatic than necessary.

Rae nudged my shoulder with a smile. "Stop it. I've bitten you harder. And we should be working."

"We are. We're dilligizing."

"That's not a word."

"Okay, fine. We're due dilligenting."

"Also not a word." Her smirk turned to a chuckle.

"I love you smirky."

Rae's face dropped. "What did you say?"

It was like a gun went off. My heart and brain broke out into a sprint. "What?" I threw up my hands. "There was no comma! Your nickname is not 'Smirky'." I took a deep breath as the color returned to Rae's face. "Let me rephrase. I *enjoy* it when I make you smirk."

Rae took a deep breath. "Okay. Sorry. I thought you meant something else."

"Right. Your mistake," I said, smiling. I waved her ahead. "Let's go, Smirky. Dilligentation is about to happen."

"Not a thing," she said, chuckling.

I huffed as we walked past Nathan's, the boardwalk creaking beneath our feet. "Fine. Employees are part of your checklist, are they not?"

"They are."

"Well, then. You're getting to know your favorite employee."

Rae said, "I already know everything I need to know about you."

I stopped to face her with hands on hips. "Oh, do you? Didn't you think you knew me when we first met? Sexist jerk, was it? And then you thought I was like everyone else. That proved to be quite false, didn't it? Clothed and unclothed."

"Okay, now you're getting a little carried away. Where are we going, by the way? It's a little too early for hot dogs, isn't it?" Rae asked, nodding to Nathan's.

"You didn't seem to mind this morning." I put up my hand for a high five. Rae did not complete it. I dropped my hand in sadness and said, "Fine. It's probably best not to eat before the Cyclone."

Rae stopped dead in her tracks and stared at the wooden coaster in the distance. "The Cyclone? That doesn't look too stable. I'm just not big on wooden rollercoasters."

"You seemed quite pleased on one last night. High five!" I threw up my hand and again, it was left incomplete.

"Shut up," she said, breaking out into laughter.

I nudged her forward by the small of her back. "I know it doesn't look great, but they use a lot of wood glue and nails. Plus, it's good to almost die every once in a while. It makes you want to live your best life."

"No. You don't understand. I don't handle roller coasters well."

"You'll be fine."

We headed deeper into the park. It was reasonably empty given the park had just opened for the season and it was late morning during the week. We walked straight onto the ride.

Rae stiffened as we approached the cart.

"You'll be fine. Let's sit in the front. It's the most fun."

She said nothing. In hindsight, I'm wondering if perhaps she could not speak. There's a reason they call it 'The Cyclone'. The thing whips around like no other. Certainly, there are faster roller coasters, but this less-than-modern marvel has perhaps the greatest speed-to-inability-to-seem-ingly-handle-said-speed ratio of any ride I've ever been on. And once it got going, Rae said more than enough.

"I hate you. I hate you. I hate you," she whispered, as the roller coaster took off slowly.

"You'll be fine. It's a New Yorker rite of passage. Most survive."

"That's not funny, dick face," she said, no hint of a smile.

I laughed in shock. I was about to protest. My face was anything but, however, we met the first drop. I threw my hands in the air as the wind whipped, the cool spring air bringing tears to my eyes.

Rae shrieked, "Holy mother fucker, you son of a bitch bastard fuck nut!" And a lot of other stuff that would make a hooker blush.

I broke out into laughter as the coaster accelerated into a tight curve and another string of curse words ensued, and didn't stop until the ride squeaked to a jolting stop. I continued laughing even as the lap harness opened and we got out. I offered Rae a hand, but she slapped it away. I investigated her ghost-like face as it slowly regained color.

"Are you okay?" I asked, seriously.

"I told you," she said, annoyed.

"I'm sorry. I didn't realize you'd be so scared. I just thought you were gonna puke on me. I had no idea that marvelous monstrosity was about to ensue."

"I'm glad you enjoyed it," she said, her words seeping with sarcasm.

"Well, I did, but I think the kids behind us might need therapy."

"You don't care that I was scared and now that I'm mad?"

"I do care, but I am also oddly fulfilled. My life could end right now and it would be complete."

Rae rolled her eyes as I wrapped an arm around her. "You are…one of a kind," she said.

"Thank you."

"I didn't mean that as a compliment."

"Well, I'm taking it as one, and there's nothing you can do about it." I tickled her chin as she glared at me. "Come on, Smirky. Let me buy you lunch. Nathan's has the best fries on the planet and you get to eat them with a mini pitchfork. It's ah-mah-zing," I said with a strange accent, just for fun.

"If I'm Smirky, you're Jerky."

"You're angry. I get it, but let's get some bacon cheese fries and then work off the calories later."

"I don't like cheese on my fries."

"That's weird, but okay. I guess I can buy you your own. I'm losing track of how many dates this is."

Rae stopped short. "No dates. We are not dating." She leaned toward me and whispered with some 'tude, "This is a fling. Not dating. And this is a business meeting."

"Admit we're dilligizing or I'll tell your father we're dating," I said, holding in a smile.

"He would kill you."

I shrugged as we approached Nathan's. "He seemed to like me at the conference."

"Because he didn't know—"

I finished her sentence, "We were dating?"

"Not dating. Didn't know I had…sexual interest in you."

"I am very sexually interesting." I nibbled on her ear, getting her to smile. "At least admit that."

"No."

I held up my hand and snapped my finger at a passing woman in her thirties, pushing a baby stroller. "Hi there! Do you find me sex—"

Rae's fingers squished my lips shut. She pulled my hand down and whispered, "You are sexually interesting."

Through still-squished lips, I said, "Thank you." I waved to the woman and said, "Sorry, thought you were someone else." She frowned and continued on her way.

"Jerky."

"Maybe you're right," I said. "But you love me." My eyes bulged. "It. You love my jerkiness. I'm a bad boy. Chicks love bad boys."

"You're a sexually interesting mamaluke."

"I'll take it."

We grabbed lunch and sat down at a table for two. It was quiet, still early for lunch, and the park.

I speared a golden-brown crinkled fry doused with cheese and speckled with bacon, utilizing the handy red pitchfork, and popped it into my mouth. "Am I wrong? The. Best. Fries. The crinkle is amazing."

Rae nibbled on hers and shrugged. "They're too stubby. I like mine longer."

I swallowed a laugh. "Oh, I know baby. You thanked me profusely for that."

Rae's face rivaled the ketchup's rich red color. She whisper-shouted, "There are people around. I was talking about french fries."

"You're even adorable when you're embarrassed."

We sat and chatted for a while, finishing up lunch. I stared out the window and said, "It's starting to pick up." I turned back to my food, about to fork the final fry, but I found nothing but a glob of cheese. "What the..." I looked at Rae, who covered her mouth while chewing.

"Hey! You just said you didn't like these."

"That one didn't have cheese."

"They are pretty damn good. For non-Italian food, it's top notch. I have to admit it, Italians can't beat the French on this one."

Rae shrugged, seemingly not impressed. "We've got latkes with applesauce. It's not too shabby. We're not even going to talk about how many amazing knishes I've eaten."

I bit the inside of my cheeks to keep from laughing. "You may not want to spread that around so much. You might start to get a reputation."

She huffed by didn't say anything.

I threw up my hands. "Okay. You got us on potatoes, but since we're on starchy carbs, not only do we crush you on pasta, we crush you on rice. You can't beat risotto."

Rae smirked. "Yeah, you guys win diabetes."

"There's my girl!" I said with faux enthusiasm, and then shrugged. "That's why we need the loose track suits. It's a vicious cycle. You wanna go dilligize over by the games? I pretty much can crush you at all of them, but let's just play for fun. Maybe I'll win you something."

"Maybe I'll win *you* something." Rae poked me hard in the chest.

I rubbed my chest, a pained look on my face. "I prefer doing the poking."

She ignored me, shaking her head, as we made our way toward the games. We arrived at Whopper Water, a water gun/hose shooting race with strange yellow Pikachu-looking figures atop each target. Stuffed unicorns, lions, giraffes, and frogs hung from the walls.

I slipped into the chair next to Rae and paid the attendant. "Let's have two rounds. She's gonna want a rematch."

"In your dreams."

"Not really. In my dreams, you actually do whip me."

"Shut up," she said, laughing.

"Ready?" the man asked from behind the counter.

Rae nodded and a bell rung. Water surged from each hose. I lined mine up and held it steady. I peeked over at Rae. Her eyes bore into the target, water disappearing into the hole, her tongue out the side of her mouth in concentration. It was almost as adorable as the dimples. She was intense. I returned my gaze to the target and said without looking, "As you know, I control hoses very well."

She ignored me until her obviously rigged Pikachu stood taller than mine. The bell rung again, and the water petered to a stop. Rae thrust her hands in the air. "Victory is mine, sucka!"

I cracked my knuckles. "Well done. Well done. I'm a little rusty, I guess."

The game started again. This time, I was winning. I

grabbed both handles of the water gun and lined it up like a laser. Water disappeared into the hole with authority. But in no time, the bell showed my loss.

Rae thrust her fists in the air and screamed, "Girl power! Feel the female burn."

I scrunched up my nose. "That doesn't sound like you won. It just sounds like you have the makings of an S.T.D."

The attendant suppressed laughter and asked, "Miss, what prize would you prefer?"

"What would you like?" Rae asked, eyebrow raised.

I said sheepishly, "I'll have the unicorn."

The attendant frowned, but handed the mythical white and purple beast to me.

"Thank you," I said, hugging the unicorn as we walked away. "You ever wonder how unicorns are fake, but giraffes are totally real? A horse with one horn. Or a twenty-foot... vegetarian...leopard."

"Nope. Can't say that I have. Now what?"

"More games? Or back to the city for dinner and some aggressive, naked cuddling?"

Rae shrieked, "What the heck is aggressive, naked cuddling?"

"Making the bacon. Mattress dancing. What do you call it?"

"Yentzing."

I used my sexiest voice, "Ooh, baby, I wanna yentz you."

Rae laughed. "Like 'Oh, baby, I wanna make the bacon with you' is any better."

I shrugged. "I wouldn't mind a little pork."

She bumped me with her shoulder. "You're so gross."

I raised my index finger. "Yet you are engrossed. It's just a fling, right? So, let's fling it."

Rae glared at me, confused. "I have nothing to fling."

"I'll do the flinging."

"You're so romantic," Rae said with a chuckle.

"You're the one who doesn't want the romance. You just want the man-ce. Tell me when to turn on the rom and I'll do it."

"You're right. And I'm just glad you didn't think this was you being charming."

We played a few more games and grabbed some funnel cake. Rae resisted any rides, which was probably a good idea since the number of kids in the crowd grew by the minute after school let out.

"You want to hit The Cyclone once before we go?" I asked.

"Funny."

"Suit yourself."

We headed back to the parking lot and slipped into my car. I glanced at the map on Waze, punched in Rae's address, and said, "To Columbus Circle!" I turned to Rae. "By the way, we have Christopher Columbus."

Rae huffed. "Is that supposed to be impressive? Very dubious past. We have Einstein."

I pulled out onto 115th street. "We have DeNiro."

Rae laughed, perhaps harder than I'd ever heard her laugh. "You're going the entertainment route? We have thousands of famous Jews in showbiz."

"I don't know. Italians are pretty solid in horror films and westerns."

"You're the only one who knows that. And we own the whole town."

"Fine. You have entertainment," I said, frowning.

She patted my knee. "Don't worry. You have Snookie and Jersey Shore. How can we Jews compete?"

I smirked. "I guess you have sarcasm, too. We have Martin Scorsese's eyebrows."

Rae broke out into laughter. "You don't care about the rest of him?"

"Not particularly. Unless he wants to turn my life story into a movie." We passed a Papa John's pizza. "That's not right. I have nothing against Papa John's, but they shouldn't be allowed in Brooklyn. What's your favorite pizza, by the way?"

"Deep dish."

My eyes found hers and I raised an eyebrow. Yeah, I know. Probably less important than paying attention to the merge onto the psychotic Belt Parkway, even so, this was important. "You mean Sicilian, right?"

"No. Chicago deep dish with the sauce on top."

"Are you a sociopath? You're a New Yorker?

"Shut up, you mamaluke."

"Hey! You're not allowed to use my words against me."

"I just did."

I huffed as we merged into traffic. "Whatever. So, who knew business could be so fun?"

"I'm pretty certain this was a lame attempt at a date?"

"It was pretty unprofessional to steal my french fry."

Rae said, "Disagree."

"One thing I'm sure we can agree on is that we will not be honeymooning at Six Flags." I cringed after I said it and quickly added, "Kidding. I'm kidding, of course."

Rae said nothing for a moment.

"What are you thinking?"

"Stop doing that or we have to stop doing this."

I huffed. "I'm sorry. I was kidding."

"You have to realize it's nothing to do with you. It's me. My family. It will never work. Because of me. Who I am. Who my family is. Would your family feel any different about me and my family?"

"No. You're right. But…"

"What?" Rae asked.

"How could you be so right for me, but so wrong? And why are we okay with this being the way it is."

Rae shrugged. "Let's forget about what can't happen and enjoy what can happen."

"Like what?" I asked, annoyed.

"Things that are so right, but so wrong?"

I laughed unexpectedly. That's what I loved about Rae. She always surprised me. And yeah, I said love. At least to myself.

———

Rae's Deal Notes

- Live in the present moment, but don't lose sight of long-term plan and the consequences of poor decisions. ~~Even when he feels so right. And looks so right wrapped in bed sheets...~~
- Read: Emotional Intelligence: A Primer.
- Read: A Guide to Long-Term Decision Making.

CHAPTER
Twenty~Five

THE RELATIONSHIP TENSION persisted until we made it to the bedroom and then it all faded away. I spent another night at Rae's apartment. If I didn't typically leave so early for work and Benny and Frankie party so late, I'd probably have a lot of answering to do. I'd been paying our neighbor to walk Jean-Claude on the sly. Mrs. Clark was a widow with a yappy Yorkie, who Jean-Claude seemed to tolerate well enough. She was a stealthy old bird, and the boys hadn't realized yet. I was about twenty percent concerned she'd walk in on one or both without pants on, but a night with Rae was worth the risk. At least for me. And Mrs. Clark didn't know any better.

I woke up just after six and made breakfast while Rae hopped in the shower. I had an omelet on the stovetop, bagels warming in the oven, and coffee at the ready when Rae headed toward me in nothing but a towel, her brown hair curly, wet, and flat-out sexy. I was ready for round two.

Rae said, "I smelled coffee. What's for breakfast?"

"Steak and eggs."

"I don't have any steak."

I flexed my stomach muscles with my best smolder, then

stepped toward her and kissed her. "You had eggs in the fridge and I'm the beef."

I picked her up and groaned, placing her on the countertop as I continued to kiss her. She shrieked, holding onto the top of her towel, much to my chagrin. No matter how many times I had seen her, all of her, I wanted more. Needed more.

Rae pulled back, brow furrowed. "Why did you just grunt when you picked me up?"

I thought quickly. "Umm, it was a love groan. I mean, uh, a sex groan. Not physical strain."

"Okay, I've been stress eating a little. I just needed to know. Please continue."

I kissed her neck and flipped off the stove. Sexy and sensible.

We talked in between kissing.

"We have to get to work," Rae whispered.

I tugged at her towel in between kisses. "I am working."

Rae threw her head back in pleasure and dropped some Yiddish on me. "Du farkirtst mir di yorn."

"Yes. No. Maybe?"

Rae laughed as I pulled her hips toward me and then tore off her towel.

She groaned. "It means, 'You'll be the death of me.' My grandmother always said it."

"Thank you," I gasped. "I'm really enjoying thinking of your grandmother as we do this. Does she have your bustiness?"

"Bubbe has big grandma knockers."

"Nonna knockers? Can we stop talking about this? I'm losing blood flow to important areas."

Rae laughed. I picked her up, careful not to groan, love groan, sex groan or otherwise, and found our way to the den couch.

"Remember when you hated me?" I asked before kissing her.

"Who says I don't still?"

"You already told me you liked me. And why are you trying to tear my sweatpants off?"

Rae chuckled, tugging at my pants. "Because I hate you in pants."

"As you wish. But I think that means you love me naked."

She didn't confirm or deny, so I was making progress.

———

After an eventful and pleasurable cardio session, we needed to carbo-load. I finished the eggs and sandwiched them up in plain bagels. Unfortunately, we were both fully dressed by that point. Rae in a blue pants suit and me in jeans and a t-shirt. I'd have to swing by the apartment before heading to the office.

I took a bite of my sandwich. "This is a great bagel."

Rae smiled. "The great work of my people."

"Soft, with a hint of vanilla. Excellent," I said, nodding with approval.

Rae nodded and offered a brief flash of dimples. "I'll let Maury know you approve."

"Who the heck is Maury?"

"Maury of Maury's Bagels, only the finest in Manhattan. Not only are the bagels amazing, but the flavored cream cheeses are to die for. And he makes a mean pizza bagel. I used to have them all the time as a kid." She raised an eyebrow and cocked her head. "Which begs the question, who owns the pizza bagel?" I loved this game we played. Maybe I should've told her we were playing it at the beginning and I wasn't just an enormous, arrogant jerk, but still. It was fun.

I scoffed. "We own pizza and we own bread. We've already established this."

"That's bullshit," Rae said, half laughing.

"Did you ever eat a bagel outside of New York?" I asked.

"No. You?"

I shook my head. "No, but I've had circles of disappointment, mislabeled as bagels."

"Yeah," she sighed. "Pizza, too, right? Except for Chicago deep dish, of course."

"Don't get me started." I took my last bite and turned serious. "So, this may be beyond fling status, so answer or don't answer, but you said you were stressed. What's going on?"

"I just need to get this deal done. My father is pressuring me. My brother is angling to run the company even though he can't or won't actually do anything, but play golf." Rae huffed, stood up, and grabbed our empty plates.

My cell phone rang in the kitchen.

"You want me to grab that?" Rae asked, disappearing.

"Yeah, please."

She headed back into the dining room, staring at my phone. "It's Sam Bennington from Impact Ink. Why would he be calling?"

"Oh, you can leave it," I said, nonchalant. "Let it go to voice mail."

Rae offered me the phone and asked again, "Why is he calling?" It wasn't accusatory, but it wasn't chipper, either.

"I met him at the conference. We exchanged cards."

Rae pursed her lips together. "I can tell when you're lying."

"Why would I lie about it? Everything I told you is true."

She crossed her arms. "What are you *not* telling me?"

I huffed. I didn't want to lie to her, but I feared her wrath, too. "Look, it's not a big deal. I reached out to him as a backup plan, but really for verification on the valuation of the business. Just to make sure."

Rae's voice rose an octave. "He's going to buy your business?"

I stood up and put my hands on her shoulders, but they didn't stay long as Rae karate chopped them away. "Rae. They're not buying the business."

"Is this why you've been stalling on signing the deal?"

"No." Maybe. "Even if I was, how is it any different from what you've done?"

She crossed her arms, glaring at me. "We weren't sexing when I was doing it."

"Sexing?" I asked, eyebrows raised and suppressing laughter.

"You know what I mean."

"No. Show me."

Rae turned her back on me. "I'm being serious. I'm upset. This deal is important to me."

I rubbed her shoulders without her breaking any of my bones. Progress. "Me, too. And so are you."

"This is not about us. It's about the business."

"Okay. Let's discuss that. Have you done what's right for you?"

"Yes. And my family and the business."

"I've done nothing different." I turned her around and stared into her eyes. I needed to see them. See her reaction. I shrugged, playing it cool. "Besides, this is just a fling to you, right?"

Rae bit her lip and then said, "It's more than that and you know it."

"I know it with every fiber of my being. I'm crazy in love with you, Rae Kane."

"Don't say that," she said, annoyed.

"I just did," I said, smiling. "It's time I met your Bubbe. Or at least see a picture of her knockers."

She angry-laughed. "Shut up. This is serious. We're totally screwed."

I caressed her face and when she looked up at me, I kissed her like she'd never been kissed before. I'm Italian. That's just how we do it.

But Rae was right. We were totally screwed.

———

Rae's Deal Notes

- ~~Holy shit- he loves me! Holy shit-he loves me? How do I feel? I know how I feel when I'm with him. I've never felt this way. I love being with him…I at least know that. This is going too far. But I don't want it to stop.~~
- Research Sam Bennington- Impact Ink on website. LinkedIn.

CHAPTER
Twenty-Six

TIME SLOWS to a stop when I'm with Rae. Like some wizard or ancient mystic cast a spell and everything and everyone around us is frozen. And it's just me and her. Competing. Challenging. Laughing. Loving.

My car was on the fritz, so I somehow convinced her to stay the night at my place. It was a Thursday, so the stunads would be out late drinking, and she would leave Friday morning undetected. At least, that was the plan.

I lay beside Rae on my bed just after six on Friday morning. I moved the hair from her face and caressed her bare shoulder. I couldn't read her expression. The Italian curse of dealing with unemotional people.

I whispered, "What are you thinking about?"

She smiled. "I'm thankful for you. I...feel loved by you. It's maybe the first time I've ever felt this way in any relationship. When I'm with you, it's fun, exciting..."

"Pleasurable?" I asked, cautiously optimistic.

"Very pleasurable." She huffed. "And then it's back to reality."

I shrugged. "Fuck reality."

"I can't. It's my life. Everything I've worked for. My father is asking about our deal. Wondering why it's taking so long. Wondering if I have the chops to get it done."

"What did you tell him?"

"I told him you're taking your sweet-ass time."

"Well, I have a sweet ass. But your hands already know that."

"I'm being serious." Tears welled up in Rae's eyes.

"Okay. I'm sorry. Why are you so upset?"

The tears streamed heavier. "Do you know how hard it is to get taken seriously as a woman in the business world, especially when people think your father hands you everything?"

"No. I don't cross-dress anymore..." I stopped myself from continuing the joke. "I'm sorry. I don't know. I mean, I've seen it from time to time, but I've obviously never experienced it."

Rae continued, "People think that because my father's rich, that it's easy for me. When I walk into a meeting, I don't know if they respect me or my father. When I close a deal, was it me or just his last name?"

I caressed her cheek and gave her a quick kiss. "I have nothing but respect for you. How hard you work. How professional you are. Your father should be proud of you."

"Professional." She chuckled, pathetically. "As I lay here in bed with you. And I'm not sure he is."

I scoffed. "It doesn't matter. You should be proud of yourself. If you know you've earned it, it doesn't matter what your father or anyone else thinks. And I get the father thing. At least yours believes in you enough to run the business. Mine is selling ours from underneath me. Every time I look at him, I feel like he's looking back at me as if I'm not enough."

Rae nodded. "I understand that. Maybe slightly differently. Why do you think I'm so competitive? It bothers me. It hurts relationships. It keeps me from even wanting relationships. If I don't win, if I'm not the best, I wonder if my parents will discount me relative to my brother." She looked away and whispered, "Maybe not even love me."

I had never seen her so vulnerable. I had pretty much never seen her anything but bad-ass confident, kicking my butt. I can't say it was nice, but it brought depth to our relationship, whatever it was.

"Why do I have to earn my parent's love?" she asked, confused.

"You don't. And even if you did, you have mine. No achievement required."

She nodded, but said nothing.

"But there are some things I'd still like to achieve. Maybe we can try a few new things?" I asked, eyebrow raised.

Rae laughed unexpectedly. "Perfect timing, as always."

I kissed her again, tasting her salty tears. "But do you feel better?"

She smiled and wiped away her tears. "A little."

I tapped my lips in faux thought. "I'd like for you to leave here feeling a lot better." I disappeared under the blanket.

She rolled away, laughing. "Stop it."

I resurfaced, my hair likely a mess. "What?"

"I have to go."

"You'll have to sign a waiver, confirming that you denied a full servicing."

Rae smirked. "Yeah. I'll sign that when you sign my contract."

"Touché."

Rae sat up and began slipping into her clothes. "When can we take care of some business?"

"You just turned me down. Women," I said, rolling my eyes.

Rae scoffed. "Actual business."

I laughed and reached for my boxers on the floor. "Can we negotiate when I'm not naked? I feel like you have me by the balls."

"I thought you liked that?" Rae said, smirking.

I shrugged. "It depends on the situation. I want some protection. In case you decide to sell."

"Like stock options?"

"Yeah. Something that would set me up if I got let go. Professionally or personally."

Rae huffed, grabbing her pocketbook. "Leo..."

"What?"

"Nothing. I'll send you an amended agreement. How long will your lawyer take on this? Two, three months?" She headed for the door.

I hopped out of bed and intercepted her. "I'll get it done. I promise."

"Whatever."

"Kiss me."

"No," Rae said, looking away.

"You can't leave until you kiss me." I pressed my shoulder into the door.

"So, I'm your prisoner?"

"I could tie you up if you'd like more clarity."

Rae chuckled, but still annoyed. "Fine. But just a peck."

I scrunched up my nose. "Eyes closed. Full tongue. Hands free to roam wherever their fingers take them."

"Who's negotiating now?"

"I have underwear on now, so I'm less vulnerable."

Rae smiled, shaking her head. "Fine. Your terms are acceptable."

I clapped my hands, rubbed them together, and then wiggled my fingers. "Be free, my little friends." I leaned in and kissed her. I tried to steer her toward the bed, but she flexed her Rae strength and pushed back. "I have to go," she said, our lips still pressed together.

"Fine," I said, giving her one last kiss.

"Should I go out the window?" Rae asked, seriously.

I scoffed. "I'm that embarrassing? You'd rather risk a

broken femur than risk a walk of shame? You should walk out of here, head held high."

Rae patted me on the chest. "Keep telling yourself that."

I nodded in the direction of Benny and Frankie's room. "You'll be fine. The idiots are probably spooning in bliss, but let's be quiet, just in case. I mean, we probably should've thought of that last night." I threw up a hand for a high five, which was only met with an eye roll. "I love your brown eyes, even when they roll."

I opened the door, peeked out, and then led the way, Rae right behind me.

"Whoa!" Benny said, stopping short in the kitchen's doorway, wearing only boxers. He covered his nipples with his hands. "What's up with this? Can't a guy get a drink of water in peace?"

"We were negotiating," I said, quickly.

Benny eyed my boxers. "Negotiating what? Each other's private parts?" he asked, eyebrows raised.

Rae's face flushed red. She looked at me for help.

I furrowed my brow. "Where's your rent money? I think you owe me three months?"

Benny blocked his eyes and navigated his way back to his bedroom. "I saw nothing. And I'm only going to tell Frankie that you're doinking the boss."

"Three months. Not a word about this. To the grave."

Benny huffed. "Fine."

I looked at Rae and smiled sheepishly. "Head held high?"

CHAPTER
Twenty-Seven

I HAD no idea what to do about Rae. I was flat-out crazy about her. But I wasn't sure that was enough. Forgetting about the whole business thing, which was huge on its own, we had our families to think about. Our cultures. Our religions. And our elders' shortcomings in accepting all that came with the other's. There would be no acceptance. At least I didn't think so. Much as I loved my mother and grandmother, they were old school Italian. If I told them I was in love with Rae, there was a fifty percent chance they would excommunicate me and a fifty percent chance Nonna would beat me with a wooden spoon until my beautiful face looked like veal scallopini with spicy tomatoes. Neither was an outcome I wanted, but I made a note to ask my mother for said dish for Fat Friday. It was friggin' delicious.

As I walked Jean-Claude one morning before work on a crisp, early spring day, I realized what I needed to do. I needed to see the man who had experienced the rejection. The spoon beating. The excommunication. I needed to see Uncle Michael, a man I grew up with as my favorite uncle but hadn't seen in fifteen years.

I was nervous. Like walk-into-a-gangster-restaurant

nervous after you backed into a car while parallel parking outside said restaurant. I sat in my car outside Uncle Michael's two-story, white and black colonial, my knee shaking. At least he wasn't living in a cardboard box. I gripped the steering wheel until my knuckles whitened, took a deep breath, and then relaxed. "You got this," I said, staring into the mirror. I almost missed Benny not being there to pump me up from the bathroom stall. Albeit, it would've been kind of weird if he was in the back seat with his pants at his ankles. It wouldn't be a first, though, either.

I trudged up the empty two-car driveway, my mind racing. Were they home or maybe not done with work yet? Out at a kid's sporting event? Was I happy about that? Did I even have cousins? It's pathetic that I didn't even know.

I stood in front of the door, just staring at the doorbell, embarrassed that as a thirty-year old, I hadn't once reached out to my uncle. True, I was barely a teenager when my family turned their backs on him. Even so, it didn't feel good. I guess I had just accepted what my parents told me and by the time I was mature enough to question it, life had moved on.

Before I could ring the doorbell, the door opened. Uncle Michael stood before me, eye to eye. His wavy black hair had grayed around his temples and crow's feet manifested on his tan face as he furrowed his brow. "Leo?" he asked, surprised.

Was he happy to see me? I looked down at his Nike slides. "Yes, Uncle Michael."

"Leo!" he shrieked, pulling me in for a hug and kissing me on both cheeks. "My God! You're a grown man."

I joined in on the hug, my anxiety morphing to regret. Tears streamed down my cheeks. I cried like a little kid whose gelato had just hit the pavement. "I'm sorry," I muttered.

Uncle Michael hugged me again and patted the back of my head. "It's not your fault." It wasn't like a *Good Will*

Hunting 'It's not your fault' hug, but it was pretty close. We parted and Uncle Michael called out, "Emily! Boys!"

Boys. I had multiple cousins. Wow.

I had only seen Aunt Emily once before. He had hidden her from the family for two years and for good reason. But we dropped by Uncle Michael's house uninvited, just as Emily was leaving one day. And that was the catalyst that drove the wedge between him and the rest of us.

She was more beautiful than I had remembered. Spiraling blonde hair framed piercing blue eyes and a sprinkle of freckles across her cheeks and nose. She was probably mid-forties, but looked a decade younger.

Uncle Michael patted my shoulder and said, "Em, I'd like you to meet my nephew, Leo."

I offered a smile and stuck out my hand for a shake. She smiled back and embraced me in a hug instead. "It's so nice to meet you."

I pulled back and said, "I'm not gonna lie. It feels weird to meet my aunt at thirty years old. Especially when you look my age."

"Oh, my goodness. I love him already," Emily said, smiling. "You don't have to call me Aunt Emily if you don't want to."

"No. I like it. Aunt Em. We could go Auntie Em like in *The Wizard of Oz*?"

"Let's not get crazy," Aunt Emily said, laughing.

Uncle Michael ushered me to a battered tan sofa in their living room and said, "Sit. Sorry for the state of this disastrous…thing, but we're waiting until the cavemen evolve to upgrade the decor. It's taking longer than expected."

"Tell me about it. Benny and Frankie live with me. The dog is the most mature beast in the place."

Uncle Michael asked, "Where the heck are the boys?"

Aunt Emily said, "They're still playing out back."

Uncle Michael and Aunt Emily plopped into a love seat

across from me. Uncle Michael said, "Okay. Let's talk without having to deal with the tornado that comes along with two boys. You can meet them later." He looked at me. "I'm elated, but surprised."

I nodded, sheepishly. I thought for a moment, not sure what to say. "I'm not sure anything has changed with the rest of the family, but I'm sorry. I was just a kid when you guys got married, but I haven't been a kid for a long time. There's just no excuse for how long this has taken, and I have to admit...I come here in desperation, although regardless of how that turns out, I'm glad I'm here."

Uncle Michael's brow pinched together. "What's going on?"

I pointed to them. "This. Déjà vu. I fell in love with a Jewish girl."

Aunt Emily said, "We're very lovable."

Uncle Michael ran his fingers through his hair and said, "You're totally screwed."

"Both true," I reluctantly admitted.

"And what did your mother say? And my mother?"

I shook my head. "Nothing. They know her, but don't know about us. Benny is the only one who knows, so I'm sure he'll trade that secret for a tray of meatballs. I'm trying to come up with a plan before that happens."

"What can we do?" Uncle Michael asked.

"I don't know. I guess I need to know if you're happy. If you'd do it all again."

"Yes," Uncle Michael said without hesitation.

"No," Aunt Emily said, smiling.

"Aunt Em's got jokes, huh?"

Uncle Michael kissed her temple. "Just one of the thousand things I love about her." Then he turned serious. "I wish I wouldn't have said some of the things I said, but I choose love over their hate any day."

"They don't hate you," I said, more hopeful than true.

"Invite me to Christmas next year."

"Maybe I will," I said, shrugging. "If I even have an invitation."

"Actually, don't. I prefer Chinese food and the movies," he said, laughing.

"Rae does that, too! It sounds amazing, but you don't want to reconcile?"

"I do, but it's not for me to make happen. I did nothing wrong."

I leaned forward, resting my elbows on my knees and my face in my hands. "What makes it all worth it? It can't just be Chinese food on Christmas."

Aunt Emily said, "No. Although the sesame chicken at Szechwan Palace is unreal."

"Noted," I said, chuckling. "I can't see myself without her. And I can't see myself without my family, either. Nonna might die on the spot."

"My family made the choice for me, but I would've made it anyway. I lost my family. And it still pains me. To see you at thirty. To have missed the last fifteen years of your life. All the kids growing up. All the holidays. All the pasta. Nonna's shrimp scampi. My God." I thought he was going to salivate, but he continued, "But I chose love. I lost my family, but I built a new one with the woman I love." He smiled at Aunt Emily as she squeezed his arm.

A sliding glass door opened in another room and feet fluttered into the house.

"Wipe your feet!" Aunt Emily called out.

"We did, Ma!" a boy's voice called out.

Uncle Michael and Aunt Emily rolled their eyes. Uncle Michael smiled. "There are some people you might like to meet."

Two boys, probably eight and ten, rumbled into the room, with their father's hair and mother's freckles. The younger boy said, "I scored two goals!"

The older clucked his tongue. "I scored six."

Uncle Michael said, "Charlie, Mikey, I'd like you to meet your cousin Leo."

I stood up and offered them a hand and a smile. "Hey guys. Great to me you."

The little one, Mikey, said with eyes bulging, "Cousin? But you're so old!"

I laughed.

Charlie asked, "Do you like soccer?"

I nodded. "Of course. We're Italian, paisano."

"My name is Charlie," he said, straight-faced.

"I know, buddy. Paisan means friend or fellow countryman in Italian. I played soccer a lot growing up."

Mikey asked, "Who's your favorite player?"

I thought for a moment, arms crossed. "When I was your age, I loved Il Pinturrichio."

Uncle Michael nodded in agreement, but Charlie scrunched up his nose. "Who?"

I laughed. "His real name was Alessandro Del Piero but they called him Il Pinturrichio after the famous Renaissance painter. Del Piero was a phenomenal forward for the Italian national team and Juventus. He was a penalty kick specialist. He could curve the ball and hit the corners, well, like one of the best soccer players ever. Goalies wouldn't even move as he painted the corners. They'd just hang their heads in shame."

Charlie asked, "How do you curve the ball?"

"Put some side spin on it. It might take some work, but I'm sure you can get it with enough practice."

Mikey asked, "Could you teach us how to curve the ball?"

"Sure."

Michael said, "Go play in the basement for a while and we'll go out into the backyard soon."

The boys disappeared down the stairs with the rumbling of what sounded like a herd of elephants.

Uncle Michael said, "You're going to be a great dad."

I sighed. "Yeah, I just have to find the right woman. Or figure out how to make her work in my life."

Aunt Emily smiled. "We figured out how to make it work. You can, too."

I leaned forward, resting my face in my hands. "At what cost?"

Uncle Michael said, "A huge one. But worth the payment."

I nodded, unsure of what to say. "Your kids are not nearly as screwed up as my brother and sister so maybe this could work."

Uncle Michael said, "Thank you? How are they, by the way? It's been so long."

"Gianna is married, with two girls and a boy. Amazing kids. Nice husband. Benny and Frankie continue their romance, holding out for the pope to allow male first cousins to marry."

Uncle Michael broke out into laughter. "You were always so funny. I can't tell you how wonderful it is to laugh with you again. But back to reality, you asked 'at what cost', but you need to shift your focus to what you will gain. Be sure she's the one. Is she?"

"I think so."

Uncle Michael said firmly, "Know so."

I shook my head. "I know so."

"Does she know?" Aunt Emily asked, laughing.

"That I don't know. And I don't think her family will react any differently than mine. I just needed to know that you're happy. That it worked. That you don't regret it."

"Not once," Uncle Michael said firmly.

Aunt Emily raised an eyebrow and then said, "There were definitely times. Just the two of us. Birthdays. Holidays. The birth of the boys. It was hard. Very hard. My family has come around. Yours. Not so much."

Uncle Michael nodded in agreement. "You're right. And I still miss my sisters and my mother. All of you. I've missed so much. But I couldn't live my life on their terms. I was in love with a Jewish girl. And still am." He admired Aunt Emily, face beaming.

I let out a deep breath. I wasn't sure what to do. They were happy. A smaller, tighter family without Nonna's shrimp scampi, but a happy family, nonetheless. "Rae says I'm meshuggeneh for even thinking it can work."

Aunt Emily chuckled. "He's speaking Yiddish. You're done for."

"I am," I said, nodding sheepishly. "Hopelessly in love."

"It's not hopeless, Leo. It works. We make it work every day."

I took another deep breath. "I have to make this work. I have to convince her. And I need to figure out how to get our parents to accept it."

"That...might be hopeless," Uncle Michael said, concerned. "At least the last part."

"Well, I have to try."

I just had no idea *what* to try.

CHAPTER
Twenty~Eight

ON SATURDAY MORNING, I readied myself in front of the bathroom mirror to meet Rae. She didn't know I was heading into the city to convince her we could make it work. I didn't know if Prince David would answer the door. Were they together? Were they yentzing? Rae wouldn't do that to me, would she? Was I crazy to have come this far not even knowing that? Was I going to give him a Sicilian sgrugnare, aka a punch in the face? Would she even be there? My mental and emotional state teetered on back and forth between agita and confidence. Either way, I had to try. I was nervous but emboldened after meeting with Uncle Michael, Aunt Emily, and the boys.

A fist pounded on my apartment door. Or was it a battering ram? I checked my watch and frowned. It was only ten o'clock. Which one of the two stunads ghosted a girl? Or swindled a muscle head?

Jean-Claude broke out into a fit of barking and scratched at the door.

"Don't answer it!" Frankie shrieked.

"Why not?" I asked, heading out to the den.

"I owe a lot of people money."

I nodded in agreement. "Yeah, me. It doesn't seem to stop you from showing up here."

Benny stepped toward the door, cracking his knuckles. "I got this." He peered through the peep hole and chuckled. "It's only Natalia. She looks upset, but—"

"Natalia?" I headed toward the door as Benny twisted the doorknob. The door was barely open a crack and Natalia burst in, tears streaming down her face.

Benny stepped to the side, hands up as if surrendering. "Whoa! Leo! Hysterical woman. What do we do?"

Frankie grabbed the dog and said, "Dude, you're Italian. Our whole lives have been dealing with overly emotional people."

I ignored him. "Natalia, what's wrong?"

She looked up at me, makeup smeared down her face. "I'm pregnant." And then buried her face in my chest.

I wrapped my arms around her reflexively. Benny and Frankie finally had nothing to say. "Umm, boys, can you give us some privacy?"

Benny eyed Frankie. "Breakfast?"

Frankie nodded. "Umm, yeah. Like yesterday." He looked at me. "Can we borrow your car? We don't have gas."

I rolled my eyes and nodded to the keys on the counter. "Take J.C." They did as they were told and disappeared quickly.

"Natalia, sit. Can I get you some water?" I ushered her to the couch and stepped toward the kitchen.

Natalia wiped the tears from her eyes and fixed her hair. Even in the mish mash of tears and mascara, she was beautiful. "How are you so calm? I'm. Pregnant. We're. Not. Married."

My body froze. Only my lips could move. "Wait, the baby's mine?"

She sniffled and stared at me with disgust. "Are you stunad? Whose else would it be?"

"I...I have no idea. We used protection. I...thought you just needed a friend to talk to."

"I don't need a friend. I need a husband. Or my father is gonna kill us both."

"Like kill kill or metaphorical?"

"Does it matter?" She buried her face in her hands, crying again.

I sat down next to her, took a deep breath, and rubbed her shoulder. "Have you told your parents?"

"Not yet. I took a test last night and one this morning. When are we getting married? It'll have to be soon."

"You dumped me. We don't love each other. Why should this change anything?"

The timing was very wrong with that question. I see that now. Natalia stood up, screaming, her hands out of her control. "It changes everything!"

I stood up, dodged a few backhands, and pulled her into a hug, half from empathy, half from self-preservation. She pounded my chest with her fists until I got control of her wrists and she went limp in my arms. My shirt absorbed more tears than Bounty that morning.

"What are we going to do?" Natalia whispered.

"This is a lot to take in. I need to think. We'll figure it out. I promise. Look at me." I tipped her chin up to look me in the eye. "We'll get through this together."

"Okay."

"Let me get you some tissues." I headed to the kitchen and nearly tore the pocket off my jeans, reaching for my phone. I texted Benny. 'Get back here now. Need help.'

I returned two minutes later with a box of tissues and handed them to her.

All Natalia said was, "When?"

"I don't know. This is big news. My brain is a having a fit right now."

A few minutes later, the boys entered tentatively, Frankie

holding Jean-Claude on a leash. Benny said, "The, umm, bathroom was busted and Frankie really had to go. Sorry to barge back in here."

Frankie nodded. "It's number two."

Benny smacked him on the shoulder. "So, go."

"Right." Frankie disappeared.

I asked Natalia, "Do you want me to take you to your parents' place?"

"I can't look at them right now. They'll know something's wrong. Take me back to Marie's."

"I'll drive her car. You follow in mine," I said to Benny, ushering Natalia to the door.

I was able to make a somewhat clean break, making a handoff to Marie with the promise I would figure it out, and soon. Of which I had no idea how to do. For her. For my family. For me and the small fact that I loved someone else.

I slipped into the passenger side of the car and said, "Let's get the hell out of here before she goes Terminator cop on my back windshield."

Benny threw the car into drive and took off. I checked behind us just to make sure Natalia wasn't bearing down on us with cyborg-like speed.

"What the hell happened?" Benny asked.

I popped the seat back and stared at the car's ceiling. "She's pregnant. I'm going to be a father. She wants to get married."

"Isn't that a gagootz in the ass?" Benny muttered.

"For once, you're right, bro. A big 'ole eggplant right up the butt." I loved the idea of being a father. Just not like this. I sat up in the chair with a grunt, my brain searching for a non-existent solution.

"Mom's gonna flip."

I stared out the window at random houses, mumbling, "Again, completely on point. Don't say a damn word. I don't know how to handle this just yet. I'll tell them when I figured it out. What am I gonna tell Rae?"

"That's not the biggest problem here, bro. You can't worry about her. That dream is over. I hope you enjoyed it."

Losing Rae before I ever really had her was soul crushing. It was too much to handle. I went numb. I lay back, sinking into the headrest, eyes closed. "My career is a giant strunza. My love life likely to send Ma into cardiac arrest. Aaaand my ex is pregnant. Just livin' my best life. I'm a schlimazel."

CHAPTER
Twenty-Nine

I COULDN'T SLEEP at all Saturday night. I kept replaying Natalia's words in my mind: 'I'm pregnant.' Would I have a son? A daughter? She wanted to get married. For the baby. For her family. For her ego. Not for me. She didn't want me. She had made that very clear when she dumped me. Was marrying her the right thing to do? Would I be happy? Did that even matter? Family first. I'd sacrifice my happiness for my child. Parents do that all the time. I wasn't even sure how to tell my parents, let alone make a decision as crazy as marrying a woman I didn't love and who didn't love me.

I rolled up to Sunday dinner, intent on dropping the bomb on my parents. Half of me wanted someone else to tell them, but in my heart I knew that would save me from nothing. I had to step up and tell them myself. At least I'd gain some semblance of respect. But I had no idea how to tell them. 'Surprise! We have a bastard child in the family!' didn't seem to hit the right tone.

As I walked up the driveway, I studied the unfamiliar red sedan parked beside my mother's Cadillac. We rarely had guests for Sunday dinner. Everyone we knew was already there.

My mother was waiting for me as I walked in the doors, arms crossed, glare on 'kill' setting.

"What's wrong?" I asked, stepping toward her.

She grabbed my arm and tugged me through the dining room and into the walk-in pantry. She closed the slatted-wood doors behind us, my backing jabbing into a shelf of non-perishables, and whisper-shouted, "How could you do this? Do this to the family?"

"Do what?" How could she know?

"We know about Natalia." Her glare seemed to glow in the semi-darkness of the pantry.

I turned away from her, rubbing my face with my hands. "I don't know what to tell you, Ma. We had sex."

"Shhh. Father Anthony is right outside."

My eyebrows bounced to the ceiling. "Why is Father Anthony here?"

"For family counsel. But don't talk about the sex in front of him."

"I think he knows how it works, Ma, even if he's never done it."

"This an enormous embarrassment."

"That Father Anthony is a virgin? Wouldn't it be worse if he wasn't?"

Tears welled up in her eyes. She poked me in the chest. "No. You. You're the embarrassment."

I huffed. "Thank you for your judgement. It's nice to see your decades of churchgoing are paying off. That's exactly what Jesus would say. Wait!" I shielded my eyes, feigning bright lights. "Lord, is that you?"

"Knock it off," my mother said through gritted teeth.

I dropped my hands in a huff. "You're a hypocrite."

"This isn't about me, you stunad."

Before I could respond, Nonna burst into the pantry like a crazed, spoon-wielding psycho, connecting with thwack after thwack as I attempted to dodge and weave the vicious attack.

My mother grabbed the spoon and stepped between me and my geriatric assailant.

"Et tu, Nonna?" I rubbed my forearm, sure it would be purple in the morning.

Nonna glared at me, arms crossed, her thick forearms putting Popeye's to shame. "You-a supposed to be-a the smart one, ya mamaluke."

"I'm sorry. I don't know what to tell you. It just happened. And how do you even know?"

"It doesn't matter," my mother said, waving away my question.

"Benny told Gia who told you?" She didn't have to confirm it. I knew it. And to be honest, my mother was right. It didn't matter.

My mother eyed me with distaste. "Let's go talk to Father Anthony."

"I'm supposed to take relationship advice from a gay priest?"

My mother scoffed. "He's not gay. He's just in touch with his feminine side." Nonna didn't seem to agree, as she eyed my mother with a raised eyebrow.

I closed my eyes and ran my fingers through my hair. I knew they wouldn't be happy, but this was going to be pure torture. "I promise you he's never touched a feminine side or a feminine anything."

"He's taken a vow of chastity, that's all."

I rolled my eyes. "Okay. Fine. Just know that I wanted to tell you myself. Talk. Just us. I don't know why he needs to be here."

My mother nudged my shoulder toward the door. "This is what you need. Guidance from the Lord."

I swallowed my pride and found my way to the den, already populated with the rest of my family. Pop, Gia, and Benny shared a couch while Aunt Franny, Uncle Freddy, and Frankie sat in a line of dining room chairs that spread across the den.

Father Anthony sat at the head of a makeshift circle, a sheepish smile on his face. He was a thin man in his early fifties. He used to wear his black hair down to his clerical collar when I was a kid, which drove the ladies wild. Little did they know they had no shot. Now said hair was atop his head in a generic buzz cut. He wore black-rimmed glasses, crooked on his thin nose. He shook my hand limply and said softly, "It's good to see you, Leonardo." He always called me Leonardo, holding the last syllable. I hated it.

I plopped into an empty chair and glared at Gia and Benny. I mouthed to Benny, "What the frig, dude?" He looked away.

My mother and Nonna sat down on each side of me. I wasn't sure if they were my support system or my guards. Because Nonna still held the wooden spoon in her hand, I kind of already knew.

Father Anthony said, "There is still hope for you, Leonardo."

"Well, that's a blessing to know," I said, my sarcasm filter failing to fully wash my words.

"God's mercy never lacks for a soul that repents. God created sex for the sacred bond of marriage."

Benny's hand covered his mouth and laughter.

"Sacred bond of marriage? Half the country is divorced," I said, shaking my head.

"We are all sinners." He looked at my siblings and said, "Some more than others."

Benny nodded in agreement.

Father Anthony continued, "The most joyous thing that can happen when a child is born out of wedlock is for the parents to marry. To bless that family with the sacrament of matrimony. To form a holy and loving family."

I interrupted, "But that's the thing, Father. We distinctly

broke up because we didn't want to be together. Why should this change that?"

Father Anthony nodded in thought. "God is merciful to those who don't choose well."

"Then he'll forgive me for not marrying her," I said defiantly.

Aunt Franny gasped. My mother wasn't breathing. Nonna's forearms seemed ready to pulverize the wooden arm rests to toothpicks.

"It doesn't work that way. You can't just do whatever you want and ask for forgiveness."

I said, "That's exactly how it works. So, I guess murderers can't be saved?"

Father Anthony sputtered, "Well...you see...the thing is..."

I stood up. "I'm done here."

Benny and Gia's eyes bulged.

"Thank you for coming, Father. I'm sorry my mother wasted your time." I headed for the door. My father was the only one to follow, stopping me after I rushed through the front door onto the grass out front.

"You're not done yet. Come back inside," Pop said, standing atop the steps, stone faced.

I threw up my hands. "For what?"

"For your mother. Your grandmother. You're going to marry Natalia. You'll do this for the family. You want a little bastard running around?"

I glared at him, arms crossed. "I feel like 'bastard' is more verb than noun."

"You think I'm being a bastard?"

"Do you prefer asshole better?"

"I'm the asshole? You're the one who's not living up to your responsibility here. You get your ass to the store and you buy the girl a ring before you shame the good Donati name."

I yelled, "I don't love her. She doesn't love me. How is that good for the baby?"

"That doesn't matter."

"Then what does? Putting up a good front for a sham marriage so you're not embarrassed?"

"You'll make it work." Pop walked down the steps and put his hand on my shoulder. "You can be pissed at me for as long as you want. Never talk to me again. I don't want that, but it's your choice. But that's the only choice in this. You must do this for your mother. The woman who has done everything for this family and you. End of story."

His words weighed heavy on me. I didn't know if he was right or not, but the responsibility, the guilt that I felt made me nod my head and whisper, "Okay."

CHAPTER
Thirty

I WENT STRAIGHT to Rae's on Sunday afternoon. I had to tell her. I needed to know what she thought. What this changed. But I couldn't formulate the words. With each floor I passed on the elevator, the gravity of the situation grew heavier in the pit of my stomach. When the door opened, I almost didn't get out. And when I found myself in front of her door, it was like my hands were shackled behind my back. Eventually, I mustered up enough courage to knock meekly on the door.

Rae opened it with a sexy smile. "Why did you need to see me so badly?" She opened the top button of her blouse. "And what do you want to see *of* me?"

I stepped into the apartment and ran my fingers through my hair. "Babe, no. It's serious."

Her face dropped. "What's wrong?"

I plopped onto the couch in front of the fireplace framed with ornate white molding. "I don't know how to tell you this."

Rae stared down at me. "Oh, God. You're gay."

I scrunched up my face. "No. Why would you…"

"You're dying. Is it cancer? A brain aneurysm?"

"I'm not sure you know those are coming. They just pop."

"Kidney failure?"

"No. Stop. Please."

"I'm sorry. It's the dayge. Agita or whatever you call it. It's hardwired in my family. What is it?"

I grabbed her hands firmly as she stood in front of me. "Natalia's pregnant," I said, my eyes staring at the floor.

Her voice rose an octave. "Your ex?"

I couldn't say the words. I nodded, my eyes scanning her face. A single teardrop ran down her face. It would've been so less bad had they streamed like a river. I waited for a moment, but she said nothing. I'm not used to silence in the presence of other people, so I didn't know what to do. I stood up and put my arms on her shoulders. "Say something."

Rae knocked my hands away. "I hate you." She swatted a glass vase filled with faux lavender from atop the mantel. I watched it as it smashed and scattered across the wood floor. This I knew how to handle.

"Okay. You're angry. I get it. Let's talk about it."

Rae chuckled pathetically. "There's nothing to talk about."

"We can talk about why you're angry. Where we go from here."

Fists on hips, Rae glared at me. "You know why I'm angry." She turned her back on me and stared out the window.

I met her at her side, neither of us saying anything, just staring at the insignificant people and cars so many stories below.

I said softly, "It's okay if you're angry. Let it out. I'm Italian. I can take it. My family yells and breaks shit all the time. I want to know how you feel. Tell me why you're so angry."

She turned to me and wiped away tears. "You made me feel."

I wasn't sure what I was expecting her to say, but not that.

"Feel what?" I tried to wrap her in my arms, but she wriggled out.

"Don't touch me."

My pulse pounded in my ears. "I'm sorry. Please tell me."

"You made me feel...everything. Alive. Loved. Challenged. Happy. Like there was somebody for me. Somebody who understood me." Admitting it all seemed to open the floodgates to fresh tears.

I fought every urge to touch her. To pull her close and comfort her. But I was the problem. "Rae. Baby. This doesn't change that. I'm still me. You're still you."

Rae asked pointedly, "Have you told your family?"

"Yes."

"And it changed nothing?"

I couldn't answer.

Rae continued, pacing in the corner. Through sniffles, she asked, "My parents would lose their shit just knowing I was dating a Catholic. Then add an illegitimate child to the mix?"

I threw up my hands. "Why would they care?"

She shook her head, seemingly in shock at my stunadity. "They would care how it looks. This was a pipe dream to begin with, Leo. This is just way too much reality. I need you to leave."

I stepped toward her, but kept my hands where she could see them. "Why can't we talk about this?" I couldn't believe this was happening.

"I don't want to talk about it. I need to process it."

"Please," I said with desperation.

"No," she said, firmly. "Go. Just go."

I stared at her for a moment, then nodded reluctantly. "At least let me help you clean up the mess." I eyed the broken glass.

"I don't need your help."

"Rae, please. I love you." A man in love is not too proud to beg.

"Love isn't enough, Leo. Goodbye." She walked to the door, opened it, and stared at me expectantly.

"Tell me you love me," I pleaded.

"Goodbye, Leo."

I took a deep breath and plodded toward the exit. I tried to hug her, but she pushed me away and out the door, which slammed in my face. I stared at the closed door for a moment, broken, gutted, empty, my heart on the other side.

———

Rae's Deal Notes

- ~~Gutted. Broken. Smarter than this. How did I let this happen? Why did this happen? This cruel universe…just when you think…start to believe… start to love…I'm numb. And so ridiculously dumb.~~
- Cancel all meetings Mon-Wed.

———

The drive home was miserable. I'm not sure what zombies feel like, but I was pretty sure that's where I was at. Every step to my apartment was a lumbering forward, empty, and awkward. Waking up the next morning and making my way out of bed felt like I was punching through the earth out of my casket, a fist of mud, rocks, and worms as I woke from my wretched dirt nap.

I was so dejected, so drained, that I actually slept past Frankie. True, my pants weren't hanging from a tree outside like after New Year's, but even so, it was a big deal. I headed out to the den just as Benny returned from walking the dog.

"I just walked Jean-Claude," Benny said, as if it wasn't his dog.

"Want a fucking medal?"

"Whoa, bro. Uncalled for." He unhooked Jean-Claude from the leash. J.C. disappeared into the kitchen. "What's up with you?"

"Sorry. My life is ruined. Thanks for telling Mom and Pop, by the way. That was...really helpful."

"I didn't tell—"

"Dude, save it. Whatever. I have much bigger issues than that."

"Well, they'll have to wait. Good news, though. Pop gave you the day off. His pinky ring guy at Whitman is expecting us at noon."

"That's ridiculous. Pop knows I don't wear pinky rings. And why would he give us the day off for that?"

Benny scrunched up his nose. "Yeah, you don't need a ring, but...Natalia does. Dad told me we needed to go ring shopping. He gave me his credit card, so you know it's serious."

I couldn't say anything. I swallowed the hurt and nodded in depressed acceptance.

Later that morning, Benny chauffeured me to the store. As he parked us in front of the small storefront just off Walt Whitman Road, he patted my knee. "Try to look a little enthused. I know you don't want to be here, but this is part of the appearance."

"When did you ever care about appearances?"

"Have you seen my hair and biceps?" Benny asked, annoyed.

"I mean, holding up family appearances," I muttered.

Benny shrugged as we got out of the car. "Well, you're the family screw up now, so I need to step up." He laughed, but then stopped when I didn't join in. "Come on, bro. That's funny."

"I'm glad you find this amusing." I hauled my useless body from the car.

Benny led me inside and said, "It'll be quick. Plus, you don't exactly have a lot of time to be picky."

"Whatever," I said, monotone. I nodded to Biagio, my father's middle-aged jeweler, who hit the Italian jewelry trifecta with gaudy authority: pinky ring, gold bracelet, and gold chain with Italian horn draped over overgrown chest hair. He wore a silk shirt that could use a few more buttons and waved as he rang up a sixty-something businessman.

Benny said, "You think you're the first person this has happened to? It doesn't mean you won't be happy. Won't build a great life. You're marrying a good woman."

I chuckled pathetically. "Yes...but not the right one."

He leaned in and whispered, "You know Mom and Dad got married and you were born seven months later, right?"

I huffed. "Shut up. Let's just get the Ring of Doom and be done with it."

"I like the *Lord of the Rings* reference, but you definitely don't have the Hobbit spirit."

I rolled my eyes and headed to the counter to look around. "I'm not a Hobbit. I'm Gollum."

"Gollum was a Hobbit."

I nodded. "Before the Ring of Doom ruined his life."

"Do you want me to just get it?"

I shook my head in a huff. "I should do it. And I can't trust you with Dad's credit card."

"Gentlemen!" Biagio came out from behind the counter, grabbed us each by the shoulders and kissed us on each cheek. "Leo, I've heard the great news. Are you excited?"

My tone seeping with sarcasm, I said, "Ecstatic. Can't you see the glow?" I encircled my dead face with my hands.

Benny said, "Let's just keep the questions ring specific."

"Got it," Biagio said, heading back behind the counter.

Benny pointed to a princess cut diamond with a solid silver band. "That one's nice. What does she like?"

I shrugged, barely looking at it. "I don't know. I know

she's a size seven. We've never even remotely discussed getting married. We dated for a few months, broke up, had three more dates, and broke up again."

Benny said, "You've known her your whole life."

I scoffed. "So have you. Do you magically know what type of ring she likes?"

"I guess not."

"What about Frankie? Do you know what he likes?"

"That's just wrong, dude."

I walked away from the counter, running my fingers through my hair while attempting to get control of my thoughts and emotions. I knew he was trying to help, but his cheery attitude was not vibing with me.

Out of the corner of my eye, I saw Benny force a nervous smile at Biagio and walk toward me. He wrapped his arm around me and whispered, "Dude, this whole thing has gotta stay under wraps. You gotta stop pretending this is your funeral. Biagio knows a lot of people."

"You make it seem like this is easy. None of it is easy."

"Leo, if there's anybody I know who can make it work, it's you. Your dedication, your sense of responsibility…You're the cheese in our family lasagna. You can make it work, you gooey bastard."

I chuckled for a quick second and then turned serious again. "I don't want to make it work. Force marriage. I just want to be happy, and this doesn't feel like that." I was heartbroken over another woman. There was no way to picture any of this in my mind that made sense or felt good, not now or ever. I didn't want to settle. Natalia didn't want me, either. She just wanted to save face, like both our families did.

"You *will* be. Come on, let's take another look." Benny eyed Biagio and chuckled. "Cold feet."

Biagio nodded and said, "Piedi freddi. You're not the first. But usually, it doesn't happen this soon."

"He's not sure she's gonna say 'yes.'"

"What—"

Benny nudged me and then pointed to a large emerald-cut diamond with a thin, diamond encrusted band. "What about that one?"

My phone interrupted before I could answer him. It was Natalia. My stomach roiled at the sight of her name. Not the feeling you want when your future bride's calling. I sent the call to voice mail and buried the phone in my pocket. "I can't do this. I just can't do this right now. Thank you, Biagio. I gotta go." I headed outside and collapsed into the car, my mind a confusing mess of depression.

Benny met me in the car, sliding into the driver's seat, but he didn't start it. "Dude, this isn't like you."

"Isn't like me how? You've never seen me forced to spend my life unhappy. This is perfectly in character with that." Neither of us said anything for a while. Finally, I said, "I told Rae about Natalia and the baby. She hates me."

Benny shrugged. "That's how most women feel about me. You'll get used to it."

I knew he was joking, but I didn't find it even remotely funny. "I may get used to Rae hating me, but I'll never get over it. Ever."

CHAPTER
Thirty~One

I SAT at a table for two with Uncle Michael at Uncle Lou's BBQ, a local joint with craft brews, all-you-can-eat ribs, and unlimited paper towels on the table. Billy Joel's *Piano Man* played softly over speakers in the background. Two beers and a half-eaten plate of nachos filled the table.

Uncle Michael said, "So, what's going on? I know something's wrong. I just don't know what."

I stared at the foam atop my beer, spinning the glass and watching it swirl. "My life is a disaster. My family doesn't understand. They've already decided for me, but I'm not sure it's what I want."

"What is it?"

I took a deep breath and exhaled long and slow. I looked Uncle Michael in the eye and said, "My ex-girlfriend, Natalia, is pregnant. I'm going to be a father. She dumped me before she knew, which I didn't fight, but now wants to get married because of the baby. My parents are obviously pushing for that, but I'm in love with another woman. I *want* to be a father. A great father. I understand the responsibility, but I don't think I should have to marry a woman I don't love and who doesn't love me. How is that good for the baby? But I also don't want to miss all the little things. And I want to be with the woman I love, who currently hates my guts."

"Wow," was all Uncle Michael said.

I laughed in frustration. "See? A disaster."

"Well, as Pat Benatar sings, 'Love is a battlefield.' She grew up fifteen minutes from here in Lindenhurst. Did you know that? That being said, Huntington is better since we have Mariah and Ralph Macchio, but not bad." He did a seated crane kick from *Karate Kid.*

I chuckled unexpectedly as he sounded like me with Rae, but then I refocused. "Thank you for the trivia question, Uncle Mike, but I've kinda got bigger issues to deal with besides prepping for Long Island Jeopardy."

"Fair enough. This is not an easy one by any stretch. We will take this one breath, one step at a time. At first I thought you were gonna ask me for money."

I shook my head. "I wish that was my problem."

"Me, too. I'd rather give you a few grand and be done with this…"

I suppressed a smile. "If only, but, while we're on the subject, I accept Venmo, PayPal, and cryptocurrency."

"I'll cover dinner. How about that?" Uncle Michael chuckled, downed the rest of his beer, and thought for a moment. "I think you have to do what's right for you and the baby."

I threw up my hands in confusion. "I know what's right for me. But how do I know what's right for the baby? How do I know what's right for both of us? Is it better to not marry Natalia, not be there all the time, but be happy with my life? Half of marriages end in divorce. Isn't it better to get it right before that? But can I still be the father I want to be if I'm not there every day? Will it hurt to miss those little moments? Will Natalia freeze me out? I'm just guessing if I try to answer these questions."

A waitress replaced our beers and placed two plates overflowing with ribs and coleslaw in front of us.

Uncle Michael said, "I know this isn't easy. Without our family involved. With them involved, Einstein couldn't solve it. Or it's just very easy. Do what they want. Do what's best for the family."

I stared down at the table in thought, scratching at a nick in the wood. "Sometimes, I think that's just what my parents say when it's best for them and they need to convince us to do something. Like selling the business."

Uncle Michael's eyebrows shot up. "Your father is selling the business? Why?"

I shrugged. "Don't know. He wants to winter in Sicily or Boca."

"Don't you run it with him?"

"Yeah."

"Why isn't he letting you take over?"

Again, a question I had no answer for. "It's the million-dollar question. Literally."

Uncle Michael licked BBQ sauce from his index finger and said, "Well, printing is a tough business. Maybe he doesn't want that for you?"

"Don't know. I've just been instructed to do what's best for the family and sell it. I haven't done a very good job of that." I chuckled pathetically. "I fell in love with the woman I'm negotiating with, and to be honest, done a lot to keep the deal from happening. For my benefit. I don't know what I'm doing. I can tell you one thing for certain. I am *not* living my best life. And I don't know how."

"Listen, Leo. You need to do what's right for you. It's your life. It should be your decision. I'm not saying don't do what your parents recommend, but you have to do what *you* think is best because you have to live with the consequences. They don't. It's easy for someone to tell you to do something that benefits them when they don't have to live with the cost."

"Family comes first. Always. I've always believed that.

Until now. Or maybe I still believe it, but which family? The Donatis, Natalia and the baby, what I could build with Rae?"

"It's a big decision. There's no getting around that. Only you can decide what's most important to you. What you can handle and what you can't. You might not have logical answers to these questions, but what feels right?"

"I don't know." I took a swig of my beer, looked at my uncle, and it just hit me. Fifteen years. I had missed out on his counsel, his jokes, his family, for what? It just felt wrong that he hadn't been there. That he'd suffered for falling in love. "I'm sorry, Uncle Michael."

His brow furrowed. "For what?"

"Our family was wrong. I'm sorry for what happened between you and my mother and Nonna."

Uncle Michael sighed. "We already talked about this. It's not your fault. I knew what was likely to happen. I'd hoped they'd come around. That was fifteen years ago. I'm still waiting." He shook his head. "Damn Sicilian women hold grudges like nothing I've ever seen in my life. And your mother is only half. Emily ignores me for ten minutes and she thinks she's winning when I hadn't even noticed. I'm used to racking up years."

I chuckled, but my smile quickly dissipated. "I don't want to lose my family. I love them." I slapped my hands down on the wooden table. "Damn them for putting me in this situation. Why can't they just let me be happy?"

"My father, as you know, was a quiet man. But when he spoke, you listened. He once told me, 'So many of the decisions we make ultimately mean very little. Less than one percent of our decisions are the ones that truly drive our lives. The key is to figure out which ones those are and to not screw them up.'"

I laughed, shaking my head in confusion. "Well, this is one of those decisions that matter. I know that, but how do I not screw it up?"

"Damned if I know," Uncle Michael said, laughing. "Look, nobody can tell you what to do. It's up to you to decide. You're going to make some people unhappy. Maybe everybody who's involved. But you have to make a decision that makes you happy. That aligns with what you value."

"I've got it," I said.

Uncle Michael eyed me with excitement.

I continued, "Witness protection." I joined him in laughter, but my mind was anything but happy. I had no idea what to do. Like he said, somebody, maybe everybody, would be unhappy. Was my own happiness worth that?

———

After we finished dinner, I didn't know where to go or what to do. I had no interest in being around other people. At least, most that I knew. I was avoiding my family. Avoiding Natalia. Everyone had questions I didn't want to answer. Couldn't answer. I found myself at an outdoor batting cage, pounding rubber baseballs into the night.

My racing thoughts dissipated with each swing, but the anger and frustration seemed to find its way into the dented metal bat as I swung harder and harder. Grunting and sweating, my hands bleeding, I collapsed to one knee, gasping for breath, and tears streaming down my face. *God damn it. What am I gonna do?*

A man's voice behind me said, "Man, that guy's crazy about baseball."

A pimply teen with long hair skirting out from a backward baseball hat eyed me with concern and confusion from outside the cage. I think he worked there. "Dude, are you okay?"

I wiped my eyes. "Yeah. Uh, spring allergies. And umm, just wanted to see if I could still crush 'em. Mission accomplished." Anything but. I stood up and studied my bloodied hands, which throbbed with pain. The kid shrugged and went on his way.

I cleaned up my hands and, still not wanting to go home, grabbed a funnel cake and a water. I found a bench in a quiet spot outside some empty cages and promised myself I would decide before my last bite. I had to move on with my life, even if none of my paths seemed all that attractive.

I took the smallest bites of my life as my mind analyzed every scenario, upside down and inside out. Should I marry Natalia? I know I'd be happy as a father, but would I be happy as a husband? No. Would I be happier with Rae? Yes. Would my family reject me? Probably. Most likely. Did Rae even want me? She hadn't taken my calls since she kicked me out of her apartment after telling her about Natalia. If Rae didn't want me, did it really matter if I was happy with Natalia? I wouldn't be happy with anyone. And at least I'd be there every day with my kid. And Natalia was a good person. She would be a wonderful mom. She was a kindergarten teacher. Maybe we wouldn't have a deep connection. She wouldn't challenge me or make me laugh, but I'd keep my family and I could find other ways to be challenged. But then I remembered the business. How could I work with Rae, knowing what we had, but couldn't have ever again? I could suck it up, do my time as contracted, and then get a different job, if I couldn't get Sam Bennington to buy us out sooner rather than later.

I popped the last bite of the fried goodness into my mouth and chewed it until it was pulverized liquid, stretching the time as long as possible. I reluctantly swallowed what was left and took a deep breath. I picked up my phone and stared at it for a moment. I took a shaky breath. *It has to be Natalia. For my family.* I dialed Biagio, the jeweler.

He answered on the second ring. "This is Biagio."

"Hey. It's Leo Donati. I wasn't sure I'd catch you."

"We're open until nine tonight. Every other day, we close at six."

I kind of wished he was closed, but there's no time like the present, as they say. I don't really know who 'they' was, but I was pissed at whomever it was. "I'm gonna swing by. I'll be there before you leave."

"Okay, Leo. See you then."

Within an hour, I had chosen and paid for a ring. I wasn't ready to propose to Natalia that night. I still had to think of the right words, and I wanted it to be special for her. Sal asked Gia to marry him when she stepped out of the bathroom at a club while Justin Timberlake's *SexyBack* was playing. I had to at least beat that.

I arrived home and tucked the ring box in the back of my sock drawer. I stared at it for a moment, envisioning asking Rae to marry me instead of Natalia. She nodded and then broke out into dimples. Our whole faux lives played out in my imagination. Wedding. Walks on the beach at Rae's Hampton house. Laughing by the fire. Kids, made years prior in front of the fire, running around the house. Growing old together, still challenging each other, still in love.

"Family first." I sighed and closed the drawer on what felt like my dream life.

CHAPTER
Thirty-Two

I NEEDED to bury the hatchet with my family and get them off my back. I showed up at my parents' house around five on Saturday night, knowing that Gia would drop the kids off with my parents for free babysitting. I walked into the house, kicked off my shoes, and headed into the den. Viola, Mia, and Sal watched *My Little Pony* from the couch while Matteo and Pop sat on the floor, rolling and throwing a mini football back and forth.

I patted the ring in my pocket nervously, as if it could've somehow disappeared.

Sal gave me a "Yo!"

Pop grunted with a head nod while Matteo wobbled over to me and wrapped his arms around my leg, equal parts hug and self-preservation.

"Hello, ladies," I said to the mesmerized girls.

The girls rushed over to me. I knelt and wrapped an arm around each of them, then stood up with a growl. I threw each over my shoulder and spun around. I used my best monster voice. "You fell into my trap. Muahahaha!"

The girls shrieked, which drew my mother, Nonna, and Gia into the room.

I put the girls down as my mother stared at me. "What are you doing here?"

"I wanted to show everybody something." I reached into my pocket.

Sal said, "We don't need to see what's in your pants."

I rolled my eyes and displayed the ring.

Gia gasped and approached for a closer look. A smile broke out across my mother's face as she nodded gently. She wrapped both arms around me, kissed my cheek, and whispered, "I knew you'd do the right thing."

Nonna pinched my cheek and shook my face as she said, "That's-a my boy."

After Sal put me through concussion protocols, necessary training to be part of the family, my father patted me on the shoulder and said, "I'm proud of you. I wish you and Natalia all the happiness in the world."

I wished for it, too. I just wasn't sure it would come true.

I procrastinated most of Sunday, telling myself that Natalia was at church, and then spending time with family. That I would interrupt them if I just dropped in, but frankly, I was nervous, and a shit-ton scared. This was my life. The rest of my life.

I tired of Jean-Claude ignoring my pleas for guidance, so I threw on my best blue suit with a matching button down, fished the ring from my sock drawer, and drove to Natalia's house. Slowly. Very slowly.

After a nosy neighbor wrote down my license plate number for parking in front of their house, apparently for too long, I made my way to the brown wooden front door of a two-story, white stucco house. I patted the ring in my pocket, contemplating my words. My stomach swirled with agita as my mind grappled with my no-win situation.

My heart pounded as I attempted to psych myself up. But the only thing coming up was lunch. I ducked behind a ten-foot Italian cypress to regurgitate half-digested chicken into a bed of mulch. I missed a lot of things from college, especially with all the recent developments and complexities of life, but puking in the bushes was not one of them. I wiped my mouth, checked my shoes, and popped a piece of gum. I wasn't sure I'd be able to go through with it after all. Uncle Michael's words rang in my ears, 'What feels right?' It wasn't hurling in the bushes, that was for sure.

I knocked on the door and was met by Mrs. Romano, who had the same jet-black hair and petite figure as Natalia. I tried not to think of the time I'd seen her topless in the lake when I was a teen, but it was impossible, being a dude. I leaned in and kissed her. "Hi, Mrs. Romano."

"Hi, Leo." She offered a tired smile.

"Is Natalia here?" I asked quietly.

"She's upstairs in her bedroom."

Mr. Romano's voice boomed grumpily from the den. "You think I should allow a man in her bedroom?"

I tread carefully. I didn't want any trouble. I could easily take his short and fat self in a fight, but with his daughter's honor at stake, I wasn't willing to risk it. I stepped into the house, closed my eyes for a moment, and then answered, "Mr. Romano, you've known me my whole life. I'm thirty years old and I think we're a little past that at this point, don't you? I need to speak with her privately."

"Fine." He waved me upstairs with the back of his hand.

I sighed, but said nothing. Mrs. Romano led me up the stairs and into Natalia's room before slipping away.

Natalia sat on her bed, arms wrapped around her knees. She looked up at me with puffy eyes. "I wasn't sure I'd ever see you again."

I huffed. "Don't be so dramatic, Nat. I'm not going anywhere."

Natalia bounced from the bed, wrapping her arms around me with a shriek.

As I stood there, I felt nothing. No excitement. No joy. No

hope for the future. Of what we might become. What our child would become. *I can't do this.*

"Wait. I'm not finished." I extricated myself from her embrace, grabbed her hands for safety as much as for her comfort, and said, "I want to raise a baby with you, but I don't think we should get married."

A wave of relief washed over me, until her face dropped in confusion. Tears streamed down her face. She tried to pull her hands from my grasp, but I squeezed tighter. She tore them away and turned from me. "How could you do this to me?"

I threw my hands up. "I'm not doing anything to you. Do you want to live in a loveless marriage?"

She turned and surged toward me. "We'll love our child."

Softly, I said, "That's not enough for me."

Natalia lay down on her bed, burying her face in her pillow.

I sighed as I sat next to her and rubbed her back. "I will be there. I promise. You'll find the right person for you and so will I, and we'll all make it work."

She turned on her side and spat, "Who's going to want an unwed mother heading for the wrong side of thirty?"

"This isn't the 50s. This isn't a scarlet letter."

Natalia pointed to the door. "Just go."

"Nat, no. I think we need to work this out more."

"There's nothing to work out! You're ruining me. Embarrassing my family. I hate you! You won't ever see my child!"

My stomach roiled. "Nat, you don't mean that. This baby is our child and I'm going to be there every step of the way."

"I don't want you around the baby. I'll find a better father. A real man."

I shook my head in disgust. When would something go right for me? "I know cooler heads will prevail at some point," I said, realizing I was talking about two Italians. "But if you are serious about what you said, know that I will fight for my rights. You can count on that. But more than that, you can count on the irrefutable fact that you can always count on me. As the father of your child. As a co-parent. As a friend."

"Get out! Get the fuck out! I hope our baby is nothing like you." She tossed a pillow at my head, which I ducked under, a reflex well-honed in an Italian household of flying spaghetti.

I knew she was lashing out in hurt, but it didn't make it any easier to hear or digest.

Was I crazy? Should I change my mind?

I took a deep breath and held firm. "Fine. You can push me away now, I get it. But you can push all you want. I will keep coming back."

She ignored me, head buried in a second pillow amid sobs. I stared at her for a moment, considered climbing out the window to avoid further confrontation with the Romanos, but took the stairs instead.

Natalia's parents stared at me as I emerged into the den from the stairs.

Mrs. Romano asked, "What happened?"

Mr. Romano asked, "Are you going to do what's right by my daughter? Our families?"

"I am, but...you might not see it that way." I inched toward the door, not knowing if he'd try to knock me out.

Mr. Romano's brow furrowed. "Which is how?"

I forced myself to look him in the eye, projecting more confidence than I truly had. "Not getting married because we don't love each other, but raising a child together with love."

His voice rose two decibels. "Who the hell do you think you are?" He nearly knocked over a lamp with a heavy hand gesture.

I headed for the door, shaking my head. "I can't do this right now."

"You're going to run away from your responsibilities, you coward?"

I turned back to Mr. Romano. "I'm not running away from anything. You just don't care what's right for me. Only for you. I want you to know something. Family is everything to me. Or I thought it was. Love is everything. Natalia and I are not getting married. It's not the family you want for us. But I promise you our child's life will be filled with love. And I will always do right by the people I love. You can hate me and push back against me, which would be a detriment to your grandchild, or you can accept that I wouldn't be the husband that Natalia deserves. I'm in love with another woman. But I will be a great father to your grandchild. I swear my life on it."

Mrs. Romano nodded, seemingly in understanding. I waited for a response, but got none until I stepped out the door.

Mr. Romano yelled after me. "This isn't over!"

"I don't want it to be," I said, simply. I lumbered down the steps, eyeing the vomit I'd left behind and added to it. *Just livin' my best life.*

———

Sunday dinner was in full swing when I arrived at my parents' house. Nonna and the al dente spaghetti wait for no one. I exhaled a shaky breath from the driveway, watching my family get situated at the table through the dining room window.

My agita level was about on par with entering the Thunder Dome. "You got this," I whispered to myself. "They'll come around. Benny would be screwed in this situation. But I'm the favorite son." I didn't really believe it, but there's no way I would've gone in there without lying to myself.

I made my way straight to the dinner table. I had to tear off the band aid immediately. It wouldn't be pretty. There would be tears. Maybe some curses in Italian. But I'd hope somehow, they'd keep it in check with the kids there.

My mother smiled from her chair at my approach. "Well?" was all she asked.

I swallowed hard as I stood behind the high-chaired Matteo at the head of the table, opposite my father. I loved the kid, but I'd use him as a human shield if I had to. "I made a decision. Not everyone will agree with it, and that's okay." Faces around the table dropped. "There was no perfect choice for everyone, but I'll make this work. I am committed to being the best father that I can be, but I can't marry Natalia. I'm in love with another woman."

My mother slumped from her chair and onto the floor with a thump. Aunt Franny and Gia shrieked. Pop rushed to Mom's side. The kids broke out in tears. Nonna grabbed the wooden spoon from the small sauce pot on the table and cleaned it with her apron, her eyes boring into me.

I rushed to my mother's side as Sal, Benny, and Frankie grabbed the kids to settle them.

Pop said simply, "You killed your mother."

My mother opened her eyes and sat up. Leaning on one hand, she smacked me across the face with the other.

I recoiled, the sting spider-webbing across my cheek. "Ma!"

She stood up, crossed her arms, and turned her back on me.

"This is my life. I get to decide." I stared at her, my chest heaving.

Uncle Freddy ushered me from the room. "Don't add to it, Leo."

Pop met me in the hallway as my mother and Nonna yelled in Italian.

"Pop, what can I do?"

He shook his head. "You ask this now? She's Sicilian. There's nothing you can do other than marry the girl."

"She's going to turn her back on me forever?"

"No. Maybe."

Uncle Freddy added unhelpfully, "Have you seen Uncle Michael at Sunday dinner in the past fifteen years?"

"But I'm her son. I'm giving her a grandchild."

Pop exhaled a deep breath. "I'll do my best to clean up this mess, but I make you no guarantees. You should go."

I held firm. "I don't want to. This is not how we do things."

"We are in uncharted territory, Leo. You being here will not help right now. It'll only stir the pot."

"I want to talk this out."

"Now is not the time," Pop said.

"When?"

Pop chuckled pathetically. "Maybe my funeral, which might be later this week, depending on how mad your mother is."

CHAPTER
Thirty-Three

AS FRUSTRATING as work had been over the past few months, it was a welcome distraction come Monday morning. Sam Bennington toured our Huntington facility first thing and then sat down with me in the conference room. He didn't seem to care all that much, but I beat him to the head of the table, just in case.

Sam loosened his tie and rolled up the sleeves of his white dress shirt. "Let's get down to business, shall we?"

"We shall," I said, stupidly.

"I'm impressed. Not with the facility. It's a print facility. I'm impressed with you, Leo. Your tech savviness, your understanding of the business, and ability to build relationships are very valuable."

I tried not to wince at the 'building relationships' part, as the only people close to me who didn't hate me were Jean-Claude, Benny, and Frankie, and they were just simple beasts.

Sam continued, "I've thought long and hard about what I want, and I want you."

"I am single and flattered, but you're not my type, Sam," I said with a straight face.

Sam laughed. "Let me rephrase. I want you as a partner."

I raised an eyebrow.

He laughed again. "A business partner. I want to buy out Donati Printing so your father can do what he wants to do and I want to give you an ownership stake in the new business and stay on as the CEO-in-waiting. A few years down the road, I moonlight as the Chairman, and you run the show."

I nodded, my mind racing. It felt good, but it was bittersweet. "I'm thankful that you're here and I welcome that opportunity."

Sam slid a piece of paper across the table. "Here is the offer sheet, highlighting the key points. 4.75x valuation on trailing twelve months EBITDA with a twenty-five percent earn-out for the next two years. Ten percent ownership for you, vesting over three years, and the title of President."

I stared at it, a smile cracking at the edge of my mouth. "This is fantastic, Sam. It's higher than the offer we have on the table. I can't see how this doesn't sway my father. And given how it benefits both him and me, I will do my best to sway him."

"One other thing," Sam said. "I want the opportunity to match if your other suitor raises their bid."

I nodded thoughtfully, thinking about what the reaction of the other suitor might be when I told her the news. *Rae is going to freak. Maybe worse than Coney Island.* "I think that's more than fair."

Sam raised an eyebrow. "You okay? I thought you'd be happier."

I forced a smile. "Yeah. Just…girl trouble. I'd ask for advice, but I don't know where to start."

"Sadly, I can't help. I've been married for thirty years and sometimes I feel like I know less now than at the beginning. I was finally figuring it out but then menopause hit. Now I'm back at square one and I freeze my ass off all night after my wife kicks the covers off."

"My problems are a bit bigger than that, so if you can't figure that out, I'll ask someone else," I said, chuckling.

"See? Wise beyond your years. Listen. Back to business. Do what's best for your family. This is more than a buyout. Yes. We would cash out your parents, but this is a partnership more than anything. You will be an owner, so you can continue to be a part of what you built and be a trusted partner for overseeing what I've built."

"How do I know you won't sell it out from under me?"

"Isn't that already happening to you? I can't make any promises, but you'd be an owner and would get paid on any deal, so you'd make a pretty penny. But I will tell you I have no intentions to sell. I have more than enough to retire on. And we are big enough where we compete pretty well with the big boys. I plan on taking an annual dividend each year, but I want this firm to continue on long after me."

I silently wished my father felt the same way about what we had built. I stood up and smiled. "Well, let me get to work."

We shook hands. Sam said, "I think this is a more than fair offer with a ton of personal upside for you. I really hope you consider it."

"I will."

I walked Sam out to the parking lot and watched him drive away, wondering how I was going to tell my father. And more important, Rae.

———

I went straight to my office without even updating Rebecca and closed the door. I knew Rae wouldn't answer my calls or texts, so I reached out to her assistant, Melanie, instead.

"Kane Printing. Ms. Kane's office. How may I help you?" Melanie asked.

"Hi Melanie. This is Leo Donati."

"Mmm, hmm," was all she said. Apparently, she was in the know.

"Can I please speak to Rae? It's about our deal."

I heard Rae's voice whisper in the background, "Tell him I'm not here."

"Tell her I hear her and I need to see her. We have some complications."

"That's an understatement," Rae said, louder.

I huffed. "Look, she's mad. I know. If she wants to cancel the deal, that's fine. Otherwise, we have things to discuss. I'd like to come in tomorrow."

Just over twenty-four hours later, I sat in a glass-walled conference room with the sweet frosted-glass switches. I flipped it back and forth, adding sound effects, until Rae walked in with an eye roll. "That's not a toy."

It was wonderful to see her face, even without the dimples. "I have nothing else to play with." Was she happy to see me? I couldn't tell.

She ignored my comment and sat down at the head of the table.

"Damn it," I said, squeezing my fist. Again. She beat me to it again.

"What?" Rae asked.

"Nothing." I looked around at the simple, yet elegant, office. White paint, glass tables, mesh-back ergonomic chairs, and fresh red roses. I nodded to the flowers. "Nice touch. Are they for you?" I asked, as nonchalant as possible.

Rae opened her laptop. "None of your business."

"So, that's a no?"

She didn't answer.

I tapped the glass table with my fingers as I waited. "Your dad strikes me more like a solid wood guy."

Rae stared at me with a raised eyebrow.

"I mean that from an interior decoration standpoint, not an exterior...dickeration point."

"Really? Dickeration point?"

"I thought the clarification was necessary."

She huffed. "My mom decorates. It keeps her busy. My dad built the empire, my mom spends it."

"Well, tell her I like what she's done with the place."

"I won't. So, I have ten minutes. Let's use them wisely."

I swallowed hard. "Right. Thank you for meeting with me, Ms. Kane. I wanted to tell you face to face that we've received an offer to buy Donati Printing at a better price than what you've offered, and a substantially better deal for me personally. Raise, stock ownership, CEO path." A small part of me expected it to feel good saying it, but it didn't.

Rae's face reddened. She spoke in a controlled, but angered voice, "I see. And who might be the other buyer?"

"That's confidential."

"Impact Ink?"

"I can't say."

She sighed, rubbed her face with her hands, and said, "I guess we're back to hating each other."

I chuckled pathetically. "I will love you until the day my family kills me. This is just business."

Rae didn't respond to my statement, but looked away from my eyes. "We can pay 4.25x EBITDA."

"I'm really not enjoying this. I promise. But it's still too low."

"What do I have to beat?"

"I think you should probably just give me your best offer and we'll see where it stands."

"4.3."

I shook my head.

"4.5x." She barely kept her composure.

"Sorry."

Rae slammed her laptop closed and stood up. "You're being incredibly childish. You're angry I rejected you, so this is how you get back at me?"

"I'm not getting back at you. I've made it very clear from the beginning, your bid was too low. And for the record, I put this in motion before you rejected me."

Rae crossed her arms and shot a laser gaze at me. "That might be even worse."

I threw my hands in the air. "I can't win."

"Not today."

"Well, in some ways, you're right. Others wrong."

She chuckled, annoyed. "You think you've gotten the best of me? What if I go after your new entity and squeeze your tiny little nut sack until you beg for mercy?"

I muttered, "I'm glad we're keeping this professional. Also, a side note, you know I don't have a tiny nut sack. I think you should put that in this meeting's minutes."

"You know what? We're done here. I'll be in touch. Probably to pull our offer."

I stood up. "After all this, you're just going to walk away?"

Her face contorted, seemingly having difficulty getting the words out. "I'm not authorized to do more. I have to talk to my father. Now, get out." Rae nodded. "There's the door."

I headed for it, but turned back. "You know, you rejected me. Every time you've stomped on me, it's just business. Now that you're finally losing, it's personal? How many times were you ahead of me? You didn't see me crying."

"I'm not crying. I'm just shocked at your lack of professionalism. How many months are we into this? Were you just stringing me along until you could find someone better?"

I stepped toward her, but stopped a few feet as she appeared more likely to meet me with a stiff backhand than loving embrace. "There is no one better. At least not for me."

"There is no us, Leo. I'm talking about the business. That's the only relationship we'll ever have. If we even want that, after this stunt you pulled. And don't bother reaching out to me. Someone else will be in touch to figure out this mess you've created."

"Rae, it doesn't have to be this way. We don't have to hate each other. I don't hate you. Could never hate you."

"This is exactly how it has to be." She grabbed her laptop, headed out of the conference room, and disappeared behind an access door without so much as a look back.

I hung my head. *Damn it.* "What did I just do?"

———

Rae's Deal Notes

- Deal is falling apart. ~~Life is falling apart. I miss him. I hate him. I don't think that's possible...~~
- Discuss new deal parameters with executive team. Impact Ink bid north of 4.5x.
- Refocus on what truly matters. Career. Deal pipeline.
- Block off time for career strategic planning.

CHAPTER
Thirty~Four

IT WAS A BIG DAY. I actually wore khakis and a sport coat. True, there was a dress code, so it wasn't my choice, but still. The Greystone Men's Club sat atop a hill overlooking the Long Island Sound to the north and a championship golf course to the south, functioning as both a yacht and golf club. So, doubly stuffy. My family was a roll-up-your-sleeves working class bunch. While I had always gotten what I needed, and Donati Printing was going to sell for two commas, sailboats, golf courses, and facelifts were out of our league. We were more soccer, baseball, and bad boob job people.

I was nervous. A fish out of water. Not to mention, meeting with Caleb Kane, Rae's father and CEO of the firm that was ruining my life in multiple ways. I sat in a common area of the club, which was none too common. A huge, well-stocked oak bar ran the course of the room, while over fifty high-back leather chairs encircled at least a dozen different coffee tables throughout.

It was just after lunch, so the golf crowd was in full swing, just having finished up eighteen holes in the morning, apparently having the minions do the real work back at the office.

Caleb Kane approached me wearing a blue pinstriped suit, a pink shirt with a white collar, and his signature diamond cufflinks and monogrammed sleeves. I stood up and met his hand for a shake.

"Mr. Kane, so good to see you again."

"Likewise, Leo. Please, sit. So glad you could make it to the club. It's spectacular, isn't it?"

"Absolutely."

"Do you play golf?"

"Not well."

"How about sailing?"

"I'm more of a rowboat kind of guy."

He chuckled.

"Is it just us? Rae isn't coming?" I asked, looking around.

"No. This is a men's club."

I nodded, trying to hide my disappointment. "Did she not want to be here, or did you want to meet at the club? I'm surprised she hasn't forced you to relinquish your membership in support of the better gender."

Caleb smiled. "She certainly has said more than enough about it. I worked extremely hard to get here. Be accepted here. The world isn't fair. Giving up my membership will not change that."

I shrugged, not really agreeing. There were some things worth sacrificing for.

Caleb continued, "And she's had her chance to get this deal done. My son is supposed to be here. Where is he?" He waved it away. "No matter. I'm sure he's in traffic or something. Let's get started. Care for a drink? Whiskey? Bourbon?"

"No. Thanks. I don't drink during the work day." It wasn't entirely true. I'd had a beer at lunch with the boys from time to time. I just didn't want to tell him that whiskey and bourbon made me sick to my stomach, and he seemed like a stiff drink snob.

"I respect that," Caleb said. "My daughter tells me you have a lot of potential as a district manager."

"With all due respect, sir, I have a lot more potential than that. If I'm being honest, it's why I haven't been so keen on this deal. I can run my family's business just fine."

Caleb chuckled. "I've seen the numbers. I'm not so sure. You don't have the scale. We've been pummeling you with pricing pressure from PremaPrint without trying very hard."

"Well, as I'm sure you can understand, my father and I don't always see eye to eye on how to run things. I was expecting to take over. When he made this deal, I wasn't happy. And I found a better one. They're willing to pay more, and I'll be the successor to the CEO."

"Well, I guess my daughter hasn't done a very good job of convincing you. I knew I should've gotten involved sooner."

I didn't like his tone or his disrespect of Rae. "Your daughter is a shark. She's been ahead of me at every turn. Sharks don't need a leash. You should've given her the freedom to get it done."

"I did. She didn't."

"No. You capped her on what she could offer. And it's going to take more. I just got lucky and found a higher bid. She was on top of me...it," I abruptly corrected, praying to the gods of sweat to leave my brow be.

"Yet here we are. It seems we still have some convincing to do. Let me tell you what it means to be in the Kane family."

I had thought of having this conversation with Caleb more than a few times, but it wasn't about joining the printing family. I pushed the thought of Rae and me ever being together from my mind and focused on his words.

"It's about success. Achievement. Prosperity. My family came to this country with nothing after World War II. We've achieved the American dream. I think our families are very much alike in that way."

I nodded in agreement. "That's part of the reason I want to keep the business in the family."

"And I want to do the same for my children. If they ever step up enough to earn it."

"You don't think Rae has?" I scoffed.

He narrowed his eyes, studying me. "You're very fond of her."

I love her. No matter how badly I wanted to say it, I couldn't. It would've only made things worse, anyway. "We started off on the wrong foot, but we've gotten to know each other throughout the due diligence process, and I respect her very much." Coney Island, Shangri-La Garden, the night by the fire, and the many nights after all ran through my mind.

"She's had her moments and was on her way, but this deal hasn't been helpful to her. You'll still be running your family business plus others in the district. You'll have stock options to take part in the business as an owner and enjoy its successes. The structure is different, but you're still getting what you want."

"Yes and no." He was partially correct, but I'd still be working for someone else. Following their rules. Their direction.

"We want you and your business to be part of our family."

"I'm not convinced you don't want us to bow down and worship you."

Caleb laughed. "That's just how it feels right now, but make no mistake, you're getting acquired. This isn't a merger of equals." He chuckled. "As if."

It wasn't like Rae was knocking down my door for us to be together, but any hope of her father ever accepting me evaporated at that moment. If he thought his business was too good to compare to mine, how would he look at me with Rae? Probably with disgust. I felt more hopeless than ever before.

Caleb downed the last of his whiskey and grimaced. "I'm

a busy man. Let's cut to the chase. Here is our final offer. This has dragged on for long enough. You have twenty-four hours to give us a decision. There are plenty of other fish in the sea, as they say."

My mind drifted back to Rae. I almost missed his offer.

"We'll pay 5x EBITDA with entrance to our executive training program for you. District manager to start. Regional potential. You should be grateful."

I nodded and chose my words carefully. "I'm grateful for the offer. I will discuss it with my father." I stood up and offered my hand. He shook it without standing up. "I'll let you know. Give Noah my regards," I jabbed.

———

As soon as I hit the Long Island Expressway, I dialed Sam Bennington from Impact Ink. He picked up on the first ring.

Sam's voice boomed through the speakers, "Leo, my boy! How are you?"

"I just got out of a meeting with Caleb Kane."

"Do you need medical attention?"

I laughed. "No. Physically unharmed. Ego shaken, but not broken."

"He's the suitor, I suppose?"

"Yes. And I wanted to share his offer with you. He offered us 5x."

"That's a good offer."

"That's what my business is worth."

"It means it's not as accretive to me, but I need a successor and there *are* synergies. I will match, but not a penny higher. I want you with us. With me."

"I appreciate that, Sam. I do. Let me talk to my father. I'm going to see him right now. I will be back in touch by tomorrow morning at the latest."

"Sounds good."

I hung up and drove straight to the office. With both players maxed out on their offers and at the same price, I could tell Caleb to pound sand and get a better personal deal and more opportunity for advancement while my dad gets paid. And paid more because of my hard work.

I walked into the office, said hello to Rebecca, and went straight to Pop's office. I peeked my head in as he hunt-and-pecked on his keyboard. "Pop, can we talk?"

He nodded. "Close the door. I've made no progress. Your mother is, well, she's pazza. A lunatic."

"That's not news, Pop, but this isn't personal. It's business."

"Shoot."

"I've gotten us a twenty-five percent increase in the offer for the company. We have two suitors at the same price. 5x trailing twelve months EBITDA."

His eyebrows shot up. "Two suitors?"

"I got the second interested to push Kane higher. But I think it's the better deal. You get what you want and Impact Ink will have me succeed the current CEO, so I get what I want, on delay." I sat back, crossed my arms, and awaited my praise.

"Well, if it's all the same to me, I'll leave the decision up to you. It seems as if you can't screw this one up."

It wasn't exactly the response I was looking for. "What's that supposed to mean?"

"Do I need to spell it out for you? You've embarrassed your mother. Your family. You had a simple path with a great young woman, you blew it up. For what?"

"For love."

"With who?"

"Rae."

His chest thrust forward and he barked, "Rae Kane? Are you insane? In what world would that work?"

"I wouldn't have made the decision I did if it was wrong.

And by the way, you're welcome. I just paid for your house in Boca. Yet you continue to discount my decision making."

"One doesn't make up for the other. Choose where you want to work and I'll sign the deal."

I stood up, shaking my head. That was the thanks I get? I just put an extra few hundred grand in his pocket after taxes and that's it? I walked out, straight to my car, and drove to the harbor in Northport.

I wasn't a sailing kind of guy, but the boats were calming to look at on a warm, spring day. The ice cream didn't hurt, either. I walked along the water's edge and then found an empty bench with a water view.

"What should I do?" I asked no one in particular. I should've grabbed J.C. for a walk in the park, but his advice wasn't exactly flowing as of late. "What am I doing with my life?" I took a lick of my black raspberry ice cream atop a waffle cone and wondered if I should be a professional ice cream eater. Maybe that would make me happy.

"Get serious," I muttered. Thoughts flooded my mind. Was I being selfish? I threw away my family. I ruined Natalia. I might never see my child. Rae hated me. I was about to crush her dreams by selling to Impact Ink. I don't want to make light of war, but I felt like I was on the Italian Front in World War II in the book *Catch-22*. My life wasn't physically at risk, but my life was at stake. My vision. My happiness. I thought of Uncle Michael's advice again, 'What feels right?' and I knew what I had to do.

CHAPTER
Thirty-Five

AT NINE THE NEXT MORNING, I stood beside my father outside of Kane Printing, the hustle and bustle of the lunch hour enveloping us.

"You sure you want to do this?" Pop asked.

I nodded. It was the right thing to do. I wasn't trying to get Rae back, if I ever had her. But if I hadn't been selfish, this deal would've closed a long time ago and she would've gotten what she deserved.

I sat beside Pop and across from Caleb, who was flanked by Rae on his left and Noah on his right. Rae wore a sharp blue pants suit, her hair twirling down to her shoulders, and simple pink lipstick. I stared at her. Couldn't take my eyes away. She met my gaze, and for a moment, I thought the walls would come crashing down, but then she looked away.

I moved on to study Noah…without the same hopes that I had for Rae. He was a handsome guy with blue eyes, curly brown hair, and a strong chin. Between that and being rich, you could understand why he didn't take things too seriously, at least by Rae's account. He didn't have to.

Caleb said, "We could've saved you the trip into the city had we met at the club."

I cut Pop off. "I won't be at any business meeting that Rae can't attend."

Noah said, "It wouldn't be called The Greystone Men's Club if they let in women."

I looked him dead in the eye. "And they're worse off for it." I looked at Caleb. "Why is he here, by the way? He's had nothing to do with this deal." Pop's eyes signaled caution, but I didn't give a shit. "I guess when you're not riding your Segway, you're riding your sister's coattails?"

Noah stuttered, but couldn't find any words while Caleb rubbed his face, seemingly stunned. "I'd like him to be here, but your point is noted."

"Fine. Whatever that means."

Pop intervened. "I know this has been a contentious deal, but we've made it to the finish line. Whatever happened is in the past."

I caught Rae's eye again. *Easier said than done.*

My father continued, "Let's move forward, as partners."

Caleb nodded. "Well said. Leo, you played the game well. You were a worthy opponent. One I'm glad is now on our team, fighting for us."

"I have something to say," I said.

Pop looked at me like, 'don't screw this up now, ya chooch.' Benny was usually on the receiving end of said stare, so I knew it well.

Caleb nodded.

I folded my hands in front of me. "We had a better deal. We chose Kane because of how well Rae represented the firm and herself. We took less, well, I took less because of that. This is her deal. She earned it."

Caleb beamed at Rae. "I'm very proud of her."

Rae smiled. Dimples. God, how I missed them.

Caleb said, "Well, we'll get the lawyers to finalize the paperwork while we eat and then we can sign."

I nodded, but then shook my head. Screw that. I had one more play to make. "I'm not signing anything."

Faces dropped. Rae's eyes bore into mine. Pop said, "Ah fanabla." Which basically means WTF in Italian.

I threw up my hands in my defense. "I meant right this minute. I have one condition."

"Yes?" Caleb asked, annoyed.

"You can sign the sales contract today. For my employment deal, Rae delivers the paperwork to me at six o'clock tomorrow night. I'll text her the address. I will sign then."

Rae frowned at me.

"What's this all about?" Pop asked.

My life. I didn't answer. "Those are my terms."

Caleb shrugged. "I guess that will be fine." He looked at Rae. "Any objections?"

Rae shook her head. "No. As long as we get the deal done."

I said firmly, "It will get done. I promise."

Caleb said, "Well, let's get legal to prep the docs and we'll bring in lunch."

"Thank you for the offer, but I can't stay," I said, standing up.

Pop frowned at me, but I didn't respond.

"Oh, that's too bad," Caleb said, most likely not meaning it.

I stood up and shook hands with all of them, feeling slightly awkward when connecting with Noah, and even more so with Rae. But I didn't want to let go of Rae. I thought she might've felt the same way, but I wasn't sure as she let go first.

"I'll see you tomorrow," I said to Rae.

Rae nodded and said, "Caleb, if you'll excuse me for a moment." She called her father, Caleb? I shook my head. It was weird, but man did I miss her weirdness.

I headed for the door, not realizing that Rae actually wanted to talk to me. She caught me in the lobby.

"Leo, wait."

I turned around, no idea what she was about to say, but hoping it was an offer to run away together.

"Thank you for having my back. If my brother didn't have a penis, he'd be worthless."

I laughed. "For an extremely articulate woman, you sure make some interesting word choices."

Rae turned up her nose at me. "Oh, God. You're so gross."

I shrugged. "I didn't say it."

"What's the deal with signing tomorrow?"

I forced a smile. "I don't want to spoil the surprise." I then realized I had to make said surprise happen.

She raised an eyebrow, crossed her arms, and whispered, "You'll be wearing pants, though?"

"You're not allowed to joke about me not wearing pants." I went to caress her face, but I caught myself, stuffed my hand in my pocket, and assessed the potential for any witnesses, my eyes darting back and forth. "I can't do this with you."

"Do what exactly? There's a million things I'm struggling with right now."

"Pretend…" *Pretend I don't love you.* I made a horrible mistake. There was no way I could work with Rae for two years. Would it get easier? I couldn't see how. My feelings for her wouldn't fade with time. It's why I did everything I did. I just had to hope that what I had planned would work.

Pop joined us in the lobby. "What're you doing? You don't just walk out of a deal like that."

"I just did."

"What is…going on?" Rae asked, confused.

"Just livin' my best life. See you tomorrow," I said to Rae, forcing my eyes from her to my father. "Good luck, Pop." I wiped a tear from my eye, headed for the elevator and pounded on the button as if it brought the car that much quicker.

———

Rae's Deal Notes

- Deal closure imminent. ~~It was so hard to see him. It's not fair. Why does there have to be so much between me and being happy? He makes me happy. So happy. Makes me feel loved. There is no one out there for me but him. But the baby? Our cultures? Is G_d laughing at us? Why does life have to be so complicated?~~
- Block off tomorrow afternoon/early evening...for what????
- Prepare integration team. Inform finance department of deal closing.

———

I couldn't go back to the office. I had no desire, no emotional energy to handle business, questions, emails, the stunads. I was done. I didn't know if I would be able to handle the next two years, but I had to find a way. Muster the strength somehow. But it wouldn't be today.

Back in Huntington, I zombie-walked Jean-Claude and then collapsed onto the couch and just lay there for two hours.

Benny came in, saw me on the couch, and checked his watch. Frankie entered with a frown.

I sat up and asked, "What are you doing here? Not that you actually work at the shop."

Benny petted Jean-Claude. "What are *you* doing here? You

actually work. Pop gave us the rest of the afternoon off. We're having a family dinner at Ma's to celebrate the deal."

"When are you moving out?" I asked.

Benny's eyes bulged. "Moving out? Why are we moving out?"

"Because you're a bunch of mama's boys with tiny little nut sacks."

"That's uncalled for," Frankie said. He nudged Benny. "But yours are kinda small."

Benny pushed Frankie back. "You haven't seen them for a decade. They've tripled. Quadrupled."

"As riveting as this conversation is, my question remains."

"Why do we have to move out?" Benny asked.

I stood up and stared out the window at the now blooming white dogwood tree, a much prettier sight than when adorned with jeans. "I've done everything for you guys. I didn't fire you like fifty times. I give you a place to stay. You eat my food. I take care of your dog. What do you do for me when I need you the most?"

They said nothing.

I turned and said, "Exactly. Your big fucking mouths couldn't say a word to support me. Get your shit out of my apartment by the weekend or pick it up by the dumpster Monday morning."

Benny sighed. "Leo—"

"Just go to your little party."

"With our little nuts," Frankie said.

I held back from punching the wall, my fist balled with fury. "It's not always a joke, dipshits! How is it possible that you don't even try, but your lives are a thousand times better than mine?"

Benny ushered Frankie to the door. "Let's go, dude. He'll chill out eventually."

"I won't."

After they left, I sunk into the couch again, not sure if I

would ever leave it. I stared at the ceiling for what must've been twenty minutes and then something clicked. As my thoughts swirled around in my head, apathy turned to anger.

"Screw this." I stood up. Jean-Claude barked. "Damn straight," I said, as if he had my back. My family was gonna hear what I had to say.

I pulled up and went straight inside, no motivational moment requirement. I was fueled by straight-up fire. I didn't even take off my shoes, the bad ass that I was. The dining room went silent. Even the kids shut up.

"What are you doing here?" My mother asked.

I forced a smile, suppressing my anger. "I'm here to celebrate with the family like everyone else. A banner day in the Donati family." I just wanted to see how she'd respond.

In a monotone voice, my mother said, "You're not welcome here."

I chuckled with anger. "Is that how you want to play this?"

She didn't answer.

I crossed my arms and blew out a deep breath. "Fine. I knew you wouldn't want me here, but I have something to say. I've earned that much in this family. I got over my pride and did what was right for the people I care about. You need to do the same. I don't need this family, but I want this family. You want to shun me, that's your choice. Family doesn't always come first. Love does. I choose love over family. You're choosing hate. You're choosing ego. You're choosing anger. This is going against our faith. Our religion."

My mother scoffed. "That's ridiculous."

"You are. With your conditional love. I can't live my life to make you happy." I looked at Pop. "I came into this business to make you happy. I could've done anything." I turned to my mother. "I dated woman after woman of your choice to make you happy." I eyed Nonna. "I eat too many carbs to make you happy. I can't do this. It's my life. My whole life. And I can't settle for the next seventy years of it." I was on a roll and couldn't stop. "You don't agree with my decision about Natalia, fine. But hate me because of it? Shun me? Are you really happy not seeing Uncle Michael for fifteen years? I'll make it right with Natalia. I will be a father to my child. I'll be the best I can at what works for me. Not you."

They met my words with nothing but silence. No yelling. No Italian mutterings. No wild hand gestures. Just dead stares.

"Am I the only one who thinks this?" I glared at Gia, Benny, and Frankie, and got nothing in return. "So much for a strong family bond. We're supposed to do everything for the family, but the family turns their backs on you as soon as you try to be true to yourself. If this is family, I don't want any part of it. I'll build my own." I stared at them for a moment, wondering, hoping that maybe someone would say something. But they didn't.

I shook my head with disgust and headed outside. The door slammed behind me. I turned when I heard it creak open again.

My father stood at the top of the steps. "Wait. I'm sorry this has happened."

I chuckled pathetically. "Not enough to say anything in front of everyone else."

He walked toward me, meeting me in the middle of the front lawn in his house shoes, a wooden-spoonable offense. "I think we were all a little shocked. I'm sorry about the company. I'm proud of what you've done. You impressed Caleb Kane. It's not easy."

"I couldn't give two shits about impressing Caleb Kane. He's an ass."

"Regardless. I'm proud of you."

"You should've trusted me. I could've run the company."

Pop rubbed his balding head. "I didn't want you to fail. We'd only be delaying the inevitable. The industry is changing faster than we could adapt. The Walmarts of printing are driving the mom and pops out of business or forcing them to sell. I thought it would be better to sell the company out from underneath you than to hand it over and have it fail. I know how much pressure you put on yourself. Know how important the responsibility to lead this family is to you."

I knew it, but I couldn't believe he was actually saying it. "You lack confidence in me that much that you know I'd fail?"

Pop shook his head, arms crossed. "I lacked confidence in the industry trends. We're getting out-competed and no matter how amazing you are, and you are amazingly talented, it couldn't make up for that. We didn't have the capital to buy someone else, so we got gobbled up. It would either be now or later at a worse price after our business deteriorated further. I didn't want you to be the CEO of nothing. I didn't want you to think I didn't have confidence in you, so I didn't tell you all this."

"You made me think you didn't have confidence in me by not telling me."

"Oops."

"Oops?" I threw up my hands and stared at the blue sky wondering when God would smite me out of my misery. "I don't even care about the business anymore, Pop. It's done. I'm a Kane Printing employee at least for the next two years, according to the agreement. This deal is the least of my problems. Mom hates me. And right now, I hate her. And Rae hates me, too, but I love her."

My list of Italian family rules had fallen apart. They had banned me from Sunday dinner. I loathed my mother, and it was mutual. I did not marry an Italian, but...I got one pregnant. I no longer believed that family always came first. I still felt it was in my best interest to not tell Nonna I was full, not that she would feed me, and I was still pretty solidly against animal print, but I realize that's not really all that important. If someone feels good in animal print, they should go for it. Live life in leopard if that's how you want to live it. Be free like the animal whose print you're wearing.

My father snapped his fingers in my face. "Leo, you with me?"

I sighed. "Yeah."

"She'll come around."

I laughed, but not because it was funny. "Are you stunad? You can't be serious. When?"

"I don't know. Maybe on her death bed. Or maybe yours if we let Nonna near the steak knives. She's been sharpening them extra these past few days."

I threw up my hands. "You know what? I don't care. She wants to be fueled by hate, that's on her. I'm in love with Rae and I'm not ashamed of it. And I'm free as a bird of this crazy family. See you around, Pop. Or not."

CHAPTER
Thirty-Six

MY MEETING WITH RAE ARRIVED. I pulled up behind Rae's car in front of Uncle Michael's house at five minutes to six. Agita outweighed my hope by a solid five to one. I had no idea what to wear, so I just went sexy casual. Jeans, a sailor blue v-neck t-shirt, and a black cargo jacket. I regretted not suiting up.

Rae stepped out of the car, meeting me on the driveway.

"Hey," I said, not sure of what else to say. I offered my hand to her. She shook it with a smirk as I studied her up and down. She wore a fitted button-down shirt dress in salmon with high-heeled black boots. My God, she looked good. Where the hell was a coat closet when you needed it?

"Where are we?" Rae studied her surroundings.

"Exactly where we're supposed to be," I said, not wanting to spoil the surprise. "Follow me."

"Which is?"

"No witches. Wizards. They'll be off to Hogwarts soon. Just waiting for their letters."

Rae rolled her eyes but followed me.

I walked up to the house and knocked on the door with Rae by my side.

Charlie and Mikey answered the door together, both smiling wide.

"Gentlemen," I said, giving the boys high fives as I stepped inside. "Rae this is Charlie and Mikey, proprietors of this establishment."

Mikey said, "She's pretty. Is she your girlfriend?"

I laughed nervously and eyed Rae. "She's very pretty."

Rae shook hands with Charlie and Mikey, her dimples on full display. She looked at me, continuing to smile. My agita disappeared.

"Mom and Dad are cooking," Charlie said.

"Can you go check on them, boys?" I asked.

They ran off with a nod.

Rae turned to me. "Why are we here? Who are these people?"

I shrugged. "I don't know, Smirky. I thought you knew them."

Rae's eyes bulged and then softened, realizing I was joking. "You picked the place."

"Oh, right," I said with a smile. The four Donatis arrived from the kitchen with smiles. "This is my Uncle Michael and Aunt Emily, and my cousins, Charlie and Mikey."

They exchanged pleasantries and then Rae studied me, confused. "I still don't know why we're here."

"Well, to sign the papers, of course. Okay if we pop into the den for a few minutes?" I asked Uncle Michael, handing him my jacket.

"Sure."

I led Rae into the den and sat down on the battered tan couch. I offered Rae the seat next to me, patting the cushion and nodded to the coffee table. "I'll sign here. Did you bring a pen?"

"No. I forgot," Rae said, sarcasm dripping from her lips.

I smiled sheepishly and returned the sarcasm. "That's tough. I'm sorry you had to come all this way. The deal's off."

"That's not even funny," Rae said, hiding her smile. She produced the paper and a pen, placing them on the coffee table.

I grabbed the pen, signed the papers, and handed them back to Rae. I looked her in the eye and said, "I'm yours." I paused for a moment and then added, "Only for two years, of course."

She looked away and then asked, "Why did we have to sign the papers here?"

"We didn't, but I wanted to. Even though you are legally required to stay for dinner, based on the contingencies laid forth in this agreement, if you don't want to stay, you don't have to. But I'd love it if you did."

"Dinner is not in the agreement," Rae said, doubtful, but scanning the papers anyway.

I reached for the papers. "Can I just amend those?"

She laughed and pulled them away. "Not on your life. I can't stay."

"Please," I said, softly. "It would mean the world to me." I added a lip quiver and sad eyes for good measure. "Surely you're tough enough to endure me for one last hour."

"Okay," she said with a chuckle.

She didn't kiss or bite my lip, but it was still worthy of an inner fist pump. I smiled and led her into the kitchen as Uncle Michael and Aunt Emily tended to the stove. I clapped my hands together and said, "Let's eat!"

Aunt Emily took something out of the oven and eyed Rae's boots. "Ooh, I like those. Are they Prada?"

"Yes. And thank you," Rae said with a smile.

I said, "Oh, Prada, is that Italian?"

Rae rolled her eyes. "Not sure."

I counted on my fingers. "Prada. Gucci. Versace. Armani, Dolce & Gabbana. I mean, do you even wanna?"

Rae scrunched up her face. "Make bad rhymes? No. I can't argue with you on Italian fashion, but I would point out that it's all negated by fat guys in track suits and gold chains."

"Don't forget the high top sneakers," Uncle Michael chimed in.

I shrugged at Rae. "That's not the dumbest thing you've ever said." I looked at Uncle Michael and Aunt Emily. "We have this thing we do."

Uncle Michael raised an eyebrow. "Careful, the children are downstairs."

I shook my head. "I mean, I call it getting to know each other's culture."

Rae crossed her arms and cocked her head, eyes on mine. "Oh, is that what we've been doing all this time? I thought it was you telling me how superior yours was to mine."

I shrugged. "It just feels that way because, well, it is."

Uncle Michael said, "I think you'll find that the Italian and Jewish cultures are very similar, and both have their strong points."

Aunt Emily whispered to Rae, "And if he doesn't agree, just use some Krav Maga."

Rae laughed. "That's what I told him. He thinks Brooklyn street fighters can take Israeli special forces."

I defended my stance. "Not straight up. I said without the hipsters and metrosexuals."

"Come, let's eat," Uncle Michael said, laughing. "Make yourself comfortable. We'll grab the food."

As we headed into the dining room, I leaned down to Rae's ear from behind her and whispered, "I've missed you."

She didn't respond. I could tell her mind was racing, but I had no idea what thoughts were running through her beautiful noggin. My agita returned with a vengeance.

The dining room was simple with a dark wood table for eight and a hutch filled with china. Rae and I sat on the far side of the table, next to each other.

Rae whispered, "Why are we here? You won't tell me."

"Okay. You already agreed to stay, so you can't leave. I want you to see there are other people like us who made it work. Uncle Michael is my mother's brother. Aunt Emily is Jewish."

Rae's face contorted, but then she forced a smile as Uncle Michael entered and placed a bowl filled with a thick, winding pasta with meat sauce. "We have pappardelle bolognese as a first course, and then a brisket that is to die for."

Aunt Emily entered with a dish of latkes and applesauce. "Don't forget the latkes, love. The brisket's almost done."

"A little pasta. Some latkes. Sounds like the best of both worlds," I said, eyeing Uncle Michael.

He nodded. "It is. We've created our own culture, a melting pot, if you will."

"Sounds like America," I said, hoping to stir Rae's patriotism, but she said nothing. "Are the boys joining?"

Aunt Emily slipped into the chair opposite Rae. "I fed the savages earlier. This is better with just the four of us. They'll join for dessert." She used tongs to scoop and serve the pasta to each of us while Uncle Michael poured some wine.

After an awkward silence, I folded my hands and angled toward Rae while everyone else ate. "So, I asked you here because I'm dying—"

"What?" Rae shrieked.

"No. I didn't mean that. I was going to say 'dying without you.'"

Rae smacked my arm. "Jerk."

"You didn't let me finish," I said, suppressing a smile. "I wanted you to see what their lives were like. The life they've created. The love they have within their family. If they could have it, so could we."

Rae nodded, but said nothing. I could sense her mind racing again. She looked to Emily. "Just because you mix the two cuisines doesn't mean their lives work. Aren't you sad the kids don't see their broader family?"

"They're totally fine. They ask questions, but this is what we know. It's more him," she said, nodding to my uncle.

Uncle Michael said, "Her family has come around. We have some excellent friends, the kids' friends' parents. We've built a new family, a life we're happy with."

Aunt Emily grabbed Uncle Michael's hand. "We couldn't imagine being with anyone else."

Michael added, "We chose love."

"How long has it been?" Rae asked.

"Fifteen years," Aunt Emily said.

"Without family," Rae finished.

"Fifteen years of love," I corrected.

Rae turned to me. "Are you willing to endure that? Not be with your family for fifteen years? No holidays? No Sunday dinners? Not seeing your nieces and nephews grow up?"

"For you?" I took a deep breath and feigned thought. "No. You're right. It's stupid. I only love you a few years' worth. Five to seven, maybe." I stood up. "Let's get the hell out of here."

Rae scoffed while everyone else broke out into laughter.

"Of course. Maybe this could be our new family dinner," I said with a shrug and sat down again. "What do you think of that?" My stomach roiled as I waited for her answer.

Rae shook her head in disbelief. "I want it to be true, but it can't be." She stood up and placed her napkin on the table. "I am terribly sorry, but I can't stay. You have been wonderful."

I stood up. "What's wrong?"

"I can't do this, Leo. You just don't live in reality."

"They're living the reality right now. For fifteen years."

"Is it David?"

Rae's voice rose a decibel. "It's never been David. I had dinner with him twice for my father's sake. It's us. We can't work." She whispered, 'I'm sorry." Then headed out of the dining room and then the front door before I could even process what had happened.

"That's not how I planned it out," I muttered to a quiet Uncle Michael and Aunt Emily.

After a moment, Uncle Michael's eyes bulged and he said, "Don't give up now. Go after her!"

I took a deep breath and rushed out of the house, but not before screaming, "Save me a latke!"

CHAPTER
Thirty-Seven

RAE'S CAR was a house away and gaining distance when I got to the front lawn. "Damn it." I patted my pockets. "Where are my keys?" They were in my jacket. There was no time. I had to make a run for it. I took off across the grass, cutting through the neighbor's yard, hurdling a garden gnome like an Olympic champion. I had a chance to catch her if I could get to her before she hit the main road. After that, fuggetaboutit.

I waved my arms as I ran down the street behind Rae's car, hoping she would stop. Willing her to stop. "Rae! Wait! Please!"

She didn't. I hoped it was because she didn't see me and not because she didn't want to see me, so I kept going, gaining on her as she slowed into a stop sign. Like clockwork, she flicked her left blinker and turned left. That's when I made my move. It was equally the dumbest and smartest move I ever made. I cut across the corner lawn on the left and then back out onto the street in a flat-out sprint.

Rae's eyes widened as I bore down on the car and then did what anyone would've done in that situation. I dove onto the hood of the Genesis, crashing onto it with a metallic thud.

I probably should've thought of a few potential cons before making my move, but hindsight is always twenty-twenty. Rae slammed on the brakes and shrieked. I grabbed for the lip of the hood, but only caught a windshield wiper as my momentum hurled me forward. The wiper snapped in my hand, and I rolled off the hood and onto the pavement below with a splat. Pain surged through my entire body as my mind tried to make sense of what had just happened.

The door opened behind me. "Leo! What the hell is wrong with you?" Rae rushed to my side.

I sat up, leaned my head against the grill of the car, and rubbed my throbbing shoulder. "I'm fine. Thank you for your concern." I handed her the windshield wiper. "You should probably get that fixed. God, I wish you had listened to me about the Vespa. That hurt."

"Why did you do that? Can you get up?"

"You know it, baby," I said, but then groaned as she helped me to my feet.

"Oh, God. Can you ever be serious?" But I could hear the worry in her voice.

I leaned on the hood to steady myself, letting go when my legs felt stable beneath me.

"I'm about to drop a whole lotta seriousness on you as soon as you see whether my spleen is hanging out. It's like fifty-fifty right now." I showed her my lower back. "Still in?"

"Yes," she said, chuckling. A car passed by, an old woman staring at us, just talking in the middle of the street. I gave her a thumbs up, but to be honest, it was just for show. My body ached. I turned back to Rae and pushed out my lower lip. "How many guys have jumped on a moving vehicle for you?"

"I wasn't even going ten miles an hour."

"You wanna try it?" I shook my head with a faux huff. "I didn't concuss myself for nothing. I promised you a serious dropping."

"Eww."

"That's not what I meant. You're so gross." I looked up at the fading, but very clear sky. "I feel like it should rain and we should make out."

"I feel like we should exchange insurance information. You dented my hood."

"A token to remember me by when I bleed out." I checked my side again. "You sure you don't see a rib popping out? It's definitely busted." I turned back to Rae. "No matter. I sacrificed my body for a reason. I know it's been established that my people are better than yours, but I'd just like to say, as far as *you* are concerned, you are...amazing. I've never met anyone like you. And I'm horribly in love with you."

Rae chuckled nervously. "That's not the best way to start."

"That's a fair point. Let me start over."

"From where?"

I smiled sheepishly. "The morning after the Hamptons?" I tapped chin, thinking for a moment, and then said, "Well, maybe the night before, because I'd like to do all that stuff again."

Rae's face softened.

I continued, "In all seriousness, you think I don't know what I'm doing, but I know exactly what I'm doing. I just don't know how it's going to turn out. Nobody does, for anything." I kicked at a pebble. "You make me want to be better. Not because I want to beat you. But because I want to be good enough for you. I like bantering with you, but if I'm being honest, I'm not sure I deserve you and I will spend every moment with you trying to be worthy of you. Just give me the chance." I grabbed her hands. She tensed, but then relaxed.

Rae huffed and said softly, "There's no way this could work, Leo."

"There is a way. And it has to do with how we're similar.

And I'm not talking about looking fabulous while naked. I know that's what you were thinking."

Rae shook her head, looking away and suppressing a smile.

I let go of one of her hands and tilted her chin to look me in the eye. "We love each other. Tell me you don't love me, and I'll never bother you again. You can marry a mohel and I'll marry a Maria with big hair in a leopard jumpsuit."

Rae chuckled and looked away. "The gold standard in Judaism, as far as I know, is not to marry a mohel."

"I know, but it just sounds good saying it. I mean, say it ten times fast."

"I don't want to do that."

I shrugged. "So then answer my question then. Do you love me? And I know when you're lying."

"When's that?"

"Come on, babe. Whenever you say your people are better than my people."

Rae scoffed. "I thought we were talking similarities?"

"See? I need you to put me back on track." I looked into her eyes and said, "Just let me love you. You need me as much as I need you."

"I do?"

"Is that a question or are you jumping to our nuptials?"

Rae pursed her lips. Was she holding a smile? "Why do I need you?"

"Because my love for you isn't based on how many transactions you complete. It's just based on you."

Her eyes welled up with tears.

I continued, "If you want to be a career woman, have at it. I'm fine if you want to be my sugar mommy, but I just want you."

She laughed and wiped away tears, but then turned serious again. "What about Natalia? The baby?"

I could sense her force field wearing down. I had to get

this right. "Are there any divorced fathers who are good fathers?"

"Yes."

I shrugged. "So, consider me that. Divorced before I made the mistake of getting married to the wrong person. I've almost literally given up everything for you. My family. My job. Tucking my son or daughter in every night. All just for the chance of you. And I would do it again. And again. Surely you have completely stupefied in love with you on your checklist?"

She laughed through tears. "I left it at home. I'll have to check it later."

"You should probably digitize that for easier reference. This is kind of an important moment. Epic fail on your part."

Rae snorted. "How do you do that to me?"

"I've done more than a few things that have left you in wonder. Care to specify?"

"Make me laugh like nobody else. Make me feel like I don't care about anything else when I'm with you. But then I think about our families."

"Things change. There's more to the world than just what we know. Forget everything else. Tell me you don't love me. Tell me you don't want to be with me. Tell me I'm not worth trying for."

"It's not that simple. It's *not* just me and you."

I rubbed her shoulder. "Do you really want to be so loyal to a family that would shun you for following your heart? Not to mention this face." I highlighted it with my hand. "Because I don't. I won't. You might as well just say yes now and save us both the trouble, because I'm gonna stalk you like Christian Grey in a hardware store."

"Stalking only works in billionaire fiction. And how do you know that?"

"Noted. I'll tell Frankie immediately. And it's none of your business what's on my Kindle."

"How can I choose between you and my family?"

I sighed and then smiled. "You're not. You're just choosing me. If they reject me, reject us, that's on them."

"But I know what they'll do."

"Your father may be a dip shit, but he loves you."

"You're marketing skills are amazing," Rae said, laughing.

"Shut up," I said, smiling. I caressed her face. "My mother and grandmother want nothing to do with me. And the rest of my family will probably just go along with it. And I'm okay with that. If they don't come around, it's a reflection on them. Not me. I mean, I have a dead-end job. I've been dumped left and right. I have a bastard on the way. That's a reflection on me. But you love me anyway. I will swear on the left arm of Sandy Koufax- I will never give up on my love for you. And we shouldn't give up on our families, either. We love them. We'll convince them together. Let me be the Jack to your Rose. Let me onto the door, baby."

"I thought you hated Rose?"

"I'm drowning without you. I've reassessed," I said, laughing. "Please." I feigned shivering.

She barely got out the words, "I don't know, Leo."

"When have you ever backed down from a challenge? You'll fight for your business, but you won't fight for me? For us? By the way, have you ever thought I should be a lawyer?"

"Because you're obnoxious?"

"Wah. No. Because I am a fabulous negotiator and consensus creator."

"No. I think you're best as my little printer's devil."

I wrapped my arms around her waist, my lips hovering above hers and our foreheads touching. "I want to know more about what that entails, but you still haven't told me the only thing that matters."

"Pasta is not soup."

I laughed. "The only other thing that matters."

Rae looked into my eyes and smiled, her dimples mesmerizing. She stood back and caressed my face. "Leo Donati, I love you beyond anything I could've possibly imagined. I will never be over you. You are a stunad mamaluke of a chooch, but I love you with all my heart."

"That makes very little sense, but I don't care, because I'm meshuggeneh about you."

Rae wiped away more tears. I tucked her hair behind her ear as another car passed, by. "Rae, at your apartment, you told me love wasn't enough. I promise you that it is."

She said, "Wherever this takes us, we'll do it together?"

I feigned frustration. "I feel like that was my idea and you stole it."

"It was a question. But we're a team. We're sharing it."

I nodded in agreement. "Will you kiss me already? I mean, you nearly killed me. I may have spoken too soon when I wished cars for your people," I said, referring to our conversation about cars en route to the east end plant tour. I rubbed my side. "If your first act of love is not going to be a kiss, how about a kidney?"

"Stop being so dramatic." Rae laughed and then caressed my face, looking up at me. "Promise me it'll be okay."

"I promise you that we'll get through this together. Although, don't hold me to that. There is a small chance I'm going to bleed out, so please kiss me immediately. Have I ever told you that Italians are the best kissers?"

Rae inched closer. "I have heard that, but in my experience, it's not fully confirmed."

"Challenge accepted."

I grabbed her face with both hands and tilted her neck to the side, adding Hollywood quality sound effects. I kissed her, dipping her nearly horizontal despite my failing spleen and kidney. Kissed her so well I'm pretty sure it made the Patron Saint of Fireworks Makers, Saint Barbara, blush. And yes, that's a thing. I returned her to her feet, gave her a moment to regroup while I held her close, and said, "I can't wait to live my best life with you."

Rae said, "I can't wait even more."

I shrugged, my face morphing to nonchalance. "Actually, I *can* wait."

Rae furrowed her brow. "I can wait longer."

"Oh, it's on," I said, laughing. "My people can so outlast your people. We have Lent. Forty days of sacrifice every year."

Rae scoffed. "We survived the ten plagues!"

"Yeah, but weren't two of them frogs and hail?" She pulled away in jest, but I wrapped her back into my arms. "I will give you hail because those suckers can hurt, but not frogs. That's just ridiculous. So I'm giving you nine plagues as a token of my love."

"That's the worst token of love I've ever heard of. For an articulate guy, you should choose your words more carefully."

I nodded sheepishly. "I have five carefully chosen words that I will say to you every day for as long as I live."

Rae smiled. "What?"

"Pasta is better than soup."

She smacked my shoulder. "It's over. I'm outta here."

"Okay. How about this? I will always love you."

She didn't have to return my words. I knew. Her dimples said it all. And then she kissed me like an Italian.

So, there you have it. My family lasagna was a mess, but all I cared about was a new recipe I could create with Rae. Would my family be some modern take on the classic, some sort of deconstructed lasagna? I didn't know. All I knew was that my best life was with her, and that together, we could get through anything.

———

Rae's Personal Notes

- Submit insurance claim for dented hood, windshield wiper. What a mamaluke!
- Scream! Take deep breath. Scream again! I'm in love!
- Research leopard print apparel. When in Rome do as the Romans do?
- Read: The Essential Guide to Italian Culture and Customs
- Create checklist for plan of attack re: parental approval ~~(69 item checklist, baby?)~~
- Hide notes from Leo…
- Live and love my life to the fullest with the stunad man I love.

The end, but definitely not end of story.

A Note From Grayson

First and foremost, thank you for reading my book! I hope you loved it. I had so much fun writing Leo and Rae's story, which is very (very, very) loosely based on my own wacky Italian family and my wife's Jewish side. I got to reconnect and deepen my appreciation for both cultures even though my carb intake tripled as my research churned out so many fabulous recipes.

I expect this will become a series. I've begun working on the outline for book two (alongside another unrelated project). Leo and Rae are in love, but that was the easy part. Now they have to convince their crazy families! Not so easy...

Anyway, I hope you enjoyed *Love and Agita!*

If you'd like to sign up for my newsletter to get updates on new releases and special deals, you can do so here:

sw3.graysonavery.com/newsletter

Italian and Jewish Glossary

Italian

Agita- Italian anxiety from the word, agitare, or to agitate. Often given to Italian women by stunad (see below) husbands or children.

Bombaloni- A delicious, stuffed dessert (custard, chocolate, or jelly) that resembles a grenade, often with hints of lemon and orange.

Capisce- You got it? Understand?

Chooch- A stupid person, meathead. My brother, Benny.

Faccia bella- Beautiful face. Something Grayson's aunt still tells him to this day, while also pinching his cheek like she's trying to tear it from said faccia bella.

Gabagool- a fabulous morphing of the word, capicola, or sliced pork shoulder.

Gagootz- An eggplant.

Gavon- A savage. Typically used in reference to how someone chows down on spectacular Italian cuisine.

Il Pinturrichio- Alessandro Del Piero, a former Italian footballer/soccer player, known for painting the corners of the goal. The nickname was inspired by the renaissance painter of the same nickname, formally known as Bernadino di Betto.

Italian family dinner effect- Government-suppressed science connecting the demise of the Italian family dinner and associated hand gesturing to a rise in global warming.

Mamaluke- Someone who does something dumb, silly, or foolish. My cousin, Frankie.

Mangia- Time to eat fabulous food.

Nonna- An Italian grandmother. May look cute, but armed and dangerous with weapons such as wooden spoons, handfuls of pasta, and laser stares.

Oreganata- A tasty mixture of bread crumbs, oregano, butter or oil, and garlic.

Paisano- Friend or fellow countryman.

Parmigiana- A spectacular combination of pick a protein (or eggplant) topped with sauce and cheese. Bake it and then thank your maker.

Pazza- Crazy. If Grayson ever opens a pizzeria, it will be called, Pazza for Pizza. He'll even allow Chicago deep dish on the menu...

Sgrugnare- To punch or bash in the face.

Sicilian Stare- When a Sicilian stares in an angry or fierce way, the intensity just shy of Medusa's stone-turning stare.

Strunza- A big shit.

Stunad- A stupid person.

Volpino- An Italian dog breed resembling a tiny, fluffy fox, or an electrocuted cotton ball.

Jewish

Bubbe- A Jewish grandma. Cute, but dangerous. Trained in psychological warfare. The Jedi Knights of guilt.

Chutzpah- Self-confidence or audacity.

Dayge- Anxiety. Labs confirm it is one of the most powerful forces in the universe.

Eyngeshparter- A stubborn person.

Knish- A tasty, fried or baked pastry stuffed with potato, and enjoyed with spicy mustard. Oy! So good.

Latke- A potato pancake cooked in oil to celebrate the miracle of Hannukah. Must be eaten with applesauce or you will die unfulfilled.

Mazel tov- A Jewish phrase meaning, congratulations or good luck. Meant to be yelled with excitement.

Meshuggeneh- A person who acts crazy or foolish…typically the person a Bubbe is complaining about.

Schlimazel- A consistently unlucky or accident-prone person.

Schmedrick- A fool or nincompoop.

Schmuck- a stupid, foolish, or unlikeable person.

Yarmulke- a thin, round skull cap worn by Jewish men.

Yiddish- a language used by Jewish people in central and eastern Europe. It is a mixture of Hebrew and several modern languages and is today spoken mainly in the US, Israel, and Russia.

About the Author

Grayson Avery is the author of Love and Agita, and The Sweet Water Circle Series, a romantic comedy series that focuses on childhood friends in their 30s and 40s as they help each other navigate the stormy waters of dating, marriage, divorce, and a whole lot of inappropriate, naughty, and downright hysterical situations.

Grayson enjoys piña coladas, but not getting caught in the rain. His passions are spending time with his family, writing, traveling to warm destinations that serve piña coladas, and baseball.

You can find him at graysonavery.com or the social media sites listed below.

f facebook.com/GraysonAveryAuthor

a amazon.com/author/graysonavery

g goodreads.com/graysonavery

BB bookbub.com/authors/grayson-avery